NEW YORK TIMES BESTSELLING AUTHOR

LYNN VIEHL

FROSTFIRE

A NOVEL OF THE KYNDRED

 SIGNET
SELECT

"Another powerful and rewarding series."
—Romance Reviews Today

3

SIGNET SELECT

$7.99 U.S.
$9.99 CAN.

ISBN 978-0-451-41302-4

5 0 7 9 9

S > EAN

continued ...

"Filled with romance, intrigue, and nonstop action, this book does not fail to satisfy."

—ParaNormal Romance
(A PNR Staff Recommended Read)

Twilight Fall

"The pace is fast and the characters strong . . . whets the appetite for more." —Monsters and Critics

"Flawed characters are Viehl's forte, and when you mix in rapidly paced plotting, the story shines with intense and dangerous emotions. . . . One highly satisfying read!"

—*Romantic Times*

"[An] intelligent and breathtaking addition to the incomparable Darkyn series." —Fresh Fiction

"Viehl scripts an excellent story in *Twilight Fall*."

—ParaNormal Romance

"An electrifying addition to this top-notch series . . . a definite must-read." —Romance Junkies

"A really good series . . . excellent." —*Affaire de Coeur*

Evermore

"Full of exciting twists and turns. . . . Viehl tells a self-contained, page-turning story of medieval vampires."

—*Publishers Weekly*

"Dual cases of unexpressed love have kept two potential mates dancing around each other. Add in guilt and remorse and this is a recipe for emotional disaster. Thankfully, Viehl knows just how to liven things up: by adding danger, treachery, and betrayal to the mix. Things never run smoothly in the Darkyn world!" —*Romantic Times*

"Lynn Viehl sure knows how to tell a hell of a story."

—Romance Reviews Today

"One of my favorites, if not *the* favorite Darkyn book to date." —Romance Reader at Heart

"Another highly satisfying chapter in the Darkyn saga."
—Vampire Genre

Night Lost

"Viehl continues to weave an intricate web of intrigue in this contribution to the amazing series. . . . I became completely engrossed in this compelling story. Lynn Viehl had me hooked from the first page. . . . Exceptional . . . I definitely recommend this marvelous book."　　—Romance Junkies

"Fast-paced and fully packed. You won't regret spending time in this darkly dangerous and romantic world!"
—*Romantic Times*

"Fans of the series will agree that Lynn Viehl is at the top of her game."　　—Alternative Worlds

Dark Need

"An exciting book and a must-read . . . frightening and creepy characters that will keep you awake late at night. Balancing the darkness is the searing heat and eroticism that is generated between Samantha and Lucan."　　—Vampire Genre

Private Demon

"Lynn Viehl's vampire saga began spectacularly in *If Angels Burn*, and this second novel in the Darkyn series justifies the great beginning. Indeed, it is as splendid, if not more, than the first one."　　—Curled Up with a Good Book

"Strong . . . a tense, multifaceted thriller. . . . Fans of Lori Handeland's Moon novels will want to read Lynn Viehl's delightful tale."　　—*Midwest Book Review*

If Angels Burn

"Erotic, darker than sin, and better than good chocolate."
—Holly Lisle

"This exciting vampire romance is action packed. . . . Lynn Viehl writes a fascinating paranormal tale."
—The Best Reviews

FROSTFIRE

A NOVEL OF THE KYNDRED

Lynn Viehl

A SIGNET SELECT BOOK

SIGNET SELECT
Published by New American Library, a division of
Penguin Group (USA) Inc., 375 Hudson Street,
New York, New York 10014, USA
Penguin Group (Canada), 90 Eglinton Avenue East, Suite 700, Toronto,
Ontario M4P 2Y3, Canada (a division of Pearson Penguin Canada Inc.)
Penguin Books Ltd., 80 Strand, London WC2R 0RL, England
Penguin Ireland, 25 St. Stephen's Green, Dublin 2,
Ireland (a division of Penguin Books Ltd.)
Penguin Group (Australia), 250 Camberwell Road, Camberwell, Victoria 3124,
Australia (a division of Pearson Australia Group Pty. Ltd.)
Penguin Books India Pvt. Ltd., 11 Community Centre, Panchsheel Park,
New Delhi - 110 017, India
Penguin Group (NZ), 67 Apollo Drive, Rosedale, North Shore 0632,
New Zealand (a division of Pearson New Zealand Ltd.)
Penguin Books (South Africa) (Pty.) Ltd., 24 Sturdee Avenue,
Rosebank, Johannesburg 2196, South Africa

Penguin Books Ltd., Registered Offices:
80 Strand, London WC2R 0RL, England

First published by Signet Select, an imprint of New American Library,
a division of Penguin Group (USA) Inc.

First Printing, January 2011
10 9 8 7 6 5 4 3 2 1

For Larissa Ione,
with much love and admiration
(I told you
that dictionary was lucky)

Only a touch, and nothing more:
Ah! But never so touch'd before!
Touch of lip, was it? Touch of hand?
Either is easy to understand.
Earth may be smitten with fire or frost
Never the touch of true love lost.

—Mortimer Collins, "Kate Temple's Song"

chimera (*kī-'mir-ə, kə-*)

Genetics: an organism composed of two or more genetically distinct tissues, as an organism that is partly male and partly female, or an artificially produced individual having tissues of several species.[*]

We must be cautious not to violate the integrity of humanity or of animal life over which we have a stewardship responsibility. Research projects that create human-animal chimeras risk disturbing fragile ecosystems, endanger health, and affront species integrity.

—Dr. William P. Cheshire, Jr., professor
of neurology, Mayo Clinic[†]

---

[*] Dictionary.com.

[†]"Animal-Human Hybrids Spark Controversy," National Geographic News, Jan. 25, 2005, http://news.nationalgeographic.com/news/2005/01/0125_050125_chimeras.html.

PART ONE

Hunger Moon

As the door to her office opened, Marla Wilkes looked up from the catalog she was perusing. The stunning good looks of the man who came in made her straighten in her chair and touch a hand to the curls of her new perm. "May I help you?"

His voice coiled around her ears like velvet ribbons. "I need to find some records."

"Well, you've certainly come to the right place." She glanced at the clock, and sighed. "But I'm afraid you're a bit late. The reference department closes at five." She picked up her pencil. "If you'd care to give me the information, I can leave it on the archive clerk's desk for first thing in the morning."

He came around her desk and pulled her out of her chair, so quickly that she hardly had time to blink. "You will find them for me."

Something burned her nose, and then spread down her throat, expanding into her chest. "Yes. I will find them."

Marla floated down the hall with him, feeling as light as the duck feathers on her best Sunday hat, and happier than a hungry schoolgirl with a basket of lardy cakes. Magician that he was, he opened all the locked doors and cabinets without using a single key. She smiled dreamily at him as he told her what he wanted, and sighed as she went to work looking for it.

"I have it," she piped up as she took a huge folder from the eighteenth-century records. "The original copy of 'The Church of St. Edward King and Confessor.' It contains all the transcripts and registers that were saved from Sutton Place."

It took an hour of slowly sorting through the crumbling pages before she found the list of names he wanted. "Here we are. A copy of the census of twelve ninety-nine. My goodness. That must have been a dreadful year. There are more than a hundred names here."

He told her which name to find, and while the old, tiny script proved difficult to make out, she read until she found the entry.

"I've got it." She ran her finger along the line. "Born twelve sixty-four, died twelve eighty-two. Victim of the plague." She squinted at the final notation, and then smiled up at him. "Fantastic news. It's right here in Surrey."

He stared at the record page for a long time. "You will take me there."

Marla retrieved her purse from her office and led him out to her Mini, and from there drove him to the ruins. She tried to chat him up along the way, but he only stared out at the passing countryside.

When they arrived at the ruins, Marla felt a bit embarrassed. Teenagers had sprayed the stone walls with some very rude words, and left behind an appalling amount of garbage. She kicked it out of his path and guided him to the back of the old sanctuary, where part of the floor remained intact under a thin layer of moss.

"It should be here somewhere. I read about it in

school." She walked along the rows of stones and bent now and then to pull back some weeds. "I think this could be it. Have a look?"

He knelt beside her, first peering at the stone and then digging his hands into it. The ancient plaque broke in two as he wrenched it out of the ground, along with great handfuls of dirt.

Marla sat on her bum and watched him work. He was beautiful when he dug, and when he plunged his hand into the hole he'd made and wrestled an odd-shaped ball from it, she clapped her hands.

"You've found it." She didn't know why he was holding the dirty old thing like that, or why it didn't make him happy. Seeing his face made her shiver a little. "That is what you wanted, isn't it?"

"Yes." He kissed the top of the ball before he carefully placed it back into the hole, and covered it over again, and fitted the broken plaque over it. "That is all I ever wanted." He stood. "All I wanted to forget." He walked away.

Marla scrambled up, hurrying after him, but as soon as she emerged from the ruins, he had gone. She turned around slowly, frowning as her happiness began to fade. After a few moments she looked at her dirty hands and then at her car. She was at the old church, which she recognized, but the last thing she remembered was being in her office.

"Good Lord." She brushed her hands off on her skirt, adding dark streaks over the odd green stains. "How did I get here?"

Marla never received any answers to her questions, but when she returned to work, she saw the caretaker talking to a constable, and hurried over to them.

"What is it?" she asked. "What's happened?"

"Oh, Miss Wilkes, I thought you'd gone for the day." The caretaker grimaced. "Someone broke into the old

archives. Busted every lock on the doors and the cabinets back there, too. Helped themselves to them old reg-
istries that they sent over from Aberdeen. Don't look
like they nicked anything, though."

Marla frowned. "I should think not. Why on earth
would anyone want to steal old church records?"

SEARCH FOR RUNAWAY TEEN HEIRESS CONTINUES

10/01/99
SANTA LUCIA, CA—Santa Lucia police and fire rescue teamed up with local volunteers to continue the
search today for sixteen-year-old Lillian Emerson, who
went missing from her family's estate on September 29.
The horse Lillian was riding at the time of her disappearance was recovered yesterday from a neighboring
property.

"He sustained some minor lacerations, but he'll be
fine," Chief of Police Ormond Teller said during last
night's press conference. "We confirmed the saddle he
was still wearing belongs to Miss Emerson."

Teller also reacted strongly to speculation the missing teen had not run away from home, as her mother
had reported to police, but instead had been attacked
during her outing and abducted. "There is not one
shred of evidence to indicate this was anything more
than an impulsive act by a thoughtless kid who likely
got thrown from her horse. We're moving up into the
hills at first light, and the rangers tell me that there are
plenty of nooks and caves up there where Lillian could
have taken shelter. I expect that's where we'll find her."

Evelyn Emerson was not among the volunteers out
searching for her daughter, as she left the state some
twelve hours after her daughter's disappearance. Wallace Bridger, Mrs. Emerson's attorney, confirmed his
client had traveled to an undisclosed location in order

to receive counseling from a person identified only as "a lifelong spiritual advisor."

Bridger also indicated that the nationally renowned interior designer felt compelled to leave in order to escape unwanted media attention, not to avoid being questioned by police for the role she may have played in Lillian's disappearance.

"Evelyn would never do anything to harm her child," Bridger told reporters. "She is a wonderful mother, a devout Christian, and has secluded herself to receive the comfort and support she so desperately needs during this difficult time."

After the death of Robert Rinehart Emerson III in 1982, Evelyn Emerson took her father's place as chief executive officer of Emerson Interiors. She has been credited with transforming the corporation from a conservative furnishings manufacturer into the highly successful parent company of such lucrative interior-decor franchises as Hearth and Home, Private Sanctuaries, and A Lady's Touch. Ms. Emerson has also personally designed the interiors of dozens of homes for important political figures, high-profile business leaders, and powerhouse celebrities, and is considered an industry leader in establishing the hottest trends in home fashions. However, little is known about Emerson's relationship with her only daughter, whom she adopted in 1982 and has since kept out of the spotlight.

Neil Huntley, Evelyn Emerson's former stable manager and an experienced rider, has been leading a group of local men up into the hills as part of the search efforts. He refused to speak to reporters or share any details as to the reason why he was fired by Emerson on the night of September 29. A source at the police department has acknowledged that Huntley was the last person to see Lillian Emerson alive, but he was seen in town at the time of the teenager's disappearance, and is not considered a person of interest in the case.

Lillian Emerson is 5 feet 5 inches tall, weighs 130 pounds, and has bright red shoulder-length hair and hazel eyes. She was last seen wearing her school uniform, a white blouse embroidered with the St. Catherine's School for Girls logo, a black and blue plaid skirt, white knee-high socks, and black loafers. Anyone with information as to Lillian's current whereabouts should contact the Santa Lucia Police Department or the Monterey County Sheriff's Office.

Chapter 1

November 30, 2009
Lake Gem, Florida

Albert Brewer had a weak chin, a low forehead, and a hooked nose, and he usually smelled like an Italian sub with too many onions on it. His petty-tyrant personality was as offensive as his insistence that everyone call him "Big Al" or "sir," but that wasn't why everyone avoided him.

It was the dandruff, Lilah Devereaux decided. Big Al had such a perpetual case of it that it lay like snowflakes in his sandy hair and on the shoulders of his shirts, and even speckled his bushy eyebrows. Whenever she stood near him, she always felt a terrible urge to itch her own clean scalp.

Today she simply stared at him, for once oblivious to his flakiness as she tried to process what he'd just told her. "I'm what?"

"You're fired, Lil," he repeated in a voice so loud it seemed to echo through the utter silence of the office. He dropped a small cardboard box on top of Lilah's desk. "I'm giving you fifteen minutes to clear out your personal belongings before I call security to escort you off the premises."

His soft brown eyes, which Lilah had always considered his only redeeming feature, shifted from her face to her breasts before he realized what he was doing and looked past her. With her earth-mother body, she'd grown accustomed to being ogled, but around her Big Al Brewer behaved like a pimpled freshman who'd just found his daddy's secret stash of porn magazines.

Maybe that was the problem. No matter how conservatively Lilah dressed, she couldn't camouflage her collection of curves. Maybe her supervisor couldn't stand having an employee who looked more like a forties pinup girl than an animal control officer.

"I don't understand," she said, careful as always to keep her emotions in check. "You're *firing* me for having a flat tire?"

"This is the third time you've punched in late for your shift," he said, and produced an index card, from which he read: "County policy states that any employee who repeatedly refuses to adhere to their scheduled work hours is subject to immediate termination."

This wasn't some practical joke; Big Al was dead serious. "But, sir, I've only been late three times in the five years that I've worked here."

"You should have known that tardies are like rollover minutes. They never go away." He gave her breasts an insulting smile. "Be sure not to take any county property with you, or I'll file a pilfering report." He turned his back on her and walked off into his office.

Lilah glanced down at the empty box, and then at the little Christmas tree one of the secretaries had put on her desk. The tiny white lights blinked around the makeshift ornaments of dog biscuits, cat toys, and beribboned birdseed bells. Was it county property? "I can't believe this. This isn't happening."

Sadie, the head clerk from the tax office, slipped into her cubicle. The dangling wreath earrings the big woman wore were swinging wildly, as if she'd run the entire way. "You all right, honey?"

"Not really." She opened her drawer and took out the gym bag with her spare uniform and hiking boots. She unloaded the uniform, which didn't belong to her, but kept the boots. "I've been fired."

"I know." The other woman lowered her voice. "Becky in resource management says it's because of the cutbacks from the state, but I think the big poop has had it out for you from day one."

"Mr. Brewer doesn't even know me. He just transferred up from Miami a month ago." Lilah removed her badge and placed it on the blotter before she picked up the little dish garden she kept by her phone. Her temper had settled, but she still felt confused. "I'm mostly on the road during my shifts. What could I have done to upset him?"

Sadie's eyes moved to the newspaper clipping someone had pinned to Lilah's day board. "Maybe it was all the attention."

The call had come in from 911 dispatch back in October, and Lilah had been the closest to the neighborhood where a four-hundred-pound black bear had been reported to be rooting through garbage cans. Because the bears were an endangered species, they were protected by the state, perhaps a little too well. Their population in central Florida had swelled over the years, until Fish and Game officials estimated there were more than three thousand roaming the huge tracts of woods in the region.

The growing number of humans moving to central Florida had resulted in a parallel population explosion, as well as a building boom, one that often encroached on the wooded areas. This was not helped by the builders, who tried to preserve some of the "country" around their developments by leaving woods and brush areas intact. As a result bears were beginning to be sighted regularly, sometimes straying into residential areas, where the smell of garbage and the presence of small pets attracted them.

Although Florida black bears had never been known to attack human beings, sightings around populated areas always generated a flurry of panicked phone calls, usually from the elderly or the terrified mothers of small children.

Lilah had tracked the animal by following the noise along with a trail of chocolate cake chunks, which led her around the back of a house. There she found an enormous male black bear standing beside a swimming pool filled with screeching, thrashing teenagers.

"I'm with animal control." She had to yell it to be heard over the kids, who instantly quieted. "Calm down. Everything is going to be okay."

At the sound of her voice the bear swung its head around to look at her, giving her an excellent view of the white froth around his mouth. She focused on his black eyes, where her ability always found the way in.

The bear didn't think in language, but in feelings, images, smells, tastes, and sounds, in strings like flashes. As she absorbed them, Lilah tagged them: hunger-trash-can-plastic-sweet-chewing-noise-moving-water-thirsty-noise-human-human-thirsty-water-human-human.

The bear had feasted, and now it simply wanted a drink.

"Shoot it!" one of the teens shouted.

"Calm down." Lilah approached the bear slowly. "He's not rabid."

The bear licked some of the sweet substance from his muzzle before he made a low, throaty sound.

"Don't you see it, you silly bitch?" a man's tight,

angry voice called from an open window in the house. "He's foaming at the mouth."

You're yelling at me while you hide inside and let your kids face a half-ton bear. "That's not foam, sir. It's cake icing," Lilah told him. "This big guy has a sweet tooth." She had already chambered a dart in her rifle; now she aimed for a harmless spot under his chin. "Time for you to take a nap."

Lilah heard the porch screen tear, but she didn't expect the small terrier that raced out to stand yapping at her target. The bear broke eye contact to inspect the tiny dog, which was lunging at him, and then lifted a paw to swat at it.

A woman shrieked out, "Muffin, no!"

Instinct made Lilah drop her rifle and dive, grabbing the terrier in her arms and rolling out of the way a heartbeat before the massive claws struck the ground. Dirt and grass flew, pelting her face as the bear turned.

The kids in the pool began to scream again, but she looked up at the confused, annoyed bear and reached into him, this time sending a single, direct thought: *Stay.*

The bear went still.

Carefully Lilah got to her feet, still holding the struggling terrier and ignoring the sound of its barking and all the human voices shouting at her. She had to maintain eye contact to keep her control over the animal, and she wasn't going to risk losing it again. *Sit.*

The bear sat on its haunches as if it were a pet.

Tucking the furious dog under her arm, Lilah backed away until she reached her rifle and picked it up. She leveled it from her waist and pulled the trigger, at the same time sending one last command into the bear's mind: *Sleep.*

The dart appeared in the bear's throat as it collapsed, closed its eyes, and went limp.

The terrier finally stopped barking and promptly peed all over Lilah's hip.

"You're welcome." Gingerly she carried him to the porch to hand him to his weeping owner, who had hysterics over the dog while not giving her children in the pool even a single glance.

Lilah had intended to use the winch on the back of her truck to haul his body onto the lift gate so she could remove him from the scene quickly. Unfortunately before she could, the kids clambered out of the pool and surrounded the bear while their disgruntled father finally emerged from safety to give Lilah a piece of his mind. Neighbors also began gathering, some of the braver ones nudging the bear with their shoes before dancing backward. By the time she managed to get some control over the scene, the first of the reporters had arrived and were sticking their cameras and microphones in her face.

WHO'S AFRAID OF THE BIG BLACK BEAR? NOT THIS LITTLE RED! The local morning edition had run the story on the front page, along with huge photos of Lilah and the tranquilized bear.

Ordinarily the capture would have been a one-day story, but it had been a particularly slow week for the local news, so the story had run every morning, noon, and night until a man donating a kidney to a woman who discovered that she was his long-lost sister finally upstaged Lilah and the bear. No video of the actual capture had been taken, thankfully, or Lilah would have been all over YouTube and made national news.

Now, as Lilah looked at the clipping, she wished for the thousandth time that she had sent the bear back into the woods.

"I didn't ask for the attention, Sadie. Besides, why didn't he fire me back when it happened?"

"Maybe he was waiting for it to die down." She looked

over the garland of artificial holly taped to the top of her cubicle before dropping her voice to a murmur. "You know Jan, his secretary? She told me that he was on the phone all yesterday morning. Swears she heard him say your name a couple times, too." Sadie's eyes softened as she watched her take an old, overstuffed envelope out of her drawer. "Oh, honey. You have to take those with you. Lord, there are so many now, aren't there?"

Lilah opened the flap and took out a few photos from the hundreds in the envelope. The first was of a black-and-white-spotted Great Dane with a lopped ear and a toothy grin, sitting between two teen boys, both of whom had their arms slung around his strong back.

"I miss Checker," she murmured as she went to the next photo, which was of a tiny black toy poodle sleeping on a sumptuous red velvet dog bed. "And Demon."

She had rescued both dogs from impossibly bad situations. Checker, the Dane, had been starved by his owner in the mistaken belief that it would make him a better guard dog. Little Demon had survived being born to an unlicensed breeder and two years of miserable imprisonment in what amounted to little more than a hamster cage.

After seeing that Checker and Demon were given the medical treatment they needed, Lilah had worked hard to place both animals in good homes. Now both were lavished with love as well as the care and attention they had been denied for so long.

She looked through a few more before forcing herself to replace the photos and close the envelope. "Guess I'll finally have some time to put these in an album."

"You can file a protest, you know," Sadie suggested, and put a hand on her arm. "There isn't one person in this office that wouldn't stand up for you, Lilah. Or you could call the papers and the TV stations. Tell them you're getting shafted by Big A-hole. It being almost

Christmas, I know people will call into the county and give them all kinds of heck."

Lilah's stomach shrank at the thought. "I've had enough publicity, Sadie." That was the truth. *And now for the lie.* "I'll find another job soon. Lots of places are hiring for the holidays."

Security showed up in the form of Billy Ray Dobe, a young trainee who had yet to be assigned a truck. Although he'd been with the county for only a few months and he barely knew her, his thin face looked as distressed as Sadie's. "Miz Devereaux, I've got to . . . Big Al says . . . "

"No problem, Bill. Oh, here." She removed her car keys from her ring before handing it to him. "You'd better put the truck in for service before you start driving it. The engine's been vibrating a lot, and I think the motor mounts need to be replaced."

Sadie took Lilah's box and shoved it into the trainee's hands. "You be a gentleman and walk her all the way out to her car, Billy Ray."

His Adam's apple bobbed. "Yes, ma'am."

Sadie enveloped Lilah in a cloud of perfume and soft arms. "If you need anything, honey, you call me, you hear?"

"I will," Lilah lied again, and hugged her back.

Everyone stood up as Billy followed Lilah out of the office. Their stares weighed on her shoulders almost as heavily as the loss of her job, but she kept her head up and her smile in place as she nodded to those she passed. Behind her, someone started clapping slowly, and then everyone was doing it, some whistling and others calling out her name.

Lilah glanced back to see the noise drive Big Al out of his office, a furious jack-in-the-box, and she paused to give him a smile. He jerked back a little, as if she'd slapped him.

No matter how many legs they had, some creatures never knew how to cope with kindness.

As soon as they were outside the building, Billy grinned at Lilah. "Big Al looked like he was about to bust a fuse, didn't he?"

"Several. Here, let me have that." She tried to take the box from him. "You don't have to walk me out to my car, Bill."

He put a protective arm up over the box. "Miz Sadie will tear my head off if I don't." He hesitated. "My mom said they're hiring now over at the market by Maplebrook. Minimum wage, but it might tide you over till you find something else."

Lilah's heart melted a little. "Thanks, Bill. I appreciate it."

"This just ain't right, Miz Dee." He shook his head as he followed her around the corner to the side lot where all the employees parked. "I mean, you're never late. Heck, you usually get in earlier than anyone else."

"Not today." Lilah stopped by the back end of a Subaru and looked around.

He stopped beside her. "I wasn't here for the bear, but I know what you did that time that Rottie got loose from the cage room and bit Doc Rivka, and all the ladies were shrieking and jumping on their desks. You just walked right on up to him like he was nothing but a yapping puppy, and made him sit, and put that muzzle on him without getting a scratch."

"He was just angry and scared." And she'd used her ability to calm him down, something she'd never put in her reports. "You should never do what I did, Bill. It was reckless."

Billy shook his head. "You got something special, Miz Dee. No matter what those critters do, you never get mad, and they never go after you. All the guys say that's why they like to send you out on the bad calls.

Mr. Brewer's crazy for letting you go." He noticed her expression. "You sure you're gonna be all right?"

"I will be." She frowned at the empty space where she had parked twenty minutes ago. "Soon as I find out who just stole my car."

Chapter 2

"I'm glad we could come to terms." Jonah Genaro shook hands with Yutaka Hashimoto while the petite Japanese man's entourage bobbed up and down in synchronized bows. "I'll have my engineers send over the specs by Friday."

"Thank you for your hospitality, Jonah. As always, you are a generous and understanding host." Hashimoto beamed at Genaro's secretary, Tina Segreta, before he glanced at his own assistant. "Schedule a meeting tomorrow morning with the factory managers. We will begin production as soon as the plans arrive." After giving Genaro a final smile, he led his people out of the office.

Genaro's secretary finished making her notes. "I'll have these transcribed in an hour, sir."

"Thank you." He sat back and regarded her. "How did your evening go?"

"As expected." Tina flipped her steno pad closed before she met his gaze. "Mr. Hashimoto seemed flattered, and was easy to please. He prefers fellatio to intercourse, and mentioned how much he likes 'tall, blond American women.' "

Genaro had hired Tina for her administrative skills, which were admirable, but also for her sexual talents, which he had personally refined over time and which had elevated her to being a formidable company asset.

However, she was petite and black-haired, which rendered her less of a temptation for Hashimoto. "Make a note of that in the file." He gave her one of his rare smiles. "You did very well, my dear."

She nodded, satisfied. "Is there anything else, sir?"

"Call Dr. Kirchner." Genaro shrugged out of his jacket and loosened his tie. "Ask him to join me in the exercise room."

"Right away, Mr. Genaro."

Showering before his workout was a waste of time, as he would only have to wash again after he finished, but it kept Kirchner waiting. By the time Genaro emerged from his private bath, the geneticist was pacing around the weight equipment.

"Eliot." He finished toweling off his face before he continued. "Hashimoto has agreed to take the contract. We should receive the first shipment by the end of the month."

"Our preparations for the move are almost finished," Kirchner said. "You should have them shipped to the new facility."

Genaro adjusted the settings on his treadmill before he started the walking sequence and climbed on. "What progress have you made with the transerum?"

"None," he said bluntly. "Since the New York operation was botched, we've only identified one new potential. Until she's classified, I won't know anything."

"I understand your frustrations, Eliot, and I share them. But now is not the time to indulge your temper." He increased the treadmill's speed to a trot. "I need you to focus on whatever it takes to make the transerum work."

"I'd be happy to, if I had what I need." Kirchner came to stand in front of the treadmill. "The progenote was stolen and lost. None of the DNA we've acquired can overcome the debilitating effects the transerum has on the subject's brain. Until we can negate it, the transerum is too dangerous to test on any of our acquisitions. We need to begin over, acquire more of the progenote and DNA from at least a dozen Primes, maybe more."

Genaro switched off the treadmill and slowed to a standstill before he stepped down. "That is unlikely to happen. You'll have to take another approach."

Kirchner's temper finally exploded.

"What would you have me do, Jonah?" the geneticist demanded. "Put an ad in the paper for superhumans to volunteer to be tested? If I'm to do the work, I must have the proper materials."

Genaro took a fresh towel from the wall rack and slung it around his neck. "Are you finished?"

Something else replaced the ferocity in Kirchner's eyes before he lost all expression. "I apologize. We've experienced so many setbacks and disappointments over the last several months that from the moment I step into the lab, I already feel defeated."

"You should follow Yutaka Hashimoto's example," Genaro said as he went to the Nautilus and set the weight pins. "He works off his frustrations through oral sex."

Kirchner, who was a celibate by preference, folded his arms. "If you provide me with what I need, Jonah, I'll personally give you head each and every morning."

Genaro had never doubted his chief geneticist's commitment to the project, but the man had no sense of humor whatsoever. "I'll look into obtaining a new sample of the progenote. In the meantime, have your people in tech step up their efforts to identify new potentials. Tell them to keep the news agencies on twenty-four-hour feed."

"They're doing that."

"Look for unusual incidents as well as miraculous recoveries," Genaro said. "The Kyndred are adept at hiding themselves, but they can't resist using their abilities, especially during emergency situations."

"Sometimes these things are just coincidences," Kirchner pointed out. "People under enormous stress are adrenaline fueled. Often it gives them superhuman strength, but it never lasts."

"We can use the mistakes as test cadavers." He glanced over as his secretary slipped into the room. "That will be all, Doctor."

Kirchner left, averting his gaze from Tina as she began to unbutton her cuffs.

The geneticist's show of distaste seemed to amuse Tina, although she didn't comment on it. Instead she stripped down to her skin and waited for Genaro's direction.

"On the bench," he told her as he took his position under the pull bars. He tested the weight and found it agreeable. "Tell me everything you did to Hashimoto last night."

Tina began relating the details of the encounter, and he timed his repetitions to the rhythm of her voice. He kept her talking until he felt the burn beginning in his muscles, and then rose and walked over to her.

"Now show me what you did to him."

"Do you need me for anything else, sir?" Tina asked once he'd finished and she'd caught her breath.

"Not today." Genaro stood, shrugging into a robe before he handed her another. "Go home and get some sleep."

She pulled on the robe. "Sir, may I make a suggestion?" When he nodded, she said, "Why don't you allow me to accompany Dr. Kirchner to the new facility?"

He frowned. "Why would I do that?"

"His loyalty to the company is essential to the project," she said. "If I go out with him, I can determine if he's been compromised in any way."

"I don't know." He thought again of the odd emotion in Kirchner's eyes. It had looked like . . . desperation. "Sex doesn't work on Eliot. You'll have to use other measures."

Tina smiled. "I can do that, sir."

"Jesus, he's one heavy dude," a young man's voice complained, grunting with effort.

A deeper voice, equally strained, snapped back. "He's dead, you dumbass. What'd you expect him to be, a feather?"

The dead man couldn't feel his weight or any part of his body. He seemed to be in a gray void, trapped between sunlight and shadow, drifting without substance or will. All he could hear was the two other men talking, the panting of their breath, and the sounds they made as they worked.

"Once we pick up the other one, then we hit the road, right?" the grunter asked.

"Yeah, and I'm driving." Metal squealed as something beneath the dead man moved. "Gimme those chains."

"Not like he's gonna jump out the back," the younger man said. "Okay, okay, don't get your dick in a knot." Chains clinked and slid across a flat surface.

Death had been his aim, the dead man thought as he floated up. The one thing that had gone right, that he had done right. He remembered the dog tags in his fist, and how tightly he had clutched them as the bullets had pelted him. He'd held on to them, even when the earth had exploded beneath him and he'd been blown into this place. They had been the last of his earthly possessions, proof of his final act of courage, the only thing he had wanted to take with him into oblivion. He couldn't feel them in his fist anymore, and that bothered him more than the voices.

"Where'd they find the big son of a bitch anyway?" the younger man asked. "Iraq?"

"Afghanistan." The older man paused to catch his breath. "Bought him from some poppy farmer who'd been using his corpse as a scarecrow."

"They hung his ass in a field to chase off birds?" He whistled. "Man, that's cold."

"They weren't trying to scare *crows*, moron." A match was struck. "At least they kept him on ice. I can't stand the ones that stink."

"So what are they gonna do? Chop him up like the others?" A thud sounded, and the young man yelped. "Shit, Bob, I was just curious."

"You ask too many questions, Joey."

The dead man silently agreed. He didn't want to know what was going to happen to his remains.

Coward.

The new voice made the harsh word sound soft, almost like an endearment. He tried to move away from it, but the void held him fast, now another prison from which he would never escape. He didn't want to hear her words, but they encircled him, manacles of silk and sweetness.

You have run from everything. Hiding in your battlefields and wars. Roaming the world like a fugitive. Now you would give them your life.

He hadn't given them anything. He'd made a trade so that he could find some peace. *I am already dead. I died in battle.*

No, you did not. The voice lashed at him. *You know it. Death does not provide a listening post.*

He had been so sure this time. . . . *I feel nothing.*

You will not allow yourself to feel. You are too afraid of what will happen if you do. That makes you a coward.

He had been many things because of his pride, some so reprehensible they had forever stained his soul. He knew it; she knew it. But he had never been spineless. He had fought his entire life against that indignity.

Then why are you here? she asked, her voice turning sly. *This is not your end. This is nothing but retreat. Surrender. Despair.*

"Give me the keys," Bob said, obliterating her voice from the dead man's head. "If you've gotta piss, hit the john now. And no more soda. Once we get on the road with the other one, we can't stop."

"Yeah, but what if we get pulled over?" Joey asked suddenly. "I mean, the truck says cold storage, man, not dead bodies. Trooper looks back there, sees them, we're going to jail."

"That's why I'm driving, asshole. So we *don't* get pulled over." Keys jingled and a metal door slammed into place. "Hurry up," Bob said, his voice fainter now. "We've only got an hour to get her before the shit we used wears off."

Joey muttered something indistinct that trailed off as he moved away.

Did you hear him? she asked. *You have an hour left.*

He had eternity, as far as he was concerned, but he had to make one last request. *You must let me go. I want it to end.*

She laughed. *I never held you here. Your pride, your stubbornness, they were your jailers. You might have freed yourself a thousand times if not for them.*

As you say. She had always burned him with her truth, but never as deeply as she did now. *What difference does it make?*

You will be free of them now. But only if you choose to live.

What have I to live for?

Not for me, she assured him. *For her.*

Chapter 3

The big, burly sheriff's deputy who brought Lilah home wanted to personally check inside her house, but while refusing seemed ungracious, if not a little suspicious, she turned him down. He asked again if there was someone he could call to come and stay with her.

"The guy stole my car, Deputy, not my license or my house keys," she assured him. "He got some Staind CDs, an old blue sweater, and a transmission that occasionally slips in reverse." And her only means of transportation, but she'd deal with that tomorrow.

The cop smiled a little, but he had the sharp, tired eyes of a veteran. "Was your registration in the glove box? That would have your home address on it."

"I always keep it in my purse." Along with her fake insurance card and every other piece of phony identification she possessed. "Can you tell me what happens now?"

"We'll list your car and plates on our database and alert the patrols." He handed her a business card with his name and phone number. "You can call me to check on the status, but unless he's stopped or ditches the car, we probably won't recover it. Your insurance should take care of replacing it."

It would if she actually had some. "Thank you."

"Not a problem. Keep your chin up." He touched the brim of his hat and left.

Once she had closed and locked the door, Lilah pressed her brow against it and released a long breath. This wasn't the worst day of her life, but it would do fine as runner-up. Slowly she turned around. She hadn't decorated for Christmas yet, and in the last of the sunlight from the windows, what furniture she had looked scruffier than usual. She'd tacked up a few cheap but pretty posters of landscapes on the bare walls, and made curtains from some old tablecloths she'd found at a rummage sale, but the rest of her possessions looked cheap or worn-out. Even her old Toshiba, sitting on the card table she used as a desk, appeared ready for the laptop graveyard.

Although it was risky, she always left her computer out in the front room and switched on, and checked it right before she left and again as soon as she arrived home. Vulcan had sent her an encryption program so complicated that only a genius hacker could access it, and the moment he did, the computer would release a vicious virus that would destroy the contents of its hard drive in seconds.

Now she sat down with the laptop in the dented, slightly rusted folding metal chair she'd rescued from a Dumpster, and clicked on the Internet icon, waiting patiently for her dial-up to connect her. Vulcan thought she was crazy not to install high-speed, but she actually preferred the lag. It gave her time to think, and if for any reason she needed to break the connection, she could simply yank the phone cord out of the wall jack.

No one was in the protected chat room they used, but Lilah knew as soon as she signed on, alerts would go out to the rest of the group. Sure enough, an avatar with a bubbling beaker appeared a few moments later.

Del, everything all right?

Lilah smiled sadly before she began to type. *Not really. Bad day here. One problem after another.*

Paracelsus typed in a sad face and *Anything I can do?*

She knew some of her Takyn friends were wealthy; while they kept their real-life identities and locations confidential, and never bragged about their situations, they sometimes let things slip. She knew Paracelsus collected antiques and lived part of the year somewhere on the beach. He was always the first to offer funds to anyone in the group who was in trouble. She was also fairly certain he and the others knew she wasn't rolling in it, as her most frequent request was for advice on how to fix things she couldn't afford to replace, like the laptop, her water heater, her transmission. . . .

Del? Serious problems?

She bit her lip. Losing her job and her car in one day was probably nothing more than bad luck and a lousy coincidence, but she couldn't shake off the sense of unease. And if she'd learned anything since her ability had manifested, it was to trust her instincts. *I'm not sure, but I think I need to take off for a while. Go visit some of the family.*

He knew she was, like all the Takyn, an orphan. *When are you leaving?*

The only place she could rent a car tonight was the airport, and she didn't have enough cash on her to cover the cab fare. *Tomorrow morning, first thing. I'll probably be on the road for a couple days.* Hopefully her credit card limit would hold out for as long as it took to find a new place to live.

You'll check in, let me know how you are?

They always kept tabs on one another, especially when they relocated. It wasn't a matter of friendship as much as it was survival. But as uneasy as she was, Lilah doubted anyone was coming after her now. From what Jezebel and Aphrodite had told her about GenHance, they shot first and never asked any questions. If the bastards at the biotech firm *had* discovered what she was, they would have grabbed her, not her car.

Absolutely, she typed.

Once she signed off, Lilah went to the kitchen and made a peanut butter and banana sandwich and a mug of hot chocolate, both of which she carried back into her bedroom. She switched on the Weather Channel and curled up on her bed, nibbling at the sandwich as she watched Jim Cantore offer details on a massive snowstorm moving inland from the Rockies, and the various ways in which the residents of six different states would be affected by it.

"You should tell them to move to Florida, Jim," she said to the television. "Just don't mention the hurricanes, the tornadoes, or the floods."

The ancient chenille bedspread she'd found at a church rummage sale kept her warm, and the hot drink and the food made her drowsy. Although Lilah suspected her sleepiness was more from depression and mental stress than real exhaustion, she resisted it. She still had some chores and lockup to do before she went to sleep. She didn't know why she felt so exhausted, but her body didn't even want to twitch, much less move.

She still had . . .

The dreams she had that she remembered were sometimes a little odd but never frightening; if Lilah had ever had a nightmare, she'd forgotten it the moment she woke. Mostly she dreamed of walking through different places, like through city streets and garden parks, across broad fields, and along empty roads. Wherever she went, it was always night, and she was always alone; no one else populated her dreams. She'd often wondered if it was some subconscious way of retreating from the world of people, the only creatures she really did fear.

What made the dreams seem odd was not the locations but the emotions Lilah felt as she moved through them. Once she passed the front display window of an art gallery, and stopped to examine the featured painting, a lovely and minutely detailed landscape of a vineyard with sun-gilded dark grapes. Normally it would have given her pleasure, as she preferred realistic art, and the artist had done an amazing job, almost to the point of making it look like a photograph. Yet while she stared at it, she felt a surge of uncharacteristic hatred welling up in her, and at one point felt like smashing in the glass with her fists.

Another night she walked through a school yard, and passed some swings that were swaying in the wind. She thought of ghost children, playing in the night, and began to smile at her own whimsy. A wrenching grief struck her then, so hard she almost doubled over. She ended up running away from the playground as if she couldn't bear the sight of it.

Both times the emotions went almost as quickly as they came over her, but the feeling of wrongness lingered. She had no reason to hate vineyards or kids. She enjoyed a glass of wine now and then, and while she didn't plan on having any children of her own, she thought they were one of the few universally wonderful things in life, like puppies and kittens.

Because Lilah trusted the safety of her dreams more than she did a bank vault in the real world, the rectangular cube of white walls that closed in around her didn't alarm her. She reached out to touch one of them and discovered the whiteness was not paint but hard-packed snow. When the icy crystals burned her fingers, she drew back her hand and turned around, looking for a way out.

A black wolf stood watching her, its light gray eyes steady, its muzzle pulled up around long, sharp white fangs. It didn't make a sound, but its muscles bunched under its frost-covered pelt as if it was prepared to spring.

Lilah reached out with her ability, trying to find a way in, but the wolf's eyes were as impenetrable as their prison.

"I'm not going to hurt you," she said out loud. "I'm trapped here, too."

The wolf lowered its head, sniffing at the ice beneath their feet before regarding her again, this time with slightly less aggression. It still didn't trust her, but it wasn't going to attack unless she provoked it.

Lilah slowly dropped down, crouching before the wolf so that she appeared smaller and less threatening, and held out the back of her hand in silent invitation.

The wolf moved then, circling to her right, showing off the lean, strong body of a male in his prime. As he moved behind her, it took all her nerve not to glance back. She could feel the heat of his breath on her neck, the brush of his icy fur against the thin fabric of her nightshirt. Then he moved in front of her, his cold nose first sniffing and then nudging her extended hand.

She turned it palm up, moving her fingertips through the rough silk of his fur. Although he was caked in frost, he felt deliciously warm, and smelled of woodsmoke and cedar. The rare privilege of being able to touch such a creature gave her so much pleasure she almost purred with it.

Finally the light gray eyes lifted to her face, and Lilah tried again to reach into his mind, but this time something pushed her back and then kept coming, passing through her eyes and reaching into her own mind, as if the wolf was doing the same to her.

The presence became a dense shadow, blocking out

her senses to everything but the wolf's eyes. *Who are you?*

Hearing speech-thought from an animal shocked and delighted her into replying with the same. *Lilah. My name is Lilah.*

I am Guide.

Guide. She knew animals didn't think of themselves or others as named creatures; even dogs responded to names only as a command word they were accustomed to. *What are we doing here, Guide?*

You came here. You are like me.

I'm dreaming of this place, she told him. *It's not real. Are you asleep somewhere?*

Asleep. He seemed to struggle with the word. *No. I do not sleep. I am injured. Captured.*

She hadn't seen any wounds on his body, and had no sense of pain, but she could feel his emotions. Like a human, Guide felt bewildered and vulnerable, unable to understand what was happening to him. But beneath that confusion was something much darker, a vast and snarling rage, unlike anything she'd ever felt from another living thing. It roiled in him, twisting in the cage of his control, struggling to free itself. If it did, Lilah sensed, he would attack anything that moved, even her.

It's all right. She tried to soothe him with her hands, stroking his bristling ruff. *Can you wake from this sleep? Can you get away and hide until you heal?*

I am trapped here. Guide lifted his head. *There were others. Men. They chained me. They did things to me. But not enough. Not nearly enough.*

What things?

They put things in me. Changed me from what I was. I have lost myself.

He had wanted to die, and Lilah couldn't blame him. To be captured and experimented on was the worst fate for anything born in the wild. *If you're alive, you still have a chance to get away.*

What is there to live for?

She looked around, suddenly understanding why she was dreaming of this frigid, featureless box. This must be how the wolf saw his cage—somehow Guide was projecting his subconscious view into her mind. *You know there is more to the world than this.*

Once there was.

The walls of snow melted away, and Lilah found herself standing on a cliff overlooking the sea.

She didn't recognize the place, although it stirred something inside her, something she didn't want to think about now. *Is this your home?*

It is where I was before . . . His thoughts dissolved into a wordless tangle of anger and regret.

She knelt down beside him, curling an arm around his neck. *Is there another place you can show me?*

The cliffs darkened and rose even higher, stretching up toward the sky. At the same time the rock they stood on dropped, flattening and spreading into a flower-speckled meadow. Although it was night, and the meadow appeared deserted except for some fireflies, Lilah felt another presence, one that remained out of sight while it watched them.

She stood and turned around, and while she saw nothing familiar, she had a definite sense of déjà vu. *I think I know this place.* She glanced down at the wolf. *Where are we?*

I have no name for it. Guide lifted his head and sniffed the air. *There were others here. Outcasts like me. They gathered here to be safe. But they would not let me come near them.*

He was lucky that he hadn't been killed. Pack animals like wolves rarely welcomed rogues into their territory. *Maybe you were meant to gather your own pack.*

He stiffened, and the mountain valley shrank in on them and became the snow cage. *They have come for you.*

Me? The abrupt transition made her a little dizzy, and she sat down on the floor beside him. *Why?*

I am not all they want. Guide nuzzled her hair. *They come for you. You must wake now. You must escape before they take you.*

In her mind Lilah saw through his eyes again, this time through an open rectangle of dark space. She glimpsed the back door of a house, and the two figures standing outside it. The smaller of the two was fiddling with the lock while the other whispered to him. The bigger one was holding what looked like a shaving-kit case and a large black plastic garbage bag. The stock of a handgun protruded from his waistband.

Lilah watched as the big man unzipped and opened the case, revealing a syringe and a bottle of clear liquid. *This isn't happening. This is a dream.*

I am not dreaming, the wolf told her. *But I cannot move yet. I am too weak. I cannot stop them.* He nudged her urgently. *Lilah. If you do not wake now, they will have you. Hurry.*

Lilah tried to wake then, the terror of what was happening only too real, but she couldn't escape the wolf's prison. The taste of the hot chocolate she'd drunk came back to her, sweet but chalky, and the way she'd fallen asleep in the middle of the day. They must have been watching her, long enough to learn her routine, to guess she would make herself a cup of hot chocolate when she came home as she always did. The gun was for if she hadn't.

I can't wake up, she told the wolf. *I've been drugged.*

The image of what he was seeing vanished from her mind, as if he'd closed his eyes. *Then we are both lost.*

She refused to believe that. *We're alive, and we'll be together.*

Here, where there is nothing. Guide seemed bitter. *Where we will die.*

We're not alone anymore, she assured him. *We have each other.*

You are human. His gray eyes glittered. *I am not.*

She nodded. *But I'm not all human. I'm like you. I've been changed.* Something stung her neck, and she flinched as burning sensations spread through her upper torso, turning her heart into a lead weight.

The wolf knew what had happened. *I will kill them for this.*

Don't kill anyone for me, she thought, her mind fogging. *Survive.*

Dimly Lilah felt her body sag and go limp, and then the wolf was on top of her. She wasn't alarmed by it; the weight and warmth of his body felt protective, comforting. The last thing she felt was a cold length of metal sliding over her wrist, and the whine of the wolf as he buried his muzzle in her hair.

She was barely breathing when they dropped her body next to his. He smelled the chemical odor of the sedative on her shallow breaths, and felt the laxness of her muscles where they pressed against his side. If he had been able to move, he would have lunged at the men and torn them apart, but unlike his mind his body remained dead. He couldn't even open his eyes to look at her.

But he could smell her, and feel her on his skin. Her heart still beat, and his body, it seemed, was not entirely dead.

"Shit, Bob, check out the rack on this bitch." Joey was close, bending over them, his hands busy. Cloth tore. "Look. They're real, too."

"Quit screwing with her and get the goddamn cuffs," the older man snapped. "We need to get the fuck outta here."

"Yeah, yeah." The younger man moved away, and then returned. Metal clicked. "What do I cuff her to?"

"Him. He's not going anywhere."

The clicking sound repeated, and he felt something hard and tight encircle his wrist. It had been so long since any of his senses had worked that he hardly knew what to think.

"She'll probably freeze solid before we get across the state lines," Joey said, his regret plain. "Won't be able to fuck her unless I put a woolly on my woody."

A match was struck, and he smelled cigarette smoke.

"Guess it's better she goes this way, huh?" Joey sucked in and blew out. "Pete told me what they do to them. Wouldn't want to be alive and awake for that shit they're gonna do to her. Do they really cut them up into pieces first?"

"Pete's got no business telling you anything," Bob said. "You keep running your mouth way you do, *you'll* end up in the back of one of these trucks. Gimme that tarp over there." Canvas stretched out over him and the woman. "Tuck in those sides. Hurry up. All right, that's good enough. Come on, we gotta hit the road."

The men climbed out of the truck and slammed the rolling door down, securing it with a lock from the outside. As soon as they were gone, he tried desperately to move but found he could only twitch his hand.

He concentrated, pouring every ounce of strength he had left into his arm, and slowly his hand flattened against the floor of the truck. He pushed against it, and his body shifted a fraction of an inch. He tried again, moving another inch, and then again. The truck jerked into gear, and a quick turn made his body slide against the woman. He used the momentum to fling his left arm over her.

The woman's soft, bare breasts moved beneath his arm as she took a breath into her chest and released it.

He felt the throbbing ache in his arm and hand with no small amount of pleasure. Movement and pain promised only more of the same, but he welcomed them. He was alive, and his body was slowly awakening.

As soon as he came fully back to his senses, he would free himself. And the two men who had put their hands on her would die. Slowly. Painfully.

Chapter 4

He allowed the heat of fury to burn through him before he beat it back. He could not give in to his murderous impulses, not when he was still as helpless as a newborn. They subsided, but the heat remained, and only after several moments did he realize it was coming from the body of the woman. She was warming his cold form, her skin almost hot against his—and it was growing hotter.

The back of the truck was refrigerated; a vented unit above them poured out a continuous stream of frosty air. They had kept the interior temperature so low that ice had formed on every surface. Naked as she was, the woman should have been losing body heat, not radiating it like a living furnace. The canvas the men had pulled over them was stiff from the cold, but it also seemed to be insulating them against the frigid air inside the truck. It trapped the heat she was generating, forming a cocoon of growing warmth around both of them.

Was she feverish? The drugs they had given her might be responsible, or perhaps she had been ill before the men had found her. He pressed his wrist against the smooth skin of her arm where they were cuffed together until he could feel her heartbeat. Like her breathing, it was slow but strong. Her skin felt soft, not tight, and along all the places where their skin touched, he felt dampness forming.

A woman with fever did not sweat, at least not until after the fever broke.

He tried to lift his arm but succeeded only in shifting his forearm a few inches. His hand opened against her shoulder, fingers curling over the gentle curve. She made a sound, and he forced his eyelids to open a sliver.

The truck's interior was not completely dark; some murky light from a source above them filtered through the canvas. At first it hurt to see again, his eyes burning like the blaze of red in front of him. Then he saw that it was the woman's hair, as vibrant and alive as a roaring fire.

This close he could pick out the different colors of each strand: gold, amber, copper, crimson, garnet. The length of it was straight and thick, tumbling down to disappear under her shoulder. In the sunlight the bountiful stuff must have made her head look as if it blazed.

His gaze shifted to what he could see of her face. Alabaster skin showed the tracings of deep blue where the veins scrolled at her temple; a tiny dark brown mole tried to hide in the burnished copper fringe of her lower lashes. She had wide brows and a short, straight nose; another, smaller mole sat on the cusp beneath it, almost on the edge of her upper lip. Her mouth was a lush, decadent flower blooming, her lips the color of a jeweled pomegranate.

His arm blocked his view of her body, but from what he had felt under him, she was young and healthy, her curves full and ripe. He had grown so accustomed to the starved-waif standards of beauty that being so close to such fertile lushness was like finding an orchard in the middle of the desert.

He gripped her shoulder as pain struck him again, this time from his legs, which trembled as the nerves and muscles began to twitch. Whatever they had used on him had been intended to keep him locked inside himself, and from what he had heard them say, the effect was supposed to last for as long as they kept him cold. Being warmed by the woman's body heat must be neutralizing the drugs.

No, it is more than that. He had not cared to come back to himself before; he had been patiently waiting for the final release. He had already given himself to Death in his heart, or they would never have been able to capture him.

Now he was dragged back to life by this woman and his need to protect her, and a part of him resented being denied oblivion again. Survival held no attraction; he was done with the business of living. Until he had gone to war for the last time, his existence had been a void, a series of empty streets and fields and pathways he had wandered, aimless and cold, a caricature of the man he had been. Not all of his dignity had been stripped from him, and in the end it had sent him overseas, into battle, determined to die as he had never been permitted to live. His last purpose, to fight the enemy and protect those who did not have his talent for killing.

She needs me now.

The men had come to Florida to take the woman; from their conversations he knew they were driving from here to Colorado. He didn't know the roads in this part of the country, but he guessed the journey would require two, perhaps three days. As long as he kept the woman warm, she might live, and at the rate his body was recovering, in another day he could regain enough mobility and strength to attempt an escape. He had no doubt he could elude the two fools abducting them; the real question was the woman and what state she would be in when she regained consciousness.

He couldn't see what bound them together, but as

needling spread up from his right arm, he felt the cold metal of the cuff the younger man had snapped around his wrist. The cuffs added another problem: Until he found the means with which to remove them, everything he did would be with her at his side, open and vulnerable to attack.

However much the men who had taken them deserved to die, he doubted she would stand by and do nothing while he slaughtered them. That narrowed his options to convincing her to help him escape.

By now the cold had retreated from his skin, leaving in its wake fresh pain as the last of his senses came to life. He clenched his jaw as his flesh crawled and stung; it felt as if he had been caught in a swarm of bees. He focused on her face, taking refuge in the slumbering, peaceful beauty there. Her lids and lashes kept him from seeing her eyes, but whatever color they were, he suspected they would be as fetching as her fiery hair, her sumptuous shape, and the generous warmth of her body.

A new sensation crept over him, one that moved under his skin and sank in, curling like a fist in his gut. That he wanted her came as no surprise to him; a man would truly have to be dead to lie beside her and feel nothing.

What shook him was the desire itself. He had not felt it in so long he had forgotten how primitive and powerful it was, how urgently it seized him in its grip. Left unsatisfied by his physical inability to serve its need, the new hunger rose into his head, battering through his defenses and engulfing him.

So relentless was the wanting that he began imagining how it would be with her, her softness under him, her eyes open, her pretty mouth smiling. He wanted to look into those eyes, to take sanctuary in her body. He would hold her to him as he forged into her, and hear her say his name as she clutched at him, his possession, his woman—

She is helpless.

His left hand convulsed, shaking as it moved to her face. He could feel the silky brush of her mouth across his palm, the whisper of her breath through his fingers.

It felt like the promise of a kiss. It sounded like a sigh of sadness.

He inched his hand down until it left her face and rested across her throat. Her pulse beat under his fingers, still sluggish but growing stronger and steadier. In a few hours she would awaken and find herself naked and bound to him, and undoubtedly that would horrify her. She would need to be calmed and told what had happened. She would depend on him to free her, to defend and watch over her, not add to her terror. And if he failed her . . .

I will snap her neck myself before I see her raped and tortured.

The thought of being forced to kill her in order to spare her suffering sickened him. He had fought in more battles than he could remember; he had made the very world his enemy, but only in this moment did he realize that he had never taken the life of a woman. He had used them occasionally for sex, discarding them as quickly as he had seduced them, but the majority of the time he simply didn't notice them. Women had never meant anything to him.

Why was this one different? What had she done to make him feel such emotions for her? They had never spoken or seen each other; he would have remembered such delicate white skin and the fiery loveliness of her hair. She was a stranger, trapped by chance in the same ungodly situation as he, and yet somehow he knew her. She had awakened a deep, slumbering part of him that seemed to recognize her, and now all he could think of was seeing the color of her eyes, and hearing her voice, and knowing her name. He wanted to tell her every-thing, all of it, every last detail of his life: the heartbreak and the betrayals, the endless years of solitude and lone-liness, the misery of chasing death only to be cheated of it over and over.

He couldn't do any of that, of course. To her he was nothing but a stranger. She didn't know him. She wouldn't care.

He understood the price. Once they escaped and reached safety, he would have to leave her. He would put her in the custody of the police, or arrange to reunite her with her family. To walk away from her would fin-ish him, he suspected, but to stay would be the greater madness.

Whatever it took, he would protect her, even from himself.

Ethan Jemmet rolled over the sag in the mattress, his hand expecting to land someplace it would want to stay. Instead he caught a tangle of damp sheets over a slighter hollow, and opened his eyes to the empty side of the bed.

He sat up, naked and pissed. The briefcase on the floor, the high-heeled shoes on the nightstand, and the white coat crumpled by the base of the lamp were gone.

So was every other trace of the woman he'd stopped last night on the road.

His father had arranged this trip and then bullied Ethan into making it, just as he did every other time he forced him to leave Frenchman's Pass.

"I don't need to go to some cop conference." Ethan had shoved the online registration paper back across the breakfast table. "I know how to do my job."

"You haven't left the pass since January, when that snowplow driver called for help." Paul Jemmet calmly dissected his pepper-speckled fried egg, neatly excising the yolk without breaking it. "A trip to the city will be good for you."

It would be torture, and they both knew it. Ethan hated everything about Denver: the traffic, the crowded sidewalks, the packed restaurants. All the weekend skiers and holiday travelers would be flooding into the hotels, so the conference wouldn't be just law enforcement—it would be a tangle of slope bunnies, board boys, and reuniting families. If there was anything he hated more than the city, it was tourists.

"The weather's been too unpredictable this year," Ethan added. "The first big snow is due in any minute."

Paul dipped a corner of one toast triangle into a tiny puncture he made in the yolk. "The forecast is clear and cold through next week."

"Dad."

Paul set down his toast and regarded him steadily: "Ethan, we've discussed this. As much as we want to keep the pass to ourselves, some of us have to maintain connections with the outside world. Now more than ever."

Ethan eyed him. "Someone else decide to move on?"

His father obviously didn't want to tell him, but after a brief silence he finally said, "The Johnsons left day before yesterday. Ben said they left everything behind, even their personal belongings. He asked Nathan—"

Ethan dropped his fork with a clatter and stood. "I'm sure he'll find them and talk them into giving life in town another try." He strode toward the door.

"Son."

He couldn't walk out on his father, not when he used that tone. "I don't want to talk about Nate."

"I'm sure you don't. Come back here." Paul waited for him to return and sit down before he added, "Ethan, as the young people say, it is what it is. There is only so much I can do, and even that is limited. When we lost the Maynards and the Tisdales last winter, our population dropped below two hundred. The town is dwindling away."

As it had been since Ethan could remember. "I can't walk around a hotel asking cops if they'd like to relocate their families up to the mountains, Dad. Especially since I know what you want from them."

"You could leave some property listings with a few Realtors," Paul said. "I've prepared a CD with descriptions and photos of all the unoccupied properties. We're going to sell them to outsiders."

This was news to Ethan. "But the town—"

"Has already approved it. Unanimously." His father offered an encouraging smile. "When you give the listings to the Realtors, you can let them know how great life is here for new residents. How friendly and welcoming our community is, especially toward single people."

"Friendly. Welcoming." Ethan folded his arms. "You really want me to say that with a straight face."

"If the town is going to survive," Paul warned, "we must bring in new residents."

Frenchman's Pass had always tolerated the occasional intrusion of an outsider, but now his father was proposing they actively recruit them. "Have you forgotten that new residents like to do things like hiking and getting in touch with nature and exploring the beauty of the mountains? How do you think they're going to react when they run into Nate and his crew? Assuming they don't first fall off a cliff or wander into one of the caves?"

"I will deal with your brother." Paul went back to eating. "The CDs are on your dresser, along with a list of the Realtors I've e-mailed. Be sure to see all of them before you leave the city."

Now Ethan got up and went to the window of the

motel room, looking through the frost whorls at the gold-edged purple sky. The sun would rise above the ranges in half an hour to outshine the stars, polish the ice-coated trees to a glassy gleam, and turn the leftover night drifts into mounds of white diamonds.

To be fair, she'd warned him she would go, just before everything had dissolved into deep, endless kisses and his hands tearing at her buttons and zippers: *I can't stay long. I have to beat the storm.*

He'd heard her, and ignored it, and when they'd made it to the bed, he'd stopped thinking altogether. He'd feasted on her, gorging himself for what he knew would be a long, empty winter, reveling in her until the night itself blurred into one long series of tangling limbs, caressing hands, and thrusting hips.

He should have arrested her, Ethan thought, his mood growing sullen as he jerked on his uniform. Her story about forgetting her license and borrowing that car from a friend had been just too damn convenient. But he'd been out of his jurisdiction and out of patience with most of the world, and she'd looked like the girl next door, right down to the fourteen freckles on her nose and the white pearl barrette holding a swatch of dark curls back from her face. Her sweet blue eyes and steady smile had tugged at him, almost pleading for forgiveness.

And he'd fallen for it, escorting her back to her motel and even accepting her offer of a cup of coffee at the next-door diner. It was at the booth in the back they'd shared when things had gone from officer and driver to man and woman.

When things had gotten out of hand entirely.

She must have sensed his interest, but she'd been too smart to try to play him. Instead she'd spoken of ordinary things: her favorite Italian restaurant back home, and the handmade pasta she'd gone there to have every Friday after work. She'd claimed she was simply a corporate secretary, a single working woman going home to spend Christmas with her sister, but Ethan caught a glimmer of something more in her voice. She wasn't traveling or vacationing; she was running. He'd figured it was from a boyfriend or husband.

He'd figured wrong.

Ethan couldn't quite recall the moment when the friendly cup of coffee had turned into serious, startling sexual attraction. She'd been listening to his description of the law enforcement conference he'd attended in Denver, and reached for the little pitcher of half-and-half at the same time he did. Their fingers had collided, almost knocking it over. Her innocent eyes had gone dark, and he'd heard her quick breath. His own heart pounded in his head.

Rather than jumping across the table, Ethan had pushed the pitcher aside to take her hand and hold on to the sensation that had clouted him as hard as a heavyweight's fist.

He felt disgusted now as he recalled how he'd barely been able to speak. "You feel that?"

She didn't want to; that was plain from the edge of her teeth worrying at her full bottom lip. Instead of telling him to forget it, she said, "I can't stay long. I have to beat the storm."

Ethan had been fully prepared to beg, but she was telling him he wouldn't have to. He turned his head to catch the attention of the waitress behind the counter. "Ma'am, check, please."

He held on to her hand, coming around the table and leading her up with him to the register. He'd used his free hand to fasten the front of her white winter coat, and pull the hood up over her dark brown curls. Then he'd walked with her to the motel, to the door of the room she had rented, and waited there as she looked up at him, unable to speak, unable to decide.

Ethan knew it couldn't happen. Not here, not with her. But he wanted it, more than anything in recent memory. Maybe in his life. *One night*, he kept thinking. *Just one night.*

"Sheriff." She sounded a little rattled. "Thank you for the coffee."

He'd reached into her coat pocket and found the room key. "Tell me good night," he suggested through his teeth as he shoved it into the lock. "Hurry."

Something shifted in her eyes before she smiled and demolished him with four words. "I don't want to."

He pushed the door open. "Then invite me in, baby."

Ethan cleared his head, jamming on his hat before scooping up the room key where she'd left it by the phone. She'd rented the room; the night manager would have her particulars. He headed toward the motel office.

"Sure, Sheriff, I remember her," the bearded college student said a few minutes later as he sorted through the guest information cards. "Nice lady. I think her last name was Anderson. No, here it is." He pulled out the card and peered at the scribbled handwriting. "Her name is Anishon. J. Anishon."

Ethan plucked the card from the kid's fingers and skimmed it. "Aniston. Damn it." He dropped the card on the counter. "Did she show you any ID? You make copies?"

"She paid cash, and she looked over eighteen. I'm only supposed to get ID on people who use charge cards." The boy frowned. "Aniston. That sounds familiar. Wait, isn't that the name of the one who was married to Brad Pitt? Before Angelina, I mean?"

"Jennifer Aniston."

"Yeah, that's her." The kid's grin lasted only three

seconds. "Oh, man. Sorry, Sheriff. I'm so used to people using 'Smith' or 'Jones' that I don't pay any attention to the normal-looking names."

Which she had probably been counting on. Ethan checked the card again and memorized the plate number before stalking out of the office and heading for his Escalade. Once inside, he booted up his dashboard monitor, typed in the license number, and sent it to CDOT. The state licensing agency sent back a registration for a UPS truck in Boulder, and a stolen-plate report filed by the fleet manager yesterday.

Ethan didn't know why she'd swapped out her plates and used a fake name at the motel, but he was going to find out. He typed up a request for every police and sheriff's office in the region to be on the lookout for J. Aniston and her car, with a notation that she was to be immediately detained and held for questioning on suspicion of grand theft auto. Just before he hit the send button, he glanced at the door to the room he had shared with her.

She had told him a little about herself last night. She'd been sprawled on top of him, her head tucked under his chin, her breasts rubbing against him as she tried to catch her breath. He'd been stroking her spine with lazy fingers and wondering if there was enough room for both of them in the room's shower. He was about to ask her to try it anyway when he realized something.

"Hey." He waited until she looked up at him. "You never told me your name, sweetheart."

"How rude of me." She propped herself up and kissed his chin. "I'm Lori. What do I call you, besides amazing, incredible, and a godsend?"

He chuckled. "Ethan. So, you have family around here?"

"Just my sister."

He felt her shoulders tense. "You two close?"

"We haven't been, but I'm trying to change that." She traced the outline of his lips. "How about you? Any brothers or sisters?"

"A brother I don't talk to, and I'm not changing that." He rolled her over onto her back and slid between her legs. "How about you and I get a little closer?"

Lori might be a liar and a car thief, but she'd been the best lover he'd ever had. While he slept, she also hadn't touched the credit cards in his wallet or helped herself to his gun, his Escalade, or his briefcase and the four hundred dollars in cash he kept stashed in it.

Slowly, cursing himself as he did it, Ethan reached out and erased the BOL he'd typed up on his one-night stand. *Bye, baby.*

He stopped to have breakfast at the diner, and sat in the same booth he'd shared with her last night. He could still smell her, although her scent was not coming from the vinyl cushions of the booth. It was all over him. He should have showered before he'd dressed; now he'd be smelling her the whole way back to Frenchman's Pass.

As Ethan paid his check, he couldn't help asking if Lori had stopped in before hitting the road. The bleary-eyed waitress, just coming off her double shift, nodded as she gave him his change.

"Came in around five, I think. Had a cup of tea and a muffin to go." She slid the cash drawer shut. "I asked her if she was all right—she looked upset—but she said she was just a little tired."

Against his better judgment Ethan drew a business card from his jacket and handed it to the waitress. "You see her again, would you give her this?"

She read the card. "You're a ways from home, Sheriff Jemmet."

He pocketed his wallet. "Heading back now."

She nodded and pinned the card up on the small cork-board next to the register. She turned back, clearly hesitant, and then said, "With you looking for her, maybe I ought to give you this." She reached under the counter and brought up a square plastic basket filled with odds and ends. From it she took a short strand of silver-linked miniatures.

"Where did you find this?"

"She dropped it on her way out. Looks like the clasp broke. By the time I saw it over there"—the waitress pointed to a spot near the entrance—"she was already gone."

Lori had taken off something from her wrist and dropped it on the nightstand. He vaguely remembered seeing a glint of silver.

"When she comes back looking for this," he told the waitress, "you give her my card and tell her to call me."

Ethan didn't examine the charm bracelet until he was back in the Escalade. It was an expensive, custom-designed piece made of pure silver and stamped in three places with maker marks, which would help him when he tracked down who had made it. From the fine, twisted links hung seven exquisite charms: a rosebud, a star, a crescent moon, a quill, a book, a crystal ball, and a cameo. Diamond chips accented five of the charms; the crystal ball had been fashioned from a dark blue moonstone.

The cameo, an oval of onyx set with a circle of rubies, had an ivory carving of a man's face in profile. He turned over the minuscule portrait and saw three words engraved in fancy script.

Essere Libero Valori.

"Italian." Ethan didn't speak the language, so he couldn't translate the phrase, but he could Google it later. It was the last word that fascinated him: *Valori.* "Valori. Lori." He repeated the name, drawing out the syllables until he realized what the English version might be. "Valerie."

He tucked the bracelet into his breast pocket, feeling a little smug now. He knew women and their trinkets, and something this personal and expensive had to be dear to her. Aside from her cheap watch, it had been the only jewelry she had worn. Whoever Lori/Valori/Valerie was, whatever she was running from, she'd be back for her bracelet. When she called him, he'd make the trip down the mountain one more time.

And then, Ethan decided, he'd slap the cuffs on her and take her back with him.

Chapter 5

A jolt brought Lilah out of the darkness and somewhat awake; she felt so sleepy she almost slipped
back at once. Something held down her chest and legs,
the weight of a heavy arm, a leg. Someone was beside
her, in her bed. Then she felt the hard, cold surface under her and wondered how she'd ended up on the floor.

Opening her eyes took a very long time, and when
she did pry her lids apart, they felt gummy, as if they'd
been sealed with defective glue. Blinking to clear her
blurred vision, she began to register other things. A blue
tarp over her, covering her from head to toe. Something
metal around her right wrist. The sense of being exposed
came from her body; she was naked. Her right arm had
gone numb, but not enough to miss the sensation of a
long stretch of warm skin over hard muscle.

A body.

She squinted in the dimness, trying to see who it was,
where she was. Short, black bristles of hair no more than
a quarter inch long covered a scalp, curved over an ear.
She shifted her gaze down, and saw part of a cheekbone,
the tapered end of a wide black brow, the jut of a hard
jaw.

A man was right next to her. A strange, unconscious
man.

A *naked* man.

Lilah swallowed against her dry throat, her head swimming with sensory overload. "Help." It came out like a cough, short and wheezing. She tried again. "Help. Me."

The head next to her face turned slowly, exposing more of his face. He opened his eye slowly, only partway, and stared at her. From the one she could see, he had dark eyes, framed by lashes beaded with drops of water. Sweat streaked his skin and collected in little pools by the bridge of his nose and the corner of his mouth. He tried to pull back, only to go still. A muscle throbbed in his cheek as his jaw shifted.

"Drugged," he breathed out, his voice more air than sound. "Taken."

"Me?" She watched his head move in a small nod. "You?" Another nod. "No. Please, no."

The man didn't say anything, but she felt something move against her neck. His fingers, stiff and clumsy. His was the arm draped across her, and he was using it to try to reassure her.

Lilah didn't dare close her eyes again. "Where? Who?"

"Truck." The lines beside his mouth deepened as he tried again to move, and managed to slide a little of his weight over her right arm. "Men. Two."

Lilah went still, listening. Now she felt the motion of the truck beneath them, heard the hum of the engine. The truck traveled at a steady speed, but she didn't hear any signs that there were men around them. She couldn't try to move until she knew for sure.

She gazed at the man beside her and swallowed against the dryness until it receded. "Are they Gen-Hance?" He nodded again, confirming her worst fears. "Where are the men?"

He shifted his eyes up toward the sound of the engine. Lilah felt his rigid body tremble, and saw pain in his eyes before he shut them tightly. He was in worse shape than she was, perhaps having some reaction to the drugs he'd been given. She moved the lead weight of her left arm, forcing it up until she felt the back of his arm under her hand, and held on as he shook.

"Easy," she said, over and over.

Gradually his convulsive movements slowed and then stopped, and he released a breath against her cheek. A moment later his left hand moved from her neck, his fingers sliding up until he cupped her cheek.

He opened his eyes, blinking away sweat that was now pouring down his face from his hairline. "Must. Escape."

Her heart constricted. "You're too sick."

Now he moved his head from side to side. "Better. Stronger. Soon."

Lilah understood the string of words. He wasn't convulsing, he was fighting the drugs—or they were wearing off. She watched him as he rested, although like her he kept his eyes open and on her face. She tested her limbs, grimacing as her right arm began to wake with a wave of pins and needles. She managed to lift it, startled by how heavy it was, and then she saw the reason why as her flexing fingers touched the backs of his.

"They handcuffed us together."

He nodded slowly.

"Jackasses." She tried to hold his hand for a moment, but they were knuckle to knuckle, so she could only rub the backs of her fingers against his. He had huge hands. "My name is Lilah." She glanced down at his neck, where the only thing he wore, a length of chain with two metal tags, lay against his skin. She could read one of them. "Walker Kimball." She looked into his eyes. "You're a marine."

Walker's expression turned curiously impassive, as if he was waiting for some negative reaction. From the beginning the war had never been popular, but Lilah knew the troops who were sent over to fight in the Middle East were never consulted as to whether they thought it was worthwhile or not. They were sent there to fight, many of them to die, in a conflict that probably made as little sense to them as it did the rest of the world.

The other tag was an enameled navy blue football helmet with the icon of a white horse with an orange mane. "Looks like you're a Denver Broncos fan, too." Lilah smiled. "Were you coming home on leave?"

"No. War." He struggled to get the next word out. "Afghanistan."

"They took you from Afghanistan? From the fighting over there?" He nodded, and Lilah felt sick. "How?"

"Wounded. Alone." And then he said one last word that chilled her to the bottom of her heart. "Sold."

Aphrodite and her other Takyn friends had told Lilah about GenHance's plans to harvest their DNA and use it to create a superhuman vaccine, one they intended to sell to factions and governments for use on their covert operatives and soldiers. Walker must have been purchased for use as a test subject; who better to experiment on than a real soldier who had been left for dead? No one would ever know what had really happened to him. The military would simply list him as one of the missing in action.

"We have to get out of here," she told him, gripping his arm with her free hand. "How much do you weigh?" She'd drag him out if she had to.

"Too much. Rest." Walker moved his hand to stroke his palm over her hair. "Soon." He gave her a small, grim smile before he repeated, "Soon."

Until that moment the enormity of the situation hadn't actually registered, but the gentle touch of his hand brought it home. He was hurt; she was helpless. They were probably going to die, and not quickly or cleanly. Lilah clenched her teeth, fighting back a sob.

"Don't cry."

Walker had shifted his head so that his lips brushed the edge of her ear, the words breathed without voice. If she had woken up alone, Lilah realized, she would have called out loud for help until the men had stopped and come for her. They'd already stripped her out of her clothes and done God only knew what to her while she was unconscious. She didn't want to think of what they'd want to do to her if they'd found her awake.

His hand was moving again, brushing over the hair at her temple, not as awkward now. She had never understood exactly what it meant to be trapped, to be powerless in the face of indifference and cruelty. The men who had drugged and abducted and stripped her had no mercy. Her feelings, her needs, didn't matter. They had denied her even the most basic decency.

It had to be worse for Walker. Left for dead while serving his country, alone and suffering, perhaps making his peace with the brevity of his life, only to have his body stolen and sold like a piece of meat . . . it was too much.

"Lilah."

She hadn't realized that she was silently weeping until she opened her eyes and looked through the shimmer of her tears. They softened his stern features, and for the first time she realized how handsome he was, like some dark angel, the light in his eyes glowing in two slivers, as if reflecting some divine flaming sword.

"Sorry." She gulped back another sob, aware that she had to guard against making any sound that might be overheard by the men driving the truck again. "Where are they taking us?"

"Denver."

She had no way to tell where they were now. Once, she'd driven straight from Lake Gem to Tupelo, Mississippi, and that had taken her twelve hours with two short rest stops. Since drugs rarely affected her as they did normal people, she guessed she had been unconscious for six, maybe eight hours. That put them in the center of Alabama. With roughly fifteen hundred miles between them and Denver, they had maybe twenty-four hours left.

In another hour or two, Lilah felt sure, the drugs would wear off completely, and she'd be able to attempt an escape. Walker wasn't Takyn like her, however, so he would need more time to recover. She might be able to free herself from the cuffs, but abandoning him was not an option. Everything depended on how fast he could shake off the drugs they'd used on him.

"Soon," he murmured, as if he were reading her mind.

He flexed his fingers against hers, and she bent her arm, bringing up their bound hands between them so she could see the cuffs. They had been cinched too tight to work off. She still felt so weak she couldn't hold their hands up longer than a minute before her muscles began to tremble.

"I'm afraid," she whispered to him.

"I know." He shifted his arm down so that he held her waist in a half embrace. "We will escape."

He could barely move, and she was still so listless she could barely think straight. "How?"

"Together."

A medieval Italian villa on an uninhabited, windswept island off the coast of Scotland should have seemed at the very least incongruous; instead it nestled like a crown jewel at the base of a treeless cliff. As the two visitors approached, the ornate marble casements and hand-glazed tile work did seem to collectively sniff over being transplanted to such wild surroundings.

Guards emerged from the gated entrance, both armed with automatic weapons, and searched the couple with brisk competence before instructing them to wait. One remained behind to watch them as the other placed a call to the main house.

"Nice place," Nicola Jefferson said as she studied the scrolled, white-painted iron gates between them and the villa. The wind coming off the sea tugged at her long ponytail of white curls. "Who did he steal it from? A pope?"

"I believe it was a gift from a grateful subject." Gabriel Seran, her companion and lover, smiled a little, his green eyes glowing with affection as he ignored the villa and kept his gaze on her face. "You are nervous."

"No, I'm not." Nick shoved her hands in the back pockets of her jeans. "Just remind me never to volunteer to be his Secret Santa."

The second guard returned, murmuring something in archaic French to Gabriel before opening the gates and escorting them to the villa's front entry, where they were met by a much bigger man.

"Welcome to *Ì Àrd*, Miss Jefferson." The blond giant bowed, but Nick noticed he never took his hand from the hilt of his sword. He turned to Gabriel and repeated the bow. "Lord Seran. I hope your crossing was without incident. He expected you to arrive yesterday."

"Richard often expects rather more than can be reasonably accomplished with such short notice." Gabriel's expression remained impassive. "Why did he summon us, Korvel?"

"My lord will explain the matter. This way, please."

The captain led them through the front of the house to a long row of stained-glass doors depicting a series of kings on thrones.

"*Ì Àrd*," Nick muttered. "What's that mean? 'I not soft'?"

"It's Gaelic," Gabriel told her. "It means 'high island.'"

Korvel escorted them through the center pair of doors out into a courtyard garden filled with broad rose-bushes and jasmine-laden trellises.

"My lord," the captain said. "Lord Seran and his *syg-kenis* have arrived."

A dark figure appeared. "Leave us, Korvel."

The captain withdrew, and Nick glanced around. The fragrance of the thousands of blooming flowers colored the air, but didn't quite mask a deeper, darker scent radiating from the cloaked man who came to stand beside the center fountain.

The last time Nick had met Richard Tremayne, high lord of the immortal Darkyn, his scent had been almost identical to that of cherry tobacco. That had been almost a year ago, under less than ideal circumstances that had changed her life forever, and (although she would never admit it) for the better. Now the most powerful immortal on the planet gave off a headier, sweeter scent, she thought, more like chocolate-covered cherries.

Nick approved of the change, but she didn't let her guard down. Richard could be as unpredictable as he was dangerous, and the only time he wasn't actively scheming was when he was unconscious.

The hood of the high lord's cloak kept his face in shadow as he turned toward them, but Nick could see the gleam of his dark eyes as he inspected Gabriel and then her.

"My lord." Gabriel bowed. "You sent for us?"

"Four days past I sent for you." Richard's voice, which he could use like a weapon on both humans and immortals, crackled with displeasure. "What kept you from attending me?"

"Oh, the usual," Nick answered before her lover could reply. "Smuggling people across borders, dodging their killers, and trying not to get our asses fried in the process. You know." She showed him her teeth. "Our little hobby."

"You could not have left her in Aberdeen?" Richard asked Gabriel.

Her lover folded his arms. "Where I go, my lord, she goes."

"And here we are," Nick added. "So, Vampire King, where's the goddamned fire?"

Nick knew she was pushing it, but she didn't care. Richard wouldn't have bothered sending for both of them if he didn't need to use her as well as Gabriel. She was the only immortal who could sense hidden or captured Kyn, and Gabriel could track anything that breathed. Whatever her lover felt he did or didn't owe to the high lord, she'd made it clear to Richard that she wouldn't be used as his personal vampire GPS.

"We have a situation in America," Richard said at last. "I need you to hunt down a Darkyn who has gone rogue." When Nick started to speak, he held up one gloved hand. "While you are there, you cannot contact Michael Cyprien or make him aware of your presence or your purpose."

Nick felt like spitting. "You have got to be kidding me."

Gabriel rested his hand on her shoulder before addressing Richard. "My lord, Michael is the American seigneur. For Nicola and me to enter his territory without his permission or knowledge—"

"—is against our laws. I know, Gabriel. I wrote the damned law." Richard sighed. "The situation is highly explosive. Were Michael to learn that this rogue was on his territory, he would have no choice but to conduct the hunt himself, alone. But I believe it is a trap, set to lure him into the hands of our enemies again. After what was done to Michael in Rome, I cannot take that risk."

"But it's fine with you if Gabriel and I get snatched instead and tortured to death?" Nick looked sideways. "Baby, we are *so* out of here."

"Wait, *ma belle amie*." Gabriel regarded the high lord. "You believe that Nicola and I can succeed where Cyprien would fail? Why?"

"It's because I can pass as human," Nick guessed. "Cyprien can't." She glared at Richard. "And neither can Gabriel, in case you forgot."

"I have forgotten nothing," Richard assured her. "But there are other reasons it must be the two of you. Very old reasons." He shifted to gaze at the water cascading from the fountain top to the rippling pool in its wide basin. "I will tell you everything you wish to know, but you must swear to me never to speak of it to another soul."

"We swear," Nick said flatly. "Okay, now tell us what the deal is."

"There have been many secret wars in which we have fought for our right to exist," Richard said slowly. "Even now, our kind still struggle for survival—as you and Gabriel have witnessed yourselves. But not every warrior goes into battle to fight for life." He pulled back his hood, revealing his part-human, part-changeling visage. "Some, my dear, go to war to die."

PART TWO

Snow Moon

How the Ahnclann Came to Be

We have always lived on the mountain. We were here before the moon-skin, before the fur-thieves, before even the oldest of the dark-hair. We saw the first eagle, and the last river of ice. We were here before things were known and named by the two-leg. The elders say that when the Master of All Things brought the mountain itself from below, we sprang up with it.

The rivers who came from the ice called us the Chahanat, but we called ourselves nothing, for we knew what we were.

In the old times before the two-leg, we hunted through the trees and above the highest cliffs, in the darkness and in the storm. We made our homes in the deepest caves, and there mated, bore our young, and grew old. The dark-hair were the first to come to the mountain, but they named us for their fear. When they found our trails, they never followed them or tried to find us in the night. Nor did the fur-thieves who came later, once we had killed enough of them.

In the old times we were many, but the fur-thieves brought pestilence that ate at us, taking our young and our old. They killed many dark-hair with the same sickness. Soon the last of the dark-hair left for the flatlands, but we could not. We were as bound to the mountain as it was to us.

While our numbers dwindled, our males began fighting over our females, but it was for nothing, for many who survived the sickness became barren, and fewer and fewer young came. There was nothing that could be done, for there were no others like us. We had watched herds and packs and flocks of other creatures die out in such ways, and we knew that our end time was upon us.

That was when the moon-skin came with their wagons, with their females and their young, and settled on the mountain. They made their own caves of cut trees and piled stones, and grew things and kept herds instead of hunting. Some of the females seemed to sense us, and left offerings of burnt meat under the trees. Kind as it was, we never touched the food, and as lonely as we were, we did not leave our hiding places. Like the dark-hair, they were two-leg, not like us.

If we had come to know them, and to let them know of us, we might have somehow warned them about the Strange One. He looked as they did, but we knew from the first time he sullied our air with his scent that he was only wearing their pale skin. Inside he was the beast, mindless and crazed, voracious with hunger although he never ate or drank.

Our elders feared him, and said he was pestilence made two-leg, and for that reason his burden and fate had to be shouldered by the moon-skins, not us. Our scouts watched, and at first he seemed to do nothing more than take refuge among them to wait out the long winter months until the snows melted and he could travel on. Then the scouts saw the moon-skins carrying out dead ones and bury them under snow and stone.

The elders feared more sickness, and drove us from our watching places to retreat into the mountain, into the very deepest caves where it could not reach us. There we stayed until the last snow, when scouts were sent out to see how the two-leg had fared. They returned to say that nearly all the moon-skins had perished, and the last two females had gone down into the valley with the Strange One. But the scouts thought that the last would also soon die, for the Strange One drank of their blood and desecrated their bodies each night.

One of the females had been particularly dear to us. Bright of hair and fair of face, she had always left some offering of meat for us under the trees. Worse, when the Strange One had come, she had been heavy with child.

Ashamed of our cowardice, we came down through the darkness, following the Strange One's unnatural scent until we found him preparing to ride out. The last of the moon-skin females lay dead and discarded by him, the pregnant bright-hair's belly ripped open. When the Strange One saw us closing in, he laughed and taunted us, hoping perhaps to frighten us away. When he saw that he could not, he tried to flee.

We brought down the monster and gutted him and his mount, but even with his entrails spilling across the ground and the crushing weight of the dead horse atop him, he would not die.

The elders told us what had to be done. So we gathered one last time, first dragging away the corpse of the horse, and then each of us in turn striking and tearing and devouring the Strange One, rending his flesh and guts and bones until there was no more of him. When it was finished, and every part of him lay in our bellies, we licked his blood from the ground and returned to the caves. There we fell one by one into the deep sleep, assured that we had brought justice for the moon-skins.

But it was not the sleep of weariness; it was the sleep of our becoming. And when we awoke, the Fury first came over us, and we were no longer the Chahanat.

For this reason it can be said that, in truth, it was the Strange One who took his vengeance on us.

SEARCH CANCELED; LOCAL RESIDENT CHARGED

10/03/99

SCARVAVILLE, OR—The Curry County Sheriff's Office has called off the search for an unknown victim of a cougar attack, and officials have charged local resident Reginald Boyce with public drunkenness and filing a false police report.

Boyce, an unemployed construction worker, phoned the sheriff's office from a roadside emergency call box yesterday and reported witnessing a cougar dragging the body of an unidentified person into the Siskiyou National Forest. Boyce told deputies that he saw the incident from the road while driving to his brother-in-law's home, and stopped to shoot at the animal several times before calling in the report.

A National Guard helicopter circled the area for several hours while forest rangers, deputies, and county S&R conducted a ground search. No evidence of the attack, the cougar, or the alleged victim was found.

Boyce, who reported to the CCS headquarters to make an official statement, was detained for questioning, and reportedly became verbally abusive with deputies when pressed for details. A source inside CCS who asked not to be named reported that Boyce insisted the cougar had been walking erect on its hind legs and had been carrying the body "like a baby." These statements, along with Boyce's adamant refusal to take a sobriety test, convinced deputies to charge him.

"I'm sorry to hear about his troubles, but Reggie likes his beers," Boyce's former wife, DeeDee, said during a phone interview. "They should have known he was drunk when he walked through the door; he always smells like an open kegger."

After being arraigned and released on bail, a sober Boyce reluctantly admitted to reporters that he has experienced several similar episodes since the breakup of his marriage.

"It seemed so real this time," he said upon leaving the city jail. "Honest to Moses, that cat walked like a man, and it was carrying the body in its arms. But it wasn't human—the thing carrying the body, I mean. I was only a hundred yards away, and I could see it had fur, and paws, and no clothes. Not a stitch on. Maybe it was Bigfoot, but all the pictures I've seen of Bigfoot, he's got dark fur. This thing was all light tan, with white on its front. Swear to God, that's what I saw."

Over the last fifty years three men have been killed by cougar attacks while hiking through the Siskiyou National Forest, according to forestry officials, with another twenty-four nonfatal attacks occurring during the same period. All the survivors of the attacks have been women hiking alone or who at the time were separated from their families; none has ever been able to give rangers any details on the incidents or the animal that attacked them.

Apparently CCS has taken at least part of Boyce's false report seriously, as Sheriff Adkins has issued a request that anyone who has seen a cougar in the area contact his office at (514) 247-3432. To report an anonymous tip to CCS, text the keyword 514CCS, along with your message, to Tip3432; or call the CCS TipLine at (512) 247-9492.

Chapter 6

"Hey there, Daddy." A long-legged working girl with hips as luscious and bouncy as her unfettered breasts strolled up to the back window of the limousine. She leaned over to offer Samuel Taske a closer view of the bountiful pale flesh exposed by her green spangled tank top. It would have had more effect on him if she weren't covered in goose bumps from the cold. "Look at you. You're some *big* daddy, aren't you? Want a date?"

Although the traffic light would be turning green any moment, inherent courtesy compelled Taske to lower the window and reply. "I already have plans, my dear, but thank you."

"Ah, come on." Small, bitter chocolate eyes sized him up in a blink. "Baby needs a decent ride tonight, and you sure look like you're all that and then some."

"Baby needs to warm up, I think." Samuel took a hundred-dollar bill from his wallet and passed it to her, watching as she made an instant deposit in her straining cleavage. "Get out of this wind and have some breakfast on me."

The light turned green, and a horn honked behind them, but Findley, Samuel's driver, only glanced back to see if the conversation had concluded.

"You giving me a Benjamin for *breakfast*?" the prostitute demanded. "What do you think I have? Caviar and champagne?"

"Not unless you want heartburn and fish breath." He nodded toward the east. "I recommend the diner around the corner. Passable omelets, but amazing coffee. Truly magnificent."

"Uh-huh." She backed away a step, but she returned the smile as well. "Whatever you say, Daddy."

"Be safe, my dear." He turned toward his patient driver. "Continue on, James."

The brief encounter with the prostitute was nothing new for Samuel. Being a blond, bearded, Asian-eyed giant made it impossible for him to escape notice wherever he went, so he never tried. His oversize physique combined with an endless amount of personal charisma attracted people like a health-care-reform town meeting drew nutcases.

The times when Samuel's magnetism became a nuisance were those when a situation demanded a certain amount of discretion or subterfuge. Under those circumstances he employed one of his few but intensely loyal staff members to act in his place, or hired a professional. Since Samuel had amassed a staggering fortune over the course of his lifetime, he could afford the best investigators and information brokers in the world.

None of them, however, had ever been able to locate or identify the woman he and the other Takyn knew as Delilah.

Findley hung up the car phone and glanced in the rearview mirror. "Mr. Dorsey on your private line, sir."

"Thank you, James." Samuel Taske picked up the cordless receiver and switched it on. "Hello, Glen. Please tell me you have some good news."

"Wish I could, Mr. Taske," the private investigator said. "My people have finished going through the last of the church's archives. They didn't find a record of any female child matching the age and description you gave me."

Taske silently cursed. "Did you have any better luck with the shelters and the volunteer agencies?"

"We found a couple of prospects," Dorsey admitted. "A Molly Perrine and Rachel Thomason, both red-haired and the correct age. But both women were born to their biological parents in county hospitals and have public birth records on file. Also, both are married and have children."

Samuel knew birth records could be falsified, but keeping a phony husband and family would be much more difficult. "Were you able to check for the tattoo?"

"Perrine likes to sunbathe in her backyard," Dorsey said. "She has a parrot in six colors on her left shoulder."

Takyn were tattooed with only one or two ink colors. "And the other woman?"

"I inspected Thomason personally; she's a beautiful girl, but other than some freckles she doesn't have a mark on her."

"Indeed." Taske frowned. "Precisely how did you accomplish this *personal* inspection?"

"We sent her a gift certificate for a free massage at an exclusive spa." Dorsey cleared his throat. "I observed her through a hidden camera in the treatment room."

Taske relaxed a little. "Very commendable of you, Glen."

"I always prefer to take the road less prosecuted, sir," Dorsey assured him. "My secretary gave me the message about the woman possibly changing jobs and relocating this week. Did you obtain this information from the same anonymous source as all the other leads?"

"Yes." He would have told the investigator that he was in contact with Delilah through the computer, but he would risk exposing the rest of the Takyn if he did so.

Dorsey was too well paid to probe further than that.

"Then I'll get to work on that. Enjoy your holidays, Mr. Taske."

"I hope you do as well, Glen." Taske switched off the phone.

Shame sank its subtle, accurate daggers into him as he stared out at the lightly falling snow. He'd always respected the anonymity of their group. It was the best safeguard they had for themselves as well as the only means of protecting one another. Their superhuman abilities made them vulnerable to exploitation and experimentation; real-life knowledge of one another was too dangerous to risk. He believed in that with all his heart.

Until a year ago, when he had learned something about Delilah that no one else in the group knew.

Samuel recalled how meek and shy Del had been in those first few months, when she would join their scheduled chats to get to know the others. Like the rest of them, she was an orphan who had been adopted through a Catholic charity. Her ability, a form of telepathy that she said allowed her to communicate with animals, had never been discovered by anyone outside the group. She had manifested at the age of sixteen after an unspecified accident. She never went into any details about her life, her adoptive family, or where she lived, but she sometimes asked advice for very mundane things, such as computer and home repairs.

None of what Delilah had revealed about herself had alarmed Samuel. Her word choices and interests indicated that she was self-educated, and he guessed she lived a simple, solitary existence on a modest income. He found her charming, if sometimes reticent and enigmatic.

Last year, just before the holidays, Delilah had begun signing into the chat room almost every night. He had

noticed only because he had been bedridden for several
weeks after badly straining his leg. Whenever he was too
crippled to get around, he used the time to do research
on the Internet. His computer was programmed to alert
him whenever any of the group signed in to chat, so he
began joining her in chat each night as well.

Delilah was equally shy with him at first, but after a
few days she began spending more time chatting with
him. Gradually he came to realize that she came to the
chat room to wait not just for him but for anyone from
the group to sign in.

Are you spending the holidays with your family? he
typed in one night.

My mother died last month, she replied. *We were
never close, but she was all the family I had.*

He had been the center of his adoptive parents' uni-
verse, and the thought of someone not knowing that
kind of love appalled him. *Please accept my condolences,
my dear.*

*It's okay. She thought I was dead. I just wish I could
have told her I wasn't.*

Sometimes the manifestation of their abilities caused
permanent rifts with their adoptive families, but Delilah
had an unusually benign gift, so it couldn't have been
that. *Were you close before?*

I tried to be. She wouldn't let me in. After typing a
string of unhappy faces, she added, *Doesn't matter. Long
time ago.*

Still, you deserve some TLC. Samuel sent her a virtual
bouquet of flowers. *I'd give you the real thing if I could,*
he typed.

You've been so nice, talking to me, she replied. *But
I'd better sign off. Have to go out of town tomorrow for
work. Wish I could send you a Christmas card. I don't
have anyone to send cards to.*

He immediately typed out the address to the remailer service he used. *This is safe, if you want to use it. Address it to Samuel Jones. Just make up the return address.*

Samuel, that's a nice name. She sent him a happy face. *Thank you.*

Delilah had stopped signing in after that, and he hadn't given any more thought to their conversation until a card had arrived two weeks later from his remailer service. He'd kept his gloves on while sorting through the mail and opening it, but as soon as he saw the name "D. Lilah" on the return address of one envelope, he couldn't resist using his ability to take a peek at the life of his mysterious little friend.

To read the history of any object, all Samuel had to do was remove his gloves and touch it, and he would see where it had been and who had handled it before him. If he let his guard down with a well-handled or antique object, he would be flooded with imagery spanning the entire existence of the piece. That ability had made him the wealthiest antique dealer in the country, but it came with a price. Like King Midas, whose touch turned everything to gold, Samuel saw the entire history of *everything* he touched.

Delilah had been the only one to touch the card, he discovered, as she had made it herself a week ago. She sat at an old folding table, painting it with a cheap set of watercolors. The room she occupied was small, the furniture yard-sale quality. She reached to dip the brush in a little tin of water, and her shirt rode up on her back, revealing the tattoo at the base of her spine.

All the Takyn had been tattooed as children with stylized animal symbols that seemed to be related to their abilities. Jezebel, the founding matriarch of the Takyn, had been inked with a golden owl, which seemed appropriate to her powerful ability to read people's darkest secrets in the same way Samuel read the history of objects. Aphrodite, a shape-shifter whom he now knew as Rowan Dietrich, had covered her two blue peacocks with black dragons. Young Taire, the runaway heiress Rowan had rescued in New York, had been inked with the head of a ram on both forearms—and she possessed telekinetic power so great that she could demolish entire buildings by thought alone.

But Delilah had not been tattooed with the figure of an animal. Instead she had a pyramid of three conjoined, dark green spirals, which Samuel had only seen once before, during a terrible vision he had experienced in one of the abandoned underground laboratories used to create the Takyn.

As his glimpse into Delilah's life faded, Samuel accessed his encrypted journals, in which he recorded everything he envisioned, opened the file on his findings at the Monterey site, and began to read.

They processed at least five hundred children here; their confusion and pain haunts everything they touched. As before, all of the documentation has been removed and only a few pieces of equipment were left. I can't go back into the dormitory rooms; the sorrow and terror overwhelms me.

I found a procedure room set apart from the others where some needles were left in an autoclave. As soon as I touched them, I saw the bastards gathered around the table, and the little red-haired toddler they had strapped on it. They didn't speak, but one of the older men grew tired of the baby's cries and sedated her with an injection directly into the base of her spine, where she was tattooed with a triangle of three green spirals.

They performed a biopsy via laparoscope and removed several ova. The lead physician then issued orders to isolate the child, whom he referred to as "Gaia," to prevent any cross-contamination from other subjects before she was released to her caretaker.

I believe that baby might have been an enhanced female who had not yet been imprinted with a specific ability; that would explain the quarantine measures. They may have used or were planning to use her ova as templates for future generations. If she survived, her genes may reveal some important clues about how the rest of us were created.

Samuel closed the file and absently rubbed his aching leg. He had never told the rest of the group about his true motives in searching the country for the hidden labs: finding a cure for his own condition. Unlike Samuel, most of the group had in some way or another made peace with what they were. They had accepted that they had to live with their unnatural psychic abilities.

But none of the others had to live with what Samuel endured. The other aspect of his ability, the one he had kept hidden from the other Takyn, gave him the precognitive ability to see into the timelines of the future, a power that he often could not control. It seemed to come over him whenever he was in close proximity to a person whose timeline had some great importance and yet was in imminent danger of being prematurely changed or terminated. He tried to save as many as he could, but often he was too late. Then he would endure the consequence of his failure: a preternatural backlash that stretched him on some psychic rack and tortured him for hours, sometimes days.

If it had been all in his head, Samuel might have learned to live with it. But failing to rescue a timeline resulted in real, physical damage to his spine, and the damage seemed to be growing more severe with each failure. He'd always hoped that eventually his precognitive ability would fade, but as he grew older, it seemed to be manifesting more often. After a failure and a particularly extended episode of suffering afterward, he finally went to a spinal surgeon for evaluation.

The prognosis had been far worse than anything he'd imagined: Thanks to the repeated injuries and his altered DNA, his immune system had begun to attack his spine. At the rate the deterioration was progressing, he had less than a year to live.

Findley guided the limousine through the automatic iron gate between two ten-foot stone walls that encircled Taske's winter home, the somewhat palatial mansion he had inherited from his parents, along with several hundred acres of woods, hills, and streams. He always wintered here at Tannerbridge because it contained his happiest memories as well as the nerve center of his private operations. Findley and his new house manager, Morehouse, were the only staff he kept on during the holidays, but both men had no plans and Taske imagined the three of them would enjoy a quiet bachelors' celebration of the season, and he would have at least a month of uninterrupted research into finding the identity and whereabouts of the elusive Delilah.

What troubled Taske the most was what he would have to do when he found his friend. He couldn't afford to ask for her cooperation and be refused, not with all that was at stake. Nor could he invite her to take sanctuary with him, which would go against the rules they had established for the group. Delilah would never agree to it. The only thing he could do was the thing he found most abhorrent, the one transgression that he knew would appall her, and for which he would never forgive himself.

As soon as Taske located Delilah, he planned to kidnap her.

After Lilah awoke, it took only a few hours for her body to free itself from the effects of the drugs. Walker also seemed to be getting a little better, but he still couldn't move freely, and harsh lines of pain etched deeper into his face as he suffered through several episodes of un-controlled tremors.

"Is it the drugs?" Lilah whispered, holding on to him after the fourth time he convulsed.

"Wearing off." The cords in his neck stood out as he seemed to be fighting against the reaction, but Lilah saw that he couldn't control his movements or stop the shakes, which traveled down his arm and pounded his fist into the floor of the truck with hard, booming thuds.

Lilah caught his wrist and pulled his hand away from the floor. "It's okay. I've got you."

The tremors gradually slowed and then stopped as Walker went limp. Exhaustion and self-disgust filled his expression.

"Hey," Lilah murmured. "Don't do that. It's not your fault."

"Everything . . . " He stopped and rested his brow against her shoulder, too tired to finish the thought.

The truck's brakes squealed as it slowed down and came to a stop. Lilah listened to opening and slamming doors, and the fainter sound of two male voices arguing. They were too muffled to make out the words, but they drifted around the truck toward Lilah's feet. Walker lifted his head, his eyes narrowing.

"Coming," he warned her. "Check us. Quiet. Don't move."

She nodded, closing her eyes and holding still. The sound of the truck door being raised made her heart quake, but Walker turned his hand and pushed his stiff fingers through hers, holding them tight.

"See?" a young male voice said. "They ain't moved. I told you, that sound was just from some boxes bouncing around."

An older voice answered him with "Shut up, Joey."

The truck bed dipped as someone climbed in. Lilah held her breath as she heard footsteps thump across the floor and the light over them was blotted out. Something prodded the tarp, a jabbing finger. It struck the knob of her elbow, which she instinctively held in a rigid position.

"It's like nine degrees back here, Bob," Joey said. "They're ice cubes now, man."

"Yeah, I guess," the man standing over her said in a deeper, disgusted voice. "I coulda sworn I heard something." A hand scraped against the canvas and then took a handful of it. "We gotta stop them from bopping around like this."

As the tarp was pulled away, Lilah felt a biting cold flash of sensation, and the warm dampness of her skin vanished under a layer of hard ice crystals that enveloped her whole body. She couldn't open her eyes now even if she wanted to; her eyelids were frozen shut.

"Nothing to tie them down with." A stiff finger prodded her breast. "Hey, she's not froze up all the way yet. Huh." That was the younger man's voice. "I wonder if she can still feel anything."

"We dosed her with enough shit to kill three horses," Bob snapped. "She's a fucking Popsicle, pinhead."

Lilah heard a grunt, and then her chest flattened as Walker's body was rolled on top of her.

"What the hell are you doing?" Bob demanded.

"You said you don't want them sliding all over the place. His weight'll keep her down." Joey snickered as he rearranged some boxes around them to keep them in place. "There. Now he's not going anywhere, are you, Marine?" He nudged Lilah's hip with his foot and brayed laughter. "This one'll stay on top of you as long as you want, baby, so you two have a real good time."

"You're a perverted twerp." Something rasped, and Bob sighed. "Christ, I feel like hell."

"You're just tired," Joey said. "Let me drive for a while. You can catch some z's."

Silence stretched out as the men hovered. Lilah didn't dare try to breathe, and her lungs felt as if they were going to burst. Finally she felt the canvas being pulled over them and the voices moved away.

"You better wake me before we cross into Mississippi," she heard Bob say as he climbed out of the truck. "If we're gonna get there before this frigging blizzard hits, we've gotta head north and take Seventy."

The truck's sliding door slammed down.

Chapter 7

Walker's body pinned Lilah's to the bed of the truck like a slab of concrete, preventing her from even wriggling beneath him. Even more frightening than his smothering weight was the rage she felt pouring from him, so deep and violent that it gripped him as tightly as the paralysis that had held him immobile. His anger drowned out everything: his reason, his self-control, even her own presence.

That inferno seemed to be bubbling up through his skin, for she could feel the layer of ice covering both of them rapidly melting; thin patches of it slid away from their limbs and fell like slush onto the floor around them.

Walker opened his eyes to see Lilah looking up at him, but he didn't seem to recognize her. Her vision blurred as the frost on her eyelashes turned to fat beads; she blinked and they slid like tears into her hair. She felt like weeping, but with him on top of her like this she could hardly breathe.

"I'm sorry," she whispered.

He moved then, grunting as he managed to prop some of his weight on his forearm, which allowed her to take a shallow breath. The shift also made her feel the stiff length of his penis pressing against her crotch. He couldn't roll away from her, not wedged in as they were by the boxes Joey had moved. Lilah knew it wasn't

Walker's fault, but the intimacy of their position made
her cringe inside. They were total strangers who were
only a few inches from having sex. She didn't want him
to see the shame she felt, so she turned her face away
from him.

A deep, guttural sound emerged from his throat as
his face dropped against her neck, and she felt the grip
of his free hand on her throat, holding her as the edge
of his teeth scraped over the pulse beneath her skin. He
didn't bite her, but a terrible panic came over her as she
realized he was fighting not to. She put a hand to his
face, lifting it so that she could see his eyes.

Her ability jumped out of her like a wild thing, trying
to grab whatever she could from his emotions.

Locked inside the rage that had taken over his mind,
two different needs tore at Walker. Lilah realized that
part of him wanted to lunge at her neck again and tear
at it; another part wanted to make the parody of the
sexual position Joey had placed them in real. He was
fighting hard to resist both, but she could sense that he
was losing.

Lilah tried to calm him with her own thoughts, and
found herself abruptly shoved back out of his mind.

His hand tightened on her throat even as he put his
mouth against her ear and spoke in a flat, tight mono-
tone. "Push me. Off. Hurry."

She couldn't use her ability to calm him because he
was human. Her throat burned from the pressure of his
fingers digging in. Only his rapidly dwindling will stood
between her and rape—or possibly death.

It doesn't have to be like this.

Some tight, bleak thing inside her that was older than
the forces ravaging Walker understood the brutal hunger and killing rage. It stood apart from them, reserved,
almost cold. It had been so long since she had felt it that

she almost didn't recognize it. It didn't care what happened to Walker, but it wouldn't let him harm her.

Now it was Lilah's turn to panic. She had to get him away from her before she lost control and did something unforgivable. But her weak limbs refused to cooperate, and he was too far gone to move.

Take him, the watcher inside her whispered. *He's yours.*

Her fingertips slid across his cheek and cupped his head. "Walker, look at me." When his dazed eyes focused on hers, she reached into him, this time giving him all her strength. "It's all right. We can do this together." Her words cost her what breath was left in her lungs, but his grip on her throat loosened. She struggled to take another breath before she wheezed, "Move to the right as far as you can. Use my arm as a brace."

With some difficulty he shifted his weight over, allowing Lilah to take another, deeper breath. As he did, she brought up her free hand and pushed at his shoulder.

"Good." The word burst from her lips as his weight pressed down on her ribs. She tugged at his shoulder, and then pushed it again. "Now . . . rock."

He had very little strength, so his movements were almost imperceptible at first, but she put her weight behind his and helped him rock back and forth, a little more each time. Her ribs began to feel like dry twigs that were being bent and nearly ready to snap, and then his body rolled over so that his back lay pressed against the boxes beside them.

"That's it." She inched one of her legs over his to keep from being rolled onto her back by the movements of the truck. They were squashed together on their sides, and she was starting to lose the feeling in the arm that was cuffed to Walker's, but she could breathe now. Her side and her throat didn't hurt too much. She also saw that some of the blind, vicious fury had faded from his expression. "Better?"

His eyes shifted toward the front of the truck. "Kill them." He almost growled the words. "Slow."

"I'd rather get away from them, fast," she said, and tried to smile. "We can get out of this, Walker. If we work together, I know we can."

He frowned at her, as if he couldn't make sense of what she was saying. "Together."

"You and me, we're a team now." She wiggled her numb arm, shifting the cuffs that bound them together. "Not like you can get rid of me yet, remember?"

"No." His confusion ebbed, and his expression grew remote. "Not yet."

He didn't know what to make of Lilah. He had bruised her, and come within a heartbeat of doing worse, but even with his hand wrapped around her throat she had shown no fear. Now she lay relaxed against him, her body as soft and easy as if they had been intimate for years. He knew she had felt his killing rage, but not once had she screamed or begged for mercy. Instead she had comforted him. As if he had been the one made to suffer.

He needed to understand this. "Lilah."

She reached up to press her fingertips against his lips, and only then did he realize the truck had stopped moving.

He listened, straining to hear the men's voices, but this time they were silent as they climbed out of the truck. He knotted his hands, sure they had heard them and were coming, but the two sets of footsteps moved forward, away from the back of the truck.

"They're gone for now." She relaxed. "If they come back, we'll have to assume the missionary position again."

She sounded brisk, as if she were discussing nothing

of importance instead of what must have been an ordeal for her.

"No more," he promised. "I will. Tear his. Head off."

She touched his cheek. "My friend, you'll have to stand in line."

After nearly being crushed under him, and coming within inches of having her throat torn out while he ravaged her body, she was smiling at him. She was calling him her friend. He didn't know what to say or think.

Lilah pushed away the canvas and looked around the interior of the truck. "What is all this stuff?" she asked, her voice low.

He regarded the stacks of unmarked boxes, their cardboard sides white with frost, and tried to remember what he had heard the men say before they had taken her.

"Supplies. Lab." He spotted a black duffel bag, a bulging garbage bag, and an aluminum case in one corner and nodded toward them. "Men. Their things."

"We should check them and see if we can find some clothes." Lilah got up on her knees and rose until their cuffed hands stopped her. "Can you try to stand?"

He was almost certain that he could, but eyed the door.

"I think we have some time before they come back. They've stopped for a meal." She wrinkled her nose. "I can smell diesel and cooking grease."

He crouched, clasping her hand in his as he found his balance. She kept her free arm around his waist to help steady him, and he fought for control of his body. His limbs felt thick and clumsy, but the maddening paralysis had gone.

"Wait," she said when he would have taken a step toward the bags. "Any dizziness? Do you feel sick?" When he shook his head, she pressed her fingers against the side of his throat. "Your pulse is still too slow. If you feel like you're going to pass out, tell me and we'll stop and rest, okay?"

He knew now that he wouldn't lose consciousness unless they drugged him again, and he would not stop or rest until they were free. But she knew nothing of him, and to dismiss her worries would likely require explanations he had no desire to make. "Okay."

Steam rolled off her skin, and she didn't seem to notice how cold it was as she moved carefully with him over to the men's belongings. He glanced down and saw that wherever she stepped on the frigid, ice-covered floor, she left a small puddle of water. Then he saw that he was doing the same. Although sweat still ran freely down their bodies, they were not wet enough to be leaving such a trail.

The soles of their feet were melting the ice on contact. Given the frigid condition of the truck's interior, that did not seem possible.

Lilah stooped to open the top of the duffel bag. "Clothes," she confirmed, glancing up at him. She removed a blue and green flannel shirt and shook it out. A small key ring fell at her feet.

"Keys!" Excited, she grabbed them and fit one into the cuffs' lock, but only the cuff around her wrist sprang open. After twisting the key several times, she frowned. "Yours is jammed, I think."

"It doesn't matter." He took it from her as she continued to search, and soon had his arms filled with men's garments. After she had found enough for him, Lilah turned to the garbage bag and untied it. From the bag she removed a pile of dark T-shirts and black jeans, all so faded most of them were gray. She shook out one T-shirt and inspected the cracked decal on the front, which depicted a pile of silver skulls around a brutal-looking long sword.

"Charming." She sniffed the fabric. "Well, at least it's

clean." She pulled it over her head before reaching for a pair of black boxers. "Do you see any jackets or shoes?"

Something dark on her lower back caught his eye, and he touched her shoulder. "Wait." He turned her away to get a better look at the bruise. Which turned out not to be a bruise at all, but a tattoo of three interlocked spirals in dark green ink. He almost touched them before he pulled back his hand. "You are marked?"

"Oh, you mean my body art," she said, her voice wry. "Yeah, it's a little odd. Norelco should pay me for the free advertising."

He bent closer. What he thought were lines were actually strings of tiny numbers, letters, and shapes. "What is it?"

"I don't know. It wasn't my idea. I've had it since I was a baby." She stepped into the boxers and pulled them up over her hips. "When did you get yours? While you were overseas?"

"I have no tattoo."

She stopped dressing and glanced up at him. "You do now, Marine. It's on the back of your left shoulder."

He turned his head as far as he could, but saw only the top of a dark blue curve.

"Don't remember it? It's two dark blue circles, and they overlap in the middle." She traced the outlines with her fingertip. "I've seen it before, but not as a tattoo. I don't know what it's called, but I think it's an old symbol for something. Maybe an astrological sign like Gemini or Pisces."

He knew what it was from her description. *"Mandorla."*

"What does that mean?"

He considered telling her, and then simply gave her the literal translation. "Almond."

"Well, the center is almond-shaped, I suppose." Her touch stilled. "There's something hard under your skin in the middle of the tattoo." She pressed gently so he could feel the small, rod-shaped object. "Were you shot in the back?"

"No." He heard the sound of the men's voices approaching the front of the truck. "They're coming." He put the bags back in place and then led her over to where the discarded canvas lay on the floor. There he waited until he heard the cab doors slam and the engine start. He tugged at her, guiding her to the back door.

"I can't jump out like this," she whispered, gesturing at her bare legs and feet.

"Not yet," he agreed, and used the noise of the truck accelerating to mask the sound of him raising the rolling door. He held it up a few inches with their joined hands as he reached outside. Once he had what he wanted and carefully closed the door, he led Lilah back to the cases.

"What were you doing?" she demanded.

"The door." His gaze shifted toward her feet. "They forgot."

"Forgot what?"

He held up the padlock in his hand. "To lock it."

Chapter 8

.

Once the GenHance corporate jet was in the air, Tina Segreta took on her usual role as hostess, and supplied Eliot Kirchner with a glass of soda water, adding a twist of lemon and enough sedative to knock out the geneticist for several hours. Since she had arranged to have the rest of his team follow them on a commercial flight, and the pilots had been instructed to stay in the cockpit, she had the doctor and the plane all to herself.

Once Kirchner had fallen unconscious, Tina carefully searched through his clothing. "Let's see what color boxers you're wearing today, Doc." She smiled a little as she opened his trousers. "Ah, the navy blue. My favorite."

Groping a brilliant scientist's flaccid genitals and searching his body cavities never thrilled Tina, but it didn't repulse her, either. Almost from birth she'd been trained to perform the most intimate tasks without emotion; it was just another part of her job. That her touch made Kirchner erect startled her only a little; perhaps the cold fish wasn't as sexless as Genaro believed him to be.

"Good to know." She patted his erection and chuckled as it bobbed. "Maybe we can do something about this before we land."

Once she had gone over every inch of his person, Tina searched Kirchner's carry-on bags and then walked from one end of the plane to the other, scanning the interior with a handheld bug detector. Only when she felt sure the plane was as clean as Kirchner did she boot up her netbook and engage the transceiver.

Genaro's face appeared on the screen a few moments later in a video call screen. "Report."

"Kirchner doesn't have anything on him." Tina had already had one of their people at the airport search the bags the doctor had checked before boarding the jet. "All he brought in his cases are a few changes of clothes and some toiletries."

"I'm glad to hear it." Genaro's expression tightened. "Chief Delaporte told me that there was a last-minute acquisition taken in central Florida yesterday. A female."

"Devereaux, the animal control officer. I remember." Tina pretended to think. "Dr. Kirchner mentioned her once or twice. I believe he flagged her from a news report about an encounter between her and a black bear."

"Why was she taken without my knowledge?"

Because Tina had destroyed every report about Devereaux that Kirchner had sent to Genaro, not that she would admit it. "I'm not sure, sir. Dr. Kirchner said only that she was the right age, had no known family members, and her identity has only existed for ten years."

"Who authorized the capture, and where is she now?"

"Let me check with Denver on that, sir." She opened another window, checking the bogus files she'd brought with her, which included fake operations reports. She might have to transmit them to Genaro, but by the time he authenticated them, she would be finished with the real reason she was traveling to Denver. She reopened the call screen. "It appears that Dr. Kirchner personally arranged the capture and transport. The female is on a truck carrying some lab supplies and a cadaver to the new facility."

"Call ahead to the facility," Genaro said. "I want

the bodies and everything on that truck thoroughly searched before Kirchner is given access."

"Yes, sir." Tina waited until Genaro terminated the video call before she logged off, and then glanced at the sleeping doctor. "You bad, bad man. You just got caught with your hand in the cookie jar."

She used the air phone to call ahead to the ground crew at the new facility, and learned that the truck wasn't expected to arrive until sometime after midnight. She couldn't help but smirk a little as she hung up the phone. Genaro had no idea that the truck would never arrive, and neither would his assistant. She was tempted to take Kirchner as well, but she suspected selling a world-renowned geneticist to the highest bidder wouldn't be as simple as bribing a couple of thugs to snatch an orphaned, friendless civil servant who'd just lost her job. She returned to her seat to review the file she had prepared on Devereaux, and then removed a mobile phone that she wasn't supposed to be carrying and hit speed dial.

"It's Tina," she said, and waited to be connected. When her employer answered, she said, "I've acquired what you wanted; we'll be arriving in Denver in a few hours. How do you want to do this?" She listened to his instructions, and then checked the balance in her offshore bank account, which had been increased by three million dollars. "I appreciate the prompt payment, and I'll see you tomorrow."

As she electronically transferred the new funds to a different account, Tina felt the last of her anxiety melt away. She'd done several similar jobs over the last five years, but this was the last, big payoff. All she had to do was finish setting up Kirchner to take the fall for stealing the bodies from Genaro as well as Tina's own disappearance, which she had meticulously planned to make it appear as if Kirchner had murdered her.

As for her other employer, by the time he discovered how Tina had screwed him, he'd be reading her obituary.

A flashing icon on the netbook's toolbar caught her eye, and Tina clicked on it. The message box that popped up displayed a tiny graphic of a red hand with the thumb tucked under the forefinger. Dread tangled with rage inside her chest as she faced the one problem she hadn't anticipated. "Goddamn it."

With one long nail she punched in a fourteen-digit code she'd never been able to forget before pressing one final button.

The call waiting for her connected instantly.

"Hello, Teresina." The young, sweet-sounding voice spoke in fluid Italian. "How are you? Have you landed yet?"

"No," Tina snapped in English. She didn't bother to ask how she had been found, and who had tapped into the encrypted computer. A glance at Kirchner told her he was still out, but she lowered her voice anyway. "What are you doing, calling me like this? Have you lost your mind?"

"I arrived in the States yesterday."

"And the first thing you do is call me? You *are* crazy." If she hadn't been so furious, she would have laughed. "Did you think we'd reminisce about the good old days? Or were you hoping that I would—"

"They know, Teresina." The cheerful voice became gentle. "They know where you are, what you've been doing, and who you work for. They know everything. They've always known. They know why you're going to Denver."

They couldn't know. No one knew.

"I'm on a business trip." Tina felt sweat beading on her upper lip and wiped it away with the heel of her hand. "I don't care. I'm nothing to them. I'm dead to them. Leave me alone."

"No, you're not." A sigh whispered over the line. "I will be in Denver in a few hours, sister, and we should—"

"You're not my sister, you stupid little bitch." Five years ago Tina had stopped looking over her shoulder, confident that she had been forgotten. She should have known they would never let her go unpunished. "Why did they send you here? One last job to make sure you're worthy of them?"

"Something like that," she agreed.

Tina realized she was so angry she was almost shouting into the phone. She turned and strode down the aisle until she took a seat in the very back of the plane, well out of earshot of the cockpit. "Did you think if we spoke that I'd help you? Or were you just hoping to make me crawl?"

"Neither, Teresina. I'm simply doing my job." She hesitated before she added, *"Pacta sunt servanda."*

She froze. "What agreements have been made?"

"I am to tell you that you have been absolved, Teresina. *Venia necessitati datur."*

Once, Tina thought, she would have sacrificed a limb to hear those words. Once. "Oh, no. *No.* You're ten years too late, Valori. I don't care what they do. *I* will never forgive them, or forget what they did to me."

"I know it is hard for you," she said. "But everything has changed now. No matter how you feel, you must return to Napoli to perform the *conclamatio."*

Which meant her brother, Tomaseo, was dead. Tina closed her eyes for a moment, reaching for calm even as she began to tremble uncontrollably. She had to clench her teeth to keep them from chattering. "How did he die?"

"It was his heart." She told Tina about the scars the doctors had found on her brother's body, wounds from an old battle that had eventually caused the aortic aneurysm to form. "He never told anyone how badly he'd been hurt, but he was proud that way. He didn't suffer. He went peacefully in his sleep. Sister—"

"Shut up. Just shut the hell up."

All the old wounds, the impossibly deep ones Tina had cauterized and covered and kept inside herself, swelled with grief. Eighteen years older and infinitely wiser and steadier, Tomaseo had been like a father to her, teaching her the ways, listening to her confessions and forgiving her so many trespasses.

She'd trespassed all over the countryside, with every dark-eyed, hard-bodied peasant boy she could tempt into meeting her in a hayloft or an olive orchard. Sex had been a drug then, her most delicious, secret vice, and she had refused to be responsible because she was supposed to get pregnant—it was her duty, her calling . . . until she had begun puking in the mornings and realized she wasn't ready to be a mother at seventeen.

Even after Tina had done the worst—the unthinkable—by getting an illegal, back-alley abortion, she had not been sorry. Her only regret was the idiot who had botched the job, causing her to nearly bleed to death afterward. Tomaseo had found her in a pool of her own blood on the floor of her room, and had rushed her to the hospital. There, when he'd learned the reason why she had hemorrhaged, he had not condemned her. He had done nothing to save her when she had been released from the hospital, either, but that didn't matter. He had been her god, and she had never really stopped worshipping him.

And now he was dead, the last living relative she had, at the ridiculously young age of forty-seven. And they had sent Valori, the no-name nothing taken from the streets, her replacement, her doppelgänger, to bring her back.

That was why they wanted her to return to the fold.

The *conclamatio*, an idiotic custom that required the dead man's family to announce his death before the *collegia* by shouting his name while horns blew. If they were so desperate to bring her back, it meant—

"Toma never had any kids?" Tina demanded.

"Unfortunately, no. His wife was unable to conceive."

"Such a tragedy," Tina sneered, suddenly feeling a little safer now that she knew she was the last Segreta. "Didn't he ever try to fuck you?"

"I was Tomaseo's friend." She said it as if she meant it. "You know that."

"No, Valori," Tina snarled. "I was his friend. His sister. His only family. You're nothing. Less than nothing. A stray bitch brought in from the streets to lap at his heels and do their dirty work."

"As you say." Her voice went flat. "The situation remains unchanged. The *collegia* are expecting you to return. You may take a few days to settle your affairs—"

"Do you think I've forgotten everything?" Tina snapped. "Nine days. I have nine days before the *novendiale sacrificium*."

"Seven," Valori corrected. "Toma passed yesterday, and it will take you another day to make the return flight."

She gritted her teeth. "Are you deaf as well as stupid? I'm not going back. *I am never going back.* You tell them that."

"It is not my place. I must carry out my orders."

"Fine." The final gauntlet had been thrown. "If you try to take me, Valori, I'll tell Jonah Genaro exactly who and what I am. I'll tell him everything. Right after I shoot you in the head."

"You misunderstand me, Teresina," she said, her voice gentle again. "I will not be taking you back to them. I was not sent here for you."

*   *   *

As Lilah hid the padlock at the bottom of the duffel bag, she could feel Walker watching her. She'd already discovered how intense he could be, but now he seemed fully focused on her, as if nothing else interested him.

Of course he was probably trying to sort out what had happened when he'd nearly lost control. She didn't blame him for whatever was going through his mind; her own thoughts were probably just as jumbled.

This is what happened: nothing. I calmed him down and he stopped before anything serious happened. He didn't mean to bruise me. He didn't want to hurt me.

Walker's reaction had been violent, Lilah knew, but even that didn't repulse her. They were alone, naked, and bound together under the worst possible circumstances. He had been in the war, and God only knew what sort of emotional toll that had taken. Now he had to cope with this ordeal; it was almost a miracle that he *had* hung on to his sanity.

As for Lilah, being treated like nothing more than a blow-up doll by that little creep Joey was the worst humiliation she'd ever experienced, but the shame was his, not hers. To him she wasn't a person, and neither was Walker. Anyone who would think it was funny to put two helpless captives in such a position wasn't worth giving another thought to—although if Walker got the opportunity to keep his promise and rip off Joey's head, Lilah felt almost certain that she wouldn't try to stop him.

What still puzzled her was why the incident had triggered her ability. Instinctively she had reached into him to try to calm him, which made no sense, because Walker was human, not an animal. He'd also somehow blocked her ability and forced her out of his mind—another first for her.

Although her psychic ability worked only on the

minds of predatory animals, she wasn't completely oblivious to human minds. Occasionally Lilah could sense the emotions coming from other people, especially if they were strong feelings like anger or fear. But other than that low-grade emotional empathy, she had no other access to their thoughts. Nor could she exercise any form of telepathic control over them.

She should not have been able to reach into Walker. She certainly shouldn't have been capable of absorbing his thoughts the way she had.

Unless they had done something to him to make him less human.

Jezebel, one of her Takyn friends, had sent out an encrypted e-mail explaining her sudden disappearance and the new Takyn she had met while evading GenHance. In it she described her encounters with Bradford Lawson, the terrifying killer who had stalked her across several states. He had been immensely strong with frightening abilities; he'd also been completely insane.

Lawson must have been one of the people GenHance experimented on, Jezebel wrote. *When I first met him, he was just a man who was in good shape. The next time I saw him, his body was much bigger, faster, and had huge, distorted muscles, as if he'd been taking some kind of super steroids. He almost didn't look human anymore.*

Lilah glanced at Walker's arms. When she'd first regained consciousness, she had seen every inch of his upper torso, and felt the rest with the lower half of her body. His muscles did seem more pronounced now. He had been paralyzed by the drugs, and perhaps the laxness had caused him to look thinner; but if he had been subjected to the same experiments GenHance had performed on Lawson . . .

Bastards.

She jerked the strings of the duffel bag to close it,

and Walker touched her hand. The unexpected contact made her start, and she looked up into the remoteness of his eyes, but there was no reading his emotions now. He seemed aloof, almost indifferent.

She almost forgot to whisper. "What's wrong?"

"You're afraid of me."

Chapter 9

His words hung in the air between them, like the white puffs of breath he'd used to say them.

"Why would I be afraid of you?" Lilah might have her doubts, but they didn't translate into fear of him, only of what their abductors might have done to him. Then she understood why he had gone glacial on her. "You didn't do anything wrong before, Walker. I knew you wouldn't, uh, hurt me."

He gave her a long look. "You know what I wanted to do to you."

"The signs were kind of unmistakable." Her face grew hot. "I know I probably look like a girl who gets around a lot, but I haven't. And I don't." She glanced down at her curves and back up at him. "Having a body like this is like owning a really hot sports car. Men think all you do is go joyriding in it night and day. But honestly, I've only taken it around the block a few times."

"Never with a stranger," he guessed.

She shook her head. "I've always been careful. With all the diseases out there, it's stupid not to be." This was too much information; his eyes were probably going to start glazing over any minute. "Anyway, no harm done. You stopped and now we're okay."

"Lilah." He turned his face so that his mouth brushed across her palm, a tender gesture that seemed at odds with his harsh expression. "You stopped me. I could not."

"It's all right. You just needed some help." Lilah didn't know how to explain her actions or her own emotions, which shifted abruptly from uncertainty and worry to a calm, cool serenity. They might not know anything about each other, but she felt connected to him now, as if those frightening moments had formed a concord between them. It should have terrified her, but once more she felt herself accepting it without a second thought. "You're a good man, Walker. A decent man."

He drew back, his gaze searching her face. "You don't know me."

That much was true. "I think I can explain why it happened. It's because of what they did to you. What they put inside you. Your injuries from the war must have triggered it." She wished she could spare him the knowledge, but it was better to tell him now than to let him go on in ignorance of his ability. "It changes you and allows you to do things that you couldn't before now. But you can learn to control it. I'll help you."

His expression blanked. "How can you help me?"

"You heard what that guy said. They deliberately gave me an overdose." She'd only ever told these things to strangers on a computer; it was much harder to tell someone in person. "I shouldn't be breathing, but here I am, still alive."

He said nothing, but watched her face closely.

Lilah took a deep breath. "Walker, I'm not exactly normal. When I was a baby, some scientists experimented on me. They altered my genes. I don't know how or with what, but it changed me. It made me stronger and able to do things ordinary people can't."

He wasn't recoiling from her; if anything, his attention sharpened. "What can you do?"

"For one thing, I can read the minds of animals." She

grimaced. "I know, that sounds like I'm some crazy pet psychic, but it's true. I know what they're thinking, and I can even keep them from hurting people. It's why I work as an animal control officer." She took a deep breath. "Anyway, that's the reason I'm not dead. I can't be killed with drugs." She met his gaze. "It's the same reason you're still alive."

His brow furrowed. "You think they did the same to me?"

She nodded and curled her fingers around his hand. "It's the reason they kidnapped me. We're going to one of their chop shops. They want to dissect me and use my genes to change ordinary people." She hesitated, and then added, "They must have already used you as one of their test subjects, to see if they could change you to be like me."

"They could not do that," he said. "They took you after. Unless . . ."

She nodded. "This isn't the first time they've done this. There are others like us, and I've become friends with some of them. We think they're trying to re-create the process that was used to change me and my friends." The truck came to a stop, and she waited until it accelerated again before she murmured, "I'm sorry. You don't deserve to be treated like this."

"You apologize to me." He seemed dumbfounded. "You forgive me."

"There's nothing to forgive." Whatever had been done to Walker wasn't his fault; he was as much a victim as she was.

The truck's wheels ran over a pothole, knocking Lilah off balance. Walker encircled her waist to keep her from falling, but as the truck picked up speed, they both slid backward toward the rear door.

"Incline," she muttered as she looked toward the front. "Did you see anything when you looked outside? Were there any roads signs?"

"Only snow and cars."

Lilah didn't know how long they had slept, and now she was afraid it was much longer than she'd originally thought. "Could you see any license plates on the cars?"

He nodded. "What state were they?"

"I don't know," he said. "White mountains behind the numbers."

"Colorado plates." Her heart sank. "That's why they stopped. We must almost be there."

"The sun is setting," Walker said. "We will go soon. Darkness will help us. Hide us . . . "

"I hope so." Lilah checked the side pockets of the gym bag, which contained a half dozen pairs of socks and several wool knit caps. She handed one of the skullies and half the socks to Walker. "They're not as good as shoes, but we can layer them."

He sat with her, bracing his back against the boxes, and with her help tugged on the socks. He had long, narrow feet with a pronounced arch, she noticed, and well-shaped toes—not something she expected to see on a soldier who had probably spent several years marching along in combat boots.

He took the socks from her and brought her right foot up onto his thigh, pausing to admire it for a moment. "You have little girl's feet."

"Unfortunately they're the only part of me that's dainty." She wiggled her own stubby toes with their short, bare nails. "These clothes won't keep us warm for long. We'll have to flag down a car or find shelter right away."

He tried to loosen the cuff still hanging from his wrist again, first tugging, and then frowning at it. "Shelter is better."

"We might get hit by oncoming traffic." She watched him roll the socks over her feet. "Maybe we shouldn't try to climb out while the truck is moving."

He scowled. "No climbing."

"You want to wait until they deliver us to the chop shop?" she countered.

"When the truck stops, we will jump."

"We don't know if they're going to stop again." She sighed. "With the ice and snow out there, we do have to wait until they stop at a traffic light. That should give us enough time to climb out."

"We are jumping."

She wriggled her feet. "Not in socks."

"I will hold you." He scooped her up and held her against his chest, with nothing supporting her weight but his arm. "Like this."

"You can't." But his arm remained rock-steady as he held her aloft. "Walker, you're still weak, and I'm no lightweight. Cut it out before you hurt yourself."

"I am strong again," he told her, sounding a little smug. "I could hold you like this for days."

It was the longest sentence he'd said to her, and it thrilled her down to her toes, but she had to be practical. "Not if you dislocate an elbow." She wriggled until he lowered her onto his lap. "You don't have to prove to me how big and strong you are." She braced a hand against his bicep, and tried to think of a diplomatic way to ask him about his size. "Have you always been in such good shape?"

He looked down at her hand. "Not like this." He flexed his arm, and the muscles moved like shifting steel under her fingers. "My body has changed. I've never been this large or so heavy." He stared at her. "What will happen to me now? Do you know?"

"Not specifically." It wasn't a lie; Lilah couldn't be sure he had been subjected to the same drugs as Jezebel's stalker, and to tell him about the killer would only worry him more. "As soon as we're safe, I'll contact my friends. They'll help us find out what's been done to you."

His reaction was abrupt and startling. "No. No hospitals. No doctors."

"My friends aren't like that," she said quickly. "All of us have had to hide what we are to prevent the government and companies like GenHance from exploiting us. We would never risk exposing you to them."

He set her aside. "I am not one of you."

Lilah wasn't about to let him push her away. "You could be."

"My friends are dead," he told her flatly. "I should be. It's what I deserve."

"You think you *deserve* to be experimented on?" Anger flooded through her, and she had to clench her jaw to keep her voice low. "You're alive, Walker. If you want to die, all you have to do is stay here. They'll mess with you for a while, but they can never let you go. As soon as they're finished, they'll kill you."

He grabbed the dangling cuffs and tried to pull them off. Lilah didn't interfere until she saw blood trickling from his wrist.

"Oh, my God. Stop. Walker, please. You're hurting yourself." Gently she uncurled his fingers from the metal and grimaced at the shallow gashes before she used the hem of her T-shirt to stanch the flow. "What were you thinking? You can't pull these cuffs apart with your bare hands."

He pulled the hem away and stared at the gashes, which were no longer oozing blood but still open and raw-looking. Then he studied the cuffs closely.

"I think they're like police issue," she added, trying to distract him from trying again, "except for the color. The cops use steel cuffs."

"Brass." He lowered his hand and looked around. "I need a lever to pry it off."

"What you need to do is get ready." Lilah stood, forcing him to do the same. "Because as soon as they slow down again, we're jumping." She felt the speed of the truck slowing. "Which would be right now."

Before he could stop her, she grabbed the interior handle of the door and yanked it up.

Joey Narda wished he'd never taken this job. If he hadn't, he'd be in his apartment right now, kicking back in his recliner and giving himself a slow lotion jerk while watching the six blondes in *Prep School Pussies IV* munch muff. Or maybe even getting a hummer from that chick Tammy who had moved in across the hall. She'd been smiling at him ever since she'd asked him to fix the leak in her sink pipe when the super couldn't be bothered. And it wasn't just because she had a great body, either; she was interested in him for real. While he'd worked on her sink, she'd asked him about his job and who he worked with, and laughed over his descriptions of Bob and the Cast-Iron Bitch who'd hired them.

Yeah, Tammy wanted him, bad. She was hot to suck on his pipe; anyone could see that.

He imagined her in those short shorts she'd been wearing that night they'd talked, and her tits bobbing as she peeled off her tight T-shirt and knelt in front of his La-Z-Boy. She had a habit of biting into the bottom half of her cherry red lips. Maybe before she blew him, she'd even talk a little dirty like the girls in the skin flicks did.

Let me suck it, Joe. It's so big and hard, and I want it. Ooooh, please, big guy, I need it. . . .

But Tammy was back in Atlanta, along with his apartment, his sofa, and his porn collection, while Joey was . . . He didn't know where the fuck he was.

He checked the GPS again, but the display still showed a cartoon car heading into nowhere with the words *signal lost* hovering over it. He should never have used it to find a faster way to Denver, and now it wasn't working at all. He'd have to reset the thing, but for that, he'd have to take it off the dashboard stand and fiddle with it, something he wasn't doing until he stopped.

When he found a place to stop.

The stupid-ass thing had told him he could shave fifty minutes off the drive if he left the highway and took some back roads, but now he was stuck on this crappy mountain going exactly nowhere. He hadn't seen any signs for the last thirty miles, which made him wonder if the narrow, two-lane road was even on the map at all. Bob would know, but Joey would punch himself in the balls before he woke up his partner and told him he'd taken a different route.

"Shoulda stayed home." As Joey massaged the half-hard bulge of his sullen dick, he slowed to a crawl and peered through the windshield. The snow had begun falling an hour ago, and now the wipers were barely keeping it from blocking the glass. "Come on, man. Show me something besides all this shit." That was when he saw the road leveling out and widening, and blew out a breath. "Okay, that's more like it."

On the other side of the cab, Bob shifted, mumbling something in his sleep.

"Keep dreaming, man; just keep dreaming," Joey murmured as he slowed and peered again through the frosty glass. A second lane appeared on the right, leading off at a steep incline into a winding trail. The GPS blipped, showing the new road with a balloon marker. When Joey tapped the balloon on the screen, it displayed the words *Frenchman's Pass* and a chevron with a tiny knife, fork, and gas pump.

"Truck stop, all right. That's what I'm talking about." Joey moved into the turn lane, but the truck's dash lights suddenly blinked on and off. At the same time, the engine began to die. "Aw, come on, not now." Without thinking, he pounded the dashboard with his fist.

"Whaaat?" Bob sat straight up, staring first at the

white windshield and then at Joey. "Where are we? Denver?"

"Not there yet." He had to keep Bob from blowing a fuse over this. "I gotta stop. Something's wrong with the engine."

His partner rubbed a hand over his face. "Nothing's wrong with the engine. Parker had it serviced before we left Atlanta."

Joey smiled nervously as the truck's dashboard went dark. "Maybe they missed something with the electrical, Bob."

"Son of a bitch." Bob yanked off his seat belt. "Don't pull onto the shoulder; there's too much fucking snow. Stay in the turn lane and put the flashers on." He peered through the windshield. "Where are we?" Without waiting for an answer, he checked his watch and snatched up the folded map from the seat between them. "We should be coming up on the exit to Denver."

"Yeah, about that." Joey ducked his head. "We're not exactly on the highway anymore."

His partner lowered the map. "*What* did you say?"

Now he was in for it, unless he talked fast. "It was the GPS, man; it screwed me up. I wanted to make better time, you know, so I hit the alternate-route thing, and it told me to take this turn off the highway and then a couple more, and then . . . Jeez, Bob, it's not my fault. I was just trying to get us there faster, man."

Bob's lips flattened. "Where are we?"

"I don't know." He hunched his shoulders. "In the mountains somewhere. Okay?"

His partner grabbed the GPS and reset it, but the screen returned to the *signal lost* screen. "Shit." After he banged it twice against the edge of the dash, it went blank. "Useless. Just like you." He threw the GPS at Joey's head.

"Motherfucker." Joey howled and clapped a hand over his ear. "What'd you do that for?"

"We're in the middle of nowhere," Bob shouted, "and you put us here, you pinhead."

"No, we're not." He rubbed his sore ear and sniffed back a stream of loose snot trying to drip from his nose. "There's some town down the road, and it's got a truck stop. I saw it on the GPS right before it died."

Bob ignored him as he tried to dial out his mobile phone. "No signal. Do you know what Parker is going to do when we don't show on time?"

"We can still call in. There's gotta be a phone in that town," Joey said, cringing when Bob made as if to throw the phone at him. "Shit, will you stop? It's not my fault the GPS sucks."

Bob went still, his eyes wide. He stared at Joey and then turned around toward the back of the cab. "Did you hear that?"

"Man, you broke my frigging ear." Joey frowned. "I don't hear nothing with this storm blowing."

"Somebody just rolled up the back door." Bob pulled the glove box open and took out the weapons he'd stowed inside. He passed a .32 to Joey before he took a Glock and tucked his hand inside his jacket to hide the weapon. "Take the other side. Unless he's holding, shoot out a knee so I can get a look at him." He glared. "And whatever you do, pinhead, don't fucking shoot me."

Joey climbed out, the icy wind scouring his face before snatching away his first breath. As he was driven back against the side of the cab, he leaned out, expecting to see flashing lights, a state trooper, something. Behind the truck was nothing but empty road, framed by snow-frosted trees and four-foot drifts.

The wind blew in his ears, so loud he could barely hear himself as he muttered, "This is bullshit, man."

He saw Bob come into view, his back toward Joey, and shuffled toward him. He stopped only when he realized Bob wasn't wearing his jacket any longer. He had on a different shirt, too, and one of Joey's skullies—

That's not Bob.

It was the stiff. There was no one else it could be. Even as his brain argued, *But he's dead, man, a Popsicle*, Joey knew it was the GI. Those GenHance doctors had pumped him full of drugs and shit, and it had resurrected him, like *Dawn of the* Fucking *Dead*.

Or he'd never been dead. . . .

She stepped out, dressed in Joey's Megadeth T-shirt and his favorite cords, her fiery hair whipping around her flushed face. In all this cold, this storm, she was hot? She met his gaze, and he fell into her eyes, those big, gorgeous eyes, like bits of the sea framed in gold. Lust dried his mouth, and crept down his throat to pour into his chest, his belly, his crotch. Automatically his gaze dropped to her rack, which stretched out two of the skulls on his tee, which made everything easy. He'd shoot the GI, and take Ginger up front with him, and have a little party with her while Bob worked on the engine.

If Bob wasn't okay with that, he'd shoot him, too.

Joey didn't feel the ice crystals peppering his face or the fact that his ears and nose had gone dead numb as he lifted his gun and started toward them. He had to have her, he thought, and squeezed off a round that somehow missed the back of the GI's head. It didn't matter that the asshole turned and saw him; he had a full clip—he'd just keep firing until the big bastard went down.

Steadying his wrist with his free hand to take better aim, Joey fired again—or tried to. The trigger didn't budge this time, and when he looked down, he saw snow swirling around his hand like a miniature white tornado. It closed around the gun and his numb fingers, solidifying into a ball of ice.

"Shit." He tried to shake it off, but the ice began to spread, creeping up both arms toward his elbows. He smashed his frozen hands into the side of the truck, shattering the ice ball and freeing one hand, but his fingers were still frozen in place around the gun.

"This ain't happening." He tried to shake the gun from his hand for a moment, and then saw the woman looking at him again as the marine picked her up in his arms. The snow hadn't touched her beautiful glowing hair or those sunlit ocean eyes . . . and suddenly nothing mattered to Joey but stopping them. "She's mine, you fuck. That bitch is mine."

The marine's lips peeled back from his teeth, and there was something wrong with them, something horribly wrong. Then the woman touched his face, and he turned and took off at a flat run toward an outcropping of rocks.

"No." Joey bolted after them, his feet slipping on the icy surface of the road. He wheeled his arms, his frozen hands like barbells, as he fought to stay upright. He had to get her back. It was the job. It was everything.

He'd die if he didn't have her.

Dimly he heard a shout from the other side of the truck, and shots firing in rapid succession. It was his partner, and he was shooting at them. Was he crazy? "Bob, don't hurt her. Bob!"

The shots ended as his partner yelled, and something unseen slammed into the other side of truck, hard enough to rock it up off one side of the tires. Joey looked ahead, and saw that the marine and the woman had vanished into the storm.

Joey's head cleared, enough for him to realize he was the one who had gone crazy. He jerked around and stumbled toward the door of the cab.

He stopped short as some massive thing emerged from behind the open driver's door. He couldn't see it clearly, but even half-blinded by tears and snow, he could tell it was huge, on all fours, its bulging body covered with blood-splattered fur.

"The fuck?" he heard his voice squeak out.

The bear or whatever it was pulled back its black lips, baring a row of glittering, gore-stained fangs. It made a low, horrible sound that blasted through the wind and sank into Joey's bones, sending a river of hot wetness down the front of his jeans.

He shook his head, only dimly aware that he'd pissed himself. He shuffled backward, falling onto his ass, scrabbling in the snow as it began to advance. "*No*," he screamed. "You get away from me. Get away." He couldn't look at it anymore, and squeezed his eyes shut. "Bob? Hel—"

Then it was on top of him, massive and crushing, and Joey's eyes flew open as he felt his ribs snapping.

Joey finally saw that he was wrong, and that it wasn't a bear at all, right before it tore off his head.

Chapter 10

Rolling up the truck's back door released a splintering, grinding sound from the rollers, too loud to be missed by their captors. As Lilah gave him a stricken look, he grabbed her up in his arms.

"That was dumb." She wrapped her hands over his shoulder. "I'm sorry, Walker."

The prospect of escape made him smile. "I'm not."

A blast of snowy wind roared in around them as he scanned the road and embankments. The emptiness surrounding them offered no safe haven; the only choice he could see was to run for the trees. He shifted her weight higher against his chest. "Hold on to me."

She shifted her hand, curled her arm around his neck, and tucked her face against the other side.

He jumped down onto the road, dropping into a half crouch and centering his weight to keep from falling. Beneath the snow he felt a thin layer of ice. Once he straightened, he carefully placed Lilah on her feet, holding her steady until she could stand on her own. A wave of heat rose between them, and he looked down to see a puddle spreading around both of them. He attributed it to exhaust from the truck until he saw how quickly patches of asphalt were emerging into view.

Somehow Lilah was generating enough heat to instantly deice the road around them.

For the first time he made out a pile of snow-covered rock, high enough to provide good cover. The dying rumble of the engine disappeared behind the squeal of cold metal as one of the truck's doors was opened, and then the other.

"Walker," she whispered. "They're coming."

He heard the one called Joey shouting at him, and felt something strike his shoulder. He turned to see the smaller man and the gun he had pointed at them, and a slow, heavy roar filled his ears. His sight narrowed, becoming a slit edged in gray, and power surged inside him.

Ice rapidly encased Joey's arm, freezing together his hands and the weapon. That should have been enough, but the force gathering inside him wanted more. It wanted flesh, and blood. It wanted to tear the little bastard limb from limb. Leisurely. Joyfully.

Lilah's warm hand turned his face to hers, and her voice wrapped around him. "Don't. We have to get away. Now."

The power ebbed as his eyes cleared and focused on her. Taking her up in his arms again, he measured the distance to the rocks. "Keep your head down."

As he ran for the outcropping, he heard shouting that ended in a short, terrified scream, eerie growls, and tearing, liquid sounds. He didn't look back, and when he reached the rocks, he dropped down behind them, holding Lilah against his chest and covering her head with his arms.

Lilah clutched his sleeve, her eyes wide as she stared up at him. "What was that?"

He touched the ends of his fingers to her lips to silence her before glancing over the edge of the rocks. He could see one dark shape, low to the ground, dragging the older man's body away from the truck and across the snow, leaving behind a dark trail. He knew it was blood from the smell carried to him on the wind. He also felt for the first time the presence of something that was not human or beast but something else. Something older, more primal. Something that felt like death itself.

And, judging by its ferocity, Death was starved.

More shadows emerged from the trees and came to join the one with the corpse. There were low, guttural sounds, and the feeding ceased. Another form emerged from the opposite side of the truck, this one bigger but lighter in color, and rose up on its back legs, at the same time seemingly dwindling.

Not shrinking, he thought. *Changing shape*.

The beast now appeared to be roughly the same size as a large human, although gray fur still covered its body, and its limbs remained in their oddly jointed dimensions. The huge muscles of its back stretched and bulged as it picked up the headless corpse of the younger man and walked into the snow to join the others.

He studied the beasts for a moment, trying to understand what they were, before sinking back down out of sight. This time when Lilah would have spoken, he clamped his hand over her mouth. He felt sure that whatever it was that had killed their abductors would not hesitate to attack them, and there were too many for him to fight off—assuming his strength was a match for the creatures.

One alone had killed and gutted two men in the space of a few heartbeats. There were at least seven now.

The ice around them thickened, blocking out the sounds of the storm. Lilah nestled against him, her body heat warming him, her scent driving away the metallic stink of blood in his nostrils. As he soaked in her warmth, ice crystals began to form an opaque white cocoon around them, enclosing them in silence.

He turned, putting his back against the frozen rock and shifting her, gathering her legs up so they didn't touch the frigid ice beneath them. Gradually the sense of the other killers faded until he knew they were miles away. Only then did he allow himself to relax a little.

"They're gone," he told her.

Lilah lifted her head and saw the cocoon for the first time. "What's this?"

"Ice."

"I can see that." With careful fingers she reached out to touch the surface of the ice bubble, scraping away some crystals before giving him an astonished look. "It's solid. How did this happen?"

He brushed a swath of red hair back from her face. "Does it matter?"

"I don't have the ability to make spontaneous igloos." She glanced down at her wet hand. "Do I?"

"It is only ice, Lilah," he assured her.

"At least it protected us." She glanced in the direction of the truck and shuddered. "What were those things?"

"I could not see them clearly through the storm." He suspected that even if he had, he wouldn't have recognized them. They had moved like nothing on this earth. "Did you hear their minds?"

"I don't know if they had minds, exactly," she said slowly. "What I felt was something that was completely focused on killing." Her throat moved. "And eating."

His own belly clenched. "Then they hunt humans as food."

"No. At least, I don't think they do." She thought for a moment. "Killing prey for food is a learned behavior. When predators in the wild are young, their mothers teach them how to kill and what to kill. Humans are never on the menu, which is why most of them try to avoid us. We're not prey to them, so we're just not that interesting."

He recalled how quickly the creature had crossed the snow. "This one took interest."

"That's the other thing I don't understand," she admitted. "It brought down two healthy men by itself, which is rogue behavior, or what an animal that lives on its own does. Only after the men were dead, other adults joined it, and it didn't try to drive them away from the kill. It let them help drag off the bodies. That's cooperative behavior."

"A starved rogue cannot cooperate?"

"Unless it and the rest of its species are schizophrenic, no." She frowned. "I don't think it was starved, either."

"Perhaps it was defending its territory." He leaned his head back and closed his eyes.

"Walker?" When he glanced down at her, she said, "We should take the truck and go before they come back."

He lifted his hand to punch a hole in the ice, but she caught his wrist and stopped him.

"Let me try something first."

Lilah placed her free hand on the ice, holding it there as she concentrated. After a few minutes, she took it away and examined the spot. "Nothing." She brought up his hand to the ice. "Put your hand against it next to mine." When he did, she focused again. He felt something coiling and uncoiling down the length of his arm, flaring hot and cold along the way. Water began dripping through their fingers, and the ice beneath their palms began to shrink outward, until their hands pushed through the bubble.

"It's not me. It's coming from you." She regarded him with troubled eyes. "But I'm making you do it, aren't I?"

He shifted their hands to another spot. "Again."

By the time they had repeated the experiment three times, there was a gaping, dripping hole in the ice cocoon. While he remained unaffected by the heat, Lilah's skin had grown flushed and damp, and sweat trickled down from her hairline.

"Whew." She tried to smile. "I could use a cold

shower." She inspected him. "You're not feeling the heat, though."

"I feel it." He wouldn't tell her that what burned inside him wanted only to push her down, spread her legs, and mount her. Instead he used his fist on the ice, widening the holes enough for them to crawl outside.

Once they emerged from the remains of the bubble, he helped her to her feet and turned toward the road.

"The truck's gone," she said, staring at the splatters and pools of blood, now frozen and quickly being covered by fresh snow. She tugged him over to the road. "How could they take the truck? I didn't hear the engine."

Neither had he, but he smelled burning fuel and saw some faint marks running across the road. "They didn't take it."

He guided her over to the other side, and they looked over the edge. A swath of broken trees and flattened brush went down several hundred feet, and stopped at a huge twisted pile of metal. All around the smoldering wreck lay torn, smashed boxes marked with the GenHance logo, some spilling out their contents on the ground.

"They must have pushed it over," Lilah said, her voice blank with shock. "Like it was nothing but a toy. But they're animals. How could they do this?"

Speculating over what the creatures had done was as useless as the truck was now. He drew her back and studied the road again, and then caught the faintest trace of warmth in the air.

"Walker?"

"I smell something." He breathed in, ignoring the stink of blood and violence and ferreting out the subtler scent beneath it. "Woodsmoke." He turned his head toward the point where the road split in two. "It's coming from there."

"That's the direction they went," Lilah said, nodding toward the dark smears still visible in the snow.

He filled his chest again, this time focusing on the smell of death. "No. They went west." He pointed to the lower peak of the pass. "That way."

Something flickered in her eyes. "You can smell their trail."

"Yes." He was frightening her, he realized, but if they were to survive this, he would have to do whatever was necessary—even lie to her. "It must be part of how they changed me, with the drugs."

Her expression cleared. "I didn't think of that. Sorry." She glanced over at the trees and shuddered. "We really need to get out of here."

He took her hand in his. "We'll follow the road into the pass. Be ready to take cover." He glanced down at their hands. "Can you keep us warm?"

She nodded, and a moment later he felt the now-familiar twining sensation spreading up from their hands. All around them the icy ground began to thaw.

He led her around the bloodied remains of the battle and around the curve, stopping briefly to study the road ahead. It lay empty and covered in a thick layer of fresh snow, with no tire marks to indicate any traffic had passed through recently.

The bitter wind buffeted them, but Lilah kept a firm hold on his hand, and through him steadily generated enough heat to keep their bodies from chilling. The storm seemed to be clearing, which helped, but by the time they had walked a mile, their clothes were dripping wet from the melting snow, and Lilah's face had grown pinched with strain.

He stopped and turned her toward him. "What is it?"

Her shoulders slumped, and the heat retreated for several seconds before she straightened and looked up at him, exhaustion clouding her eyes. "I don't think I can keep this up much longer."

The settlers who had originally built the town of Frenchman's Pass had been a group of eleven families from the East who had been drawn together by unwavering faith and new purpose. After some years of planning, saving, and preparing, they had left their comfortable homes in rural Pennsylvania and traveled to the remote mountains of Colorado. They chose the more remote, unpopulated region specifically to avoid the lawlessness and vice of the established mining camps and boomtowns.

Like so many faithful of their time, the settlers had staked their future on the dream of building the kind of community that reflected their beliefs and values. Led by a master carpenter named Josiah Jemmet, his wife, Anna, and their six sturdy children, the forty-nine settlers had set out on the arduous journey from their homes in the East in late winter, before the Mississippi could thaw.

"This is our great exodus," Josiah was fond of saying whenever a minor squabble erupted. "Let us not disappoint the Lord with how we conduct ourselves along the way."

Although they were determined to isolate themselves from the evils of the world, the settlers knew that in order to survive they would have to trade with others who did not share their values. That spring they began clearing land in the pass between the peaks and measuring out lots for a proper town, one that unlike their mountain homes would welcome strangers. While the women stayed up in the peaks to plant vegetable gardens and tend to the younger children and the livestock they had brought from back East, Josiah and a group of men and older boys spent the short summer months erecting a general store, stables, a boardinghouse, and a trading post.

When their first visitor, a trapper who lived twenty miles west, rode in, he was shocked to discover that the settlers had not brought a drop of liquor with them, nor did they have any plans to build a saloon.

"Why, a town without a saloon is like one without a jail," the old-timer had protested.

"We're not building a jail, either," Josiah assured him. "If we don't have one, we surely won't have need of the other."

The settlers continued to thrive and build until the first hard freeze arrived and sent them back up the mountain to their comfortable log cabins to weather the upcoming storms until spring. As they had during their first winter, they planned to look out for one another and gather as often as they could to discuss naming their new town. Unaware of what else had come to the pass that winter, Josiah consulted his Bible to find names for both the town and his seventh child. By March he expected to welcome Daniel or Ruth into the world, and perhaps carve a sign that read MOUNT DAVID or ABRAHAMVILLE near the entrance to the pass.

Josiah, who believed that hard work, prayer, and clean living earned a man the right to a good, long life, didn't know he would never come down from the mountain again.

There still were no saloons in the mountain town the first families had built, but 130 years had added another dozen business establishments, including two diners, a Victorian bed-and-breakfast, a local crafters' co-op, and a jail, the latter presided over by Larimer County sheriff Ethan Jemmet.

Ethan, who was finishing out his first shift since returning from Denver, had spent most of the afternoon trying not to think about runaway Lori or her bracelet, which lay curled like a tiny sleeping snake in his shirt pocket. Working the crossword puzzle from the *Sunday Times* he had picked up in Denver wasn't helping, but it kept him from issuing an all-points bulletin.

"Evening, Sheriff."

"Shem." Ethan nodded toward the cardboard boxes stacked neatly along the wall. "You're welcome to whatever you want as long as you pass it on when you're done."

" 'Preciate it."

Because the winter months cut off most regular deliveries to the town, and Internet and satellite service was spotty at best, Ethan had also brought back from Denver a hefty stock of the latest newspapers, magazines, books, DVDs, and CDs to pass around. The townspeople would share them through the dark cold months, and by spring be caught up on most of what they needed to know had changed with the outside world.

"You pick up any new Tony Bennett?" Shem asked.

"Nope, sorry. I think he's retired." Ethan frowned at the clue for fourteen across. "What's a seven-letter word for 'bootless cries to a deaf heaven'? Starts with a *T*."

"Trouble. Kinda like what we got."

He glanced up at the old man. Shem Warner had come down to Frenchman's Pass at the end of October in order to move into the boardinghouse. A loner by nature, he resented having to give up his cabin and closely guarded solitude for four months out of the year, but he knew better than to stay alone on the mountain during the winter. Even in town he kept to himself, unless he had one of his spells.

Ethan set down his clipboard and swung his worn work boots off from where he'd propped them on the edge of his desk. "You going to tell me about this trouble?"

"What I can." Shem rasped a hand over his cheek and sighed. "Outsiders, four of 'em. Coming up in a truck from the flatlands. Saw it last night in a spell I had afore I hit the sack."

Paul Jemmet considered Old Shem's spells to be nothing more than manifestations of his many, deeply ingrained paranoid fantasies. Ethan was inclined to agree, but he had never embraced science as closely as his father had, and preferred to reserve judgment until he had evidence either way.

He reined in a sigh. "When will they get here?" Shem shrugged. Of course, his spells never came with a calendar or a clock. But Ethan caught the way he shifted his eyes. "What else did you see?"

Dislike hardened the old man's voice. "Something's wrong with 'em. Two of 'em, they ain't regular folks."

He almost laughed. "Not a lot of regular around here, Shem. Maybe you got your signals crossed."

"It ain't funny," the old man flared. "I don't just see 'em, Sheriff. I feel 'em." He thumped his chest with one gnarled fist. "These two, they liked to burn a hole through me."

"All right, then. What did you feel about them?"

"Can't say. Ain't no words for it." His mouth moved as if he were sucking on something sour. "They was there with the other pair one minute, and then the next they wasn't. Like they was never there in the first place." His mouth hitched. "But Nate was. He saw 'em."

The mention of his brother brought Ethan to his feet. "Nathan never comes down off the mountain."

"He did this time. He knows all about 'em." The old man stuffed his hands in his trousers and rocked back on his heels. "Mebbe if you two weren't feuding allatime, he'd have brought 'em in."

He ignored the sarcasm. "They're still *here*?" When Shem nodded, he swore. "Why didn't you say so?"

"Just them two that ain't right." Dislike flickered in the old man's faded blue eyes as he lifted his head. "Other ones, they got et."

Ethan grabbed the mike to the radio. "Elroy, this is base."

His deputy answered a moment later. "Copy, Sheriff."

"We've got strangers on foot in the pass. I'm heading out to collect them." He set down the mike to pull on his jacket.

"Flatlanders." Elroy sounded scathing. "You want me to return to base?"

"I need you to go up to my father's place and get him." He took the gun from his desk drawer, checked the rounds, and holstered it at his side. "I'll meet you two back here."

"Don't you want to take them to the B&B and let Annie see to them?" his deputy asked.

He glanced at Shem, who shook his head. "We'll have a look at them first here."

"Copy that."

Ethan's Escalade had been outfitted for operation during the worst conditions, and as he drove down toward the entrance to the pass, he expected to feel the buffeting of the wind. But a break in the storm had apparently come along, and aside from the light powdery flakes drifting down, there was hardly a breeze stirring the snow-encrusted trees.

Twilight had already painted most of the sky deep purple, and he switched on his headlights as he peered through the icy windshield. With only one road in and five-foot drifts on either side, there was no place for two people to conceal themselves—but all he saw ahead was snow and empty road.

Unless they missed the road to town and went up the slope.

Ethan's jaw set as he reached for the radio and switched it to a frequency he hadn't used since joining the sheriff's office. "Nathan, do you copy?"

Static answered him for a long minute, but just as he was going to repeat the call, it crackled.

"What do you want?" His brother's voice sounded garbled, but not enough to disguise the anger.

"Shem stopped in to see me. Said you came down to the pass tonight." He clamped down on his own temper. "That true?"

"I was hunting."

Nathan was always hunting. "Did you come across anything unusual down by the road?"

"No."

He'd have to be direct. "What about a truck? You find any stranded motorists?"

"They weren't stranded." Static came over the channel.

Ethan swore, but he had reached the entrance to the pass, and there was no time to mince words with his brother. He pulled over, putting the truck into park as he hung the mike back on the unit.

He'd told his father after he'd taken the badge and sworn his oath that he had to enforce the law, no matter who broke it, or why. Until tonight he'd never been obliged to, but now, thanks to his damn brother, he just might have to keep that threat.

Ethan got out to walk the rest of the way to the road and see what kind of mess had been left behind. Before he had gone a few yards, he saw shadows near the trees move, and a figure separate from them.

PART THREE

Hunter Moon

"A C in English. A D in Calculus. An F in Bible Study." Evelyn Emerson dropped the report card on the gleaming marble of the coffee table. "How could you let your grades drop this much? Why didn't you ask to stay after school and do some extra credit?"

Elle almost reminded her that she had, although the nuns wouldn't allow her to do extra credit while serving out her detentions. But her mother's voice was already starting to climb toward the piercing octave she used when she was outraged. "I'm really sorry, Evelyn."

"Are you." Her mother went to the bar and poured two inches of brandy into a snifter.

Elle stayed in her penitent position on the edge of the antique love seat and stared at the pile of glossy French fashion magazines that her mother never read. The maid changed them once a week, along with the crystal vases of fresh-cut flowers that had no fragrance, and the dish of Swiss chocolates that Elle was never permitted to touch. Everything in her mother's sitting room was beautiful and polished as if they lived in a display case in a museum. In a sense it was: an ongoing exhibit of Evelyn's own genius at interior design that changed with her moods and the seasons.

Sometimes Elle imagined that they lived like dolls in a playhouse, just two figurines that were moved around and posed by some giant, unseen hand.

"Is it some boy?" her mother asked suddenly. "Is that what is responsible for this behavior?"

Elle choked back a laugh. "I go to an all-girls school, Evelyn." She hated using her first name, but her mother refused to be called Mom, Mother, or anything else. "The only time I see boys is when we drive through town, and you don't let me out of the car."

"Don't lie to me. I know how resourceful you teenagers are." Evelyn finished her drink. "Who is it, then? The brother of one of your friends? Are you meeting one of them behind my back?"

"Well, there is this really cute altar boy I see every Sunday at church, but I think he's a little young for me." She cringed as Evelyn strode over to her. "I'm kidding, I'm kidding."

"I'm not laughing," she snapped. "Neither should you, considering what your birth mother did to you."

Not my birth mother again. Elle closed her eyes. "Please, Evelyn. Don't."

"Don't what? Don't talk about her, the schoolgirl who conceived you in the backseat of some car, and abandoned you the day you were born?" Her mother made a contemptuous sound. "Don't remind you that if it wasn't for me, you'd be in some dreadful foster home, being starved or beaten or molested?"

"I'm very grateful that you adopted me," Elle said quickly. "I know how lucky I am."

"I didn't simply adopt you, Lillian." She sat down beside her and took hold of her hands. "I saved you. I gave you my name, and brought you into my home, and cared for you. I put you in the best Catholic school in the country so that you could get a decent education." She drew back, her expression hurt. "And *this* is how you repay me."

"I try, I really do." Criticizing the stern nuns who taught her would only enrage her mother, who thought that the sisters were perfect. "It's me. I'm just not that smart. I forget the rules sometimes and I speak out of turn. But I'll work harder, I promise. And I'll behave."

"I've never expected you to get straight A's, have I? All I've asked is that you do your best." Evelyn sighed. "With these grades you won't even graduate, much less get into Holy Cross."

"I know."

"Sister Maria Paul called me at work this morning." Evelyn folded her arms. "She says you're becoming incorrigible. That you're a bad influence on the other girls. She believes you'd be happier in public school."

Elle stared at the nails the nuns had clipped short. *I would be.*

She didn't realize she'd murmured it out loud until Evelyn grabbed her chin and made her look up. "Don't even think it, you stupid little twit. With a public school record, you'll never get into Holy Cross." She got up and went to the window overlooking the formal gardens.

"I know it's important to you, Evelyn." Maybe this was the right time to talk about it. "But I think you should know that I want to go somewhere else for college."

Her mother turned around. "*What* did you say?"

"You know how much I like working with the dogs and the horses." She had to talk fast now before Evelyn's temper exploded. "Every time Dr. Devereaux comes by to check on Dancer or give Royal his shots, he does ask me to help him. He says I have the touch, that animals trust me." She could see how pink her mother's face was, but she had to say the rest. "I don't want to go to Holy Cross. I'm going to apply to vet school. I want to be a veterinarian."

Evelyn seemed to wither in front of her eyes. "I should have seen this coming. You've spent half your life mucking around in that wretched barn and fooling around in the kennels."

"It's what I want to do with my life." Elle watched her mother move like a sleepwalker toward her desk. "You want me to be happy, don't you?"

"I want you to be a good girl, Lillian," she said, as she had whenever Elle defied her. "Be a good girl, and you'll get your reward."

She was so tired of hearing that. "I can be a vet and still be a good girl, can't I?"

Evelyn didn't answer her; she picked up the phone and dialed a number. "Lyle? Yes, it's Evelyn. Are you still interested in Dancer and the other horses? What are you offering?"

Elle rose. "What?"

Evelyn listened, and then nodded. "That's acceptable. You can pick them up in the morning. Yes. See the stable manager. You're quite welcome."

"Wait. Evelyn. You can't sell the horses." Elle rushed to the desk and picked up the phone. "Call him back. Tell him it's a mistake. You changed your mind. *Evelyn, please.*"

"It was foolish of me to indulge this ridiculous obsession you have with animals, but there is still time to correct the situation." Evelyn took the receiver from her and hung it back up. "There will be no more talk about being a vet, or defying my wishes. You are going to apply yourself in school, bring up your grades, and behave yourself. When you graduate, you will attend Holy Cross."

"You can't sell Dancer." Elle backed away from her.

"I've had him since he was a colt. You *gave* him to me for my birthday."

Not a flicker of pity passed over her mother's cool features. "I know you're upset now, but it's for the best. Someday, when you understand, you'll thank me for doing this, Lillian."

"For doing what? For taking away everything I care about? The only thing that makes me happy?" She was shrieking now, but she couldn't stop herself. "How could you? How could you?"

Elle ran from the sitting room and out into the reception hall, dodging around her mother's housekeeper as she raced through the dining room and into the kitchen, where the cook and two maids were preparing the evening meal.

"Miss Lillian?"

Elle didn't stop as she flung open the side door and flew outside, racing toward the barn. Huntley, the stable manager, came out of his office and blocked her path.

"Your mother just called down, miss," he said. "She wants you back up at the house."

"I'm not going back." Elle went around him and strode back to Dancer's stall. The gelding poked his head out and whickered softly as he watched her take down her saddle. When Elle turned and found Huntley standing between her and her horse, she took a deep breath. "My mother just sold Dancer and the other horses to Lyle Hamilton. He's coming in the morning to pick them up."

"So she told me, miss. I'm very sorry."

He didn't get it. "Mr. Huntley, once the horses are gone, what do you think you're going to do around here?" Before he could answer, she added, "God, what am I going to do?"

"I think you'll go back to the house, miss. I'd walk

you up, but I have to head into town now." He stuffed his hands in his pockets and rocked back on his heels. "I'll be picking up some supplies, getting a haircut and maybe a bite to eat. Probably'll take me a good two, three hours."

"Thank you, Mr. Huntley."

As soon as the stable manager left, Elle saddled Dancer and mounted him, leading him out through the back of the barn. If Evelyn saw her from the windows, she couldn't do anything to stop her. All the stable hands had gone home for the day, and Mr. Huntley's Jeep was halfway down the long drive. None of the maids could ride.

Neither could Evelyn.

Elle barely nudged Dancer with her heels before he took off, breaking from a walk into a fast lope like a rocket. She crossed the back pasture and wheeled him around to the stretch of fence separating Emerson land from the first slope of the hills beyond it.

She'd never attempted to jump a fence with Dancer, but when his muscles bunched under her, she knew they would clear it as easily as they had all the practice poles. He landed like an Olympian, keeping her safe in the cradle of the saddle as his long, strong legs tackled the slope.

Elle had to rein him in as they passed the tree line and made their way into the woods, where Evelyn had strictly forbidden her to ride. The sunlight had already begun to fade, and with no moon to light the way, she'd have to turn back.

"Or we could keep going," she said, leaning forward to rest her cheek against the roughness of his mane. The sound of her voice made him flick his ears, and he turned his head to eye her. "Would you like that, Dance? Would you ride off with me into the sunset?"

Going back meant more than losing the horse she

loved. What little freedom Elle had would be taken from her as well. She'd never go to vet school. She'd finally become the perfect doll for Evelyn to dress and pose as she pleased forever.

It was impossible to run away from home on a horse—Elle knew that—and as they came out of the trees and faced a high, rocky incline, she knew her illicit ride had come to an end. She dismounted, leading Dancer to a patch of grass speckled with dandelions. She bent to pick one that had gone to seed, and as she straightened, she silently made her wish.

I wish my mother would love me for me.

Elle puffed a breath at the dandelion, and watched the fluffy seeds burst away from the stem, spreading out on the breeze as they flew away, taking her wish with them.

Dancer lifted his head and shuffled to the side, snorting and then whinnying as he back-stepped.

"Wait a sec." Elle tried to grab the dangling reins, but he turned suddenly, knocking her away as he barreled off toward the trees. "Dancer, wait, I mean, whoa—"

The body that hit her was big, heavy, and silent, plowing her into the grass under its weight. Before Elle had a chance to breathe, she saw narrow green eyes, and then a mouth filled with sharp white teeth.

Cougar?

It hissed like a snake, its cool breath blasting her face before it dropped its head and sank its fangs into her throat.

Elle writhed under the deadweight, her scream trapped by the teeth tearing into her throat and the claws digging deep into her shoulders. All she knew was hot, tearing pain that grew so enormous it pushed her into some small corner of her mind where she could only huddle in terror.

The gush of blood from her throat bathed her and the

big cat in a wet, warm spray, and as it lifted its muzzle to strike again, Elle felt something besides the agony of her wounds: the cougar's terrible hunger.

She couldn't speak, couldn't move, and then her hand inched up and rested against the tawny fur. It felt so soft, this deadly thing, its pelt like polished silk. She didn't want her life to end, not this soon, but the wounds the cat had inflicted on her were too terrible to survive. Now that she knew the end had come, she felt only regret. If only she had been able to control the wildness inside her, she might never have ended up here, at the mercy of this beautiful, wild thing.

A rough tongue lapped at her cheek, and Elle coughed a little as the unbearable inferno of pain burned down to a glowing, incandescent heat. She counted down her heartbeats as they slowed, and felt the chill of the ground beginning to seep over her, putting out the last of the fire.

The night came then, as fast as Dancer had taken her, and Elle went gladly on her final ride.

SEARCH FOR RUNAWAY TEEN HEIRESS ENDS

10/01/00

SANTA LUCIA, CA—After a year of searching for sixteen-year-old Lillian Emerson, who vanished from her family's estate, Santa Lucia Police Chief Ormond Teller has announced that the investigation into her disappearance will be suspended.

"It is with great personal regret that I am calling off the search," Teller told reporters. "I still believe Lillian is out there somewhere, alive and well, but we have exhausted all of our leads, and our officers are needed on other cases." When asked where he thought Lillian was, Teller responded, "I can't say, but wherever that is, I don't think she wants to be found."

Like her daughter, Evelyn Emerson has also vanished from the public eye, and has not been seen since the day Lillian ran away. Ms. Emerson is now rumored to be residing in Chicago, where she runs her interior-design empire from Emerson Interiors' corporate headquarters on Michigan Avenue. Ms. Emerson has refused all interview requests, and Emerson's attorney, Wallace Bridger, has repeatedly defended his client's reluctance to talk about her daughter's disappearance.

"Evelyn has never given up hope that Lillian will come home someday," Bridger recently told reporters. "Her efforts to find her daughter have been tireless, and will continue until such time as she can confirm that Lillian is alive and well. She has no desire to put her deepest personal pain on display in order to titillate the public." When asked why Evelyn Emerson has never offered any reward for information regarding her daughter's whereabouts, as is typical in such cases, Bridger dismissed the question. "This isn't a murder or an abduction. Lillian ran away from home. It was thoughtless and cruel, but she knows she can come back whenever she wants to."

Chapter 11

The shadow moving toward Ethan became a man, and in his arms he carried the limp body of a woman. The man wore only ordinary clothes covered with new snow, and although a flannel shirt covered the woman's torso, all she had on her feet were socks. The man walked down, kicking his way through the drifts and hefting the woman up when he sank.

Ethan trotted out to meet him, inspecting him for wounds but seeing none. What he noticed was the man's shaved head, the grim set of his jaw, the flat black of his eyes. "You folks all right?"

The man looked down at the unconscious female. "I can't wake her."

"She's probably hypothermic. We need to get her inside and warmed up. We've got a doctor in town." He reached out to take the woman, stopping only when he saw the glitter in the other man's eyes. "My truck's right over here."

The man slogged out of the drift and followed him to the Escalade. Ethan opened the door to the backseat, and reached in to shove over the go-bag he stowed there. He expected the man to lay the woman inside on the seat, but instead he climbed in and held her on his lap. Ethan peeled off his parka and handed it in.

"Put it over her legs," he told him. After he got in

and started the truck, he glanced at the rearview mirror. "What's your name?"

The man returned his stare. "Walker Kimball."

Ethan noted the slight hesitation, but the man looked like he'd been battered nine ways to Sunday; he was entitled to be suspicious. "Is that lady Mrs. Kimball?"

His eyes narrowed. "Why?"

"Just curious." The man was suspicious and territorial as all hell. "You want to tell me what you two are doing out in the middle of a blizzard?"

"Our car broke down. We needed help."

Ethan could read people like open books, and knew all the small tells that indicated when someone was lying. Walker Kimball wasn't being dishonest, but he wasn't telling the whole truth.

"Were you traveling with anyone else besides your lady there?" Ethan asked.

"We were," Kimball said, "but they left us behind."

Another partial truth. "Anything else you want to tell me, Mr. Kimball?"

"She's very cold," he said, his voice tight. "Please drive faster."

Ethan nodded and stepped on the gas.

Once he pulled up to the curb outside his office, Ethan saw through the window that his father and his deputy were standing inside. "You want me to carry her in?" Before he finished the question, Kimball had already opened the door and climbed out. "I guess not."

Elroy had opened the door a gap when Kimball reached it and shouldered his way through. He inspected Ethan's office with a glance before turning to Paul Jemmet. "You are a doctor?"

"Yes." Ethan's father lifted the shirt away from the woman's face and touched her throat, frowning at the bruises under her jaw. "She's still alive, but we have to get her out of these wet clothes and warm her. Elroy, run over to Annie's and borrow some space heaters. Ethan, we'll need towels, blankets, and hot tea."

Kimball followed Paul into the back room while Elroy trotted for the door.

Ethan caught his deputy before he went out. "Ask Annie to send for Nathan. I'll be over to talk to him once we've got the woman stable."

Elroy frowned, but nodded and darted out. Ethan filled the electric kettle before he took some clean towels and a pair of chenille blankets from the storage closet.

When he joined his father and Kimball in the back, they had already stripped the woman down to her skin. Kimball took the towels from him and began gently chafing her damp limbs as Paul shifted the pad of his stethoscope over her left breast.

"How long were you out in this weather?" his father asked Kimball.

"I don't know. Half an hour, perhaps." He draped one towel over her hips and touched her side before straightening and reaching for the blankets.

"Wait on those." To Ethan, Paul said, "Go check the kettle, son."

He didn't appreciate his father sending him from the room like a misbehaving child. "Kimball, come with me. You and I need to talk."

The big man didn't even look at him. "I can't leave her."

"It'll just take a few minutes—"

Kimball took the woman's hand in his, revealing a pair of handcuffs hanging from his wrist. From the red, raw marks on the woman's arm, it was obvious that she had been cuffed to him.

Ethan folded his arms. "You mind explaining to me why you and your lady are in handcuffs?"

"We were kidnapped."

He stepped closer. "Sure you were. And I'm . . . the . . . " He halted, his tongue growing thick and useless as he looked down at the woman's face.

He heard his father saying his name, but his voice sounded miles away. All he could see was the white glistening skin, the soft ripe mouth, and the molten glory of her hair. Knowing he would be burned but not caring, Ethan lifted his hand, stretching out so that he might touch all that lovely fire.

A large, brutal hand clamped around his wrist, forcing him to look into savage black eyes. "No."

Rage shattered his wonder. "What?"

"Ethan." His father stood, stepping between and separating them. He grabbed his shoulder, turning him away from the cot to face the door. "The kettle. Call me when it's ready." He gave him a push.

Once he was outside the room, Ethan's head cleared and he spun around, only to find the door closing in his face.

"Shit." He wanted to kick the door in, but backed away, dragging a shaking hand through his hair. Whatever had taken hold of him in that room was gone, and he was in no hurry to feel it again. He retreated to the front office, where he stood over the kettle and listened to the water coming to a boil. From the moment he'd seen Walker Kimball plowing his way through the snow, he'd assumed what problems Shem had foreseen during his spell would be caused by the big man. The handcuffs and his bullshit about being kidnapped were plenty of justification. But he was wrong.

The real trouble that had come to town was Kimball's helpless, unconscious, beautiful woman.

Someone had wrapped Lilah in violets, so warm and deep and soft that they turned darkness into a bower of midnight silk. Her toes curled with pleasure as the petals crept into her sodden hair and curled around her stiff fingers, spreading warmth wherever they caressed. After the terror of waking in the truck and trying to fight through the snowstorm, she would happily stay curled up in this gentle cocoon of blooms forever. No one in that other place would miss her, no one had ever wanted or needed her, except . . .

Walker.

The violets began to melt, becoming wet beads on her skin, sliding down her cheeks and seeping between her lips, salted with sadness. Then she tasted something else, something fragrant and tart and golden-sweet, that filled her nose and trickled into her mouth, and when she swallowed, she tasted honey and lemon.

"Drink."

Walker, his hand at the back of her head, holding it up. Lilah felt the edge of a cup at her lips, and tasted the sweet warmth of the tea, and swallowed again, although some of it spilled down her chin.

"She's coming around." A strange male voice sounded pleased. "Stay with her. I'm going to have a word with my son. I'll get a cutter for those cuffs, too."

Lilah waited until the other man had left before she opened her eyes. Walker knelt beside the cot she occupied, and when he saw her eyes, he set aside the cup he was holding to her lips.

"What happened?" She tried to sit up, but he put an arm across her. "Where are we?"

"You fell unconscious from the cold. We're in the local sheriff's office. He found us before I could reach the town." Walker glanced over his shoulder before adding in a murmur, "Whatever they ask, let me answer their questions."

"We can't tell them," she said quickly. "They'll run our names and try to confirm our story, and then Gen-Hance will know where we are."

"I already told him my name was Walker Kimball," he said.

"Then you'll have to be who you are: a marine who just got back to the States," Lilah said. "I'm your girlfriend. We were driving to see your folks, and stopped to help a couple of guys who were pretending that their truck had broken down. They robbed us, handcuffed us, and threw us in the back before they took off. They were going to kill us and dump our bodies in a ravine." She thought for a moment, mentally running through all the aliases she had used. "Tell them my name is Marianne Gordon. You call me Mari. Can you remember all of that?"

"Yes." He gave her a measuring look. "You never told me your surname."

"I'll tell you anything you want to know, as soon as we get out of here," she promised, glancing over his shoulder as the door swung open. Quickly she closed her eyes and went limp.

"I'm sorry that took so long. My son can be argumentative at times," Lilah heard the smooth voice of the man she assumed was the doctor. "How is she?"

"I think she's starting to wake." Walker bent close. "Mari. Can you open your eyes?"

Lilah did her best imitation of a woman regaining consciousness, and feigned confusion as she looked up at the silver-haired man standing over them. He had a kind face, but his eyes seemed guarded. "What happened? Where are we?"

"We got away from them, my heart," Walker told her. He kissed her brow before he added, "We're safe now."

The doctor produced a heavy-duty tool that pried apart the cuff on Walker's wrist, releasing him.

"I know you've both been through a terrible ordeal," the doctor said, "but my son has some questions, and I need to examine this young lady more thoroughly."

"I will go and speak to him." Walker looked down at her. "I'll be back soon."

She nodded, and watched him leave before she looked at the doctor. "Hello." She produced a tired smile without much effort; she felt horribly weak and exhausted. "I'm Marianne Gordon."

"Dr. Paul Jemmet. I'm the local GP." He pulled up a folding chair and sat down beside the cot. "My son found you and your boyfriend out in the storm. Exposure to the cold caused you to become hypothermic and lose consciousness. I'm going to check you for frostbite, and while I'm doing that, I'm also going to ask you some annoying questions. Is that all right?" When she nodded, he smiled and picked up her hand and gently flexed her thumb. "Do you know who is now president of the United States?"

"Barack Obama."

He continued testing each of her fingers. "What month is it, Marianne?"

"December."

"And the year?" he asked as he switched hands.

"Two thousand nine."

"Why were you handcuffed to your boyfriend?"

"To keep me from getting away," she said without thinking, and hastily amended, "The men who took us knocked out Walker. They knew he was too heavy for me to lift."

Dr. Jemmet gave her a shrewd look. "Not many thieves think to pack handcuffs for a hijacking."

"I think they were involved in more than just stealing trucks and our wallets." She lifted her chin as he felt her ears. She didn't have to fake the tremble in her voice now. "They were going to kill us, Dr. Jemmet. If Walker hadn't woken up, and jumped out of the truck with me . . . "

"He's a brave man. Most soldiers are." His smile seemed more genuine this time as he shifted around to look at her feet. "Are his parents expecting you to arrive home today?"

"No, we didn't tell them Walker was back. It was supposed to be a big surprise."

"That's good." He chuckled. "What I mean is, it's good that they won't be worried. I'm afraid with this storm you two are stranded here until the snowplows can clear the main road."

"How long will that take?"

"Once the storm passes, a few days, maybe a week." He lifted the blanket, sliding it up to expose her legs. "I'm not seeing any sign of frostbite, which is good." He lowered the blanket back in place, and in the same gentle voice asked, "Marianne, did these men hurt you?"

"No, sir." She didn't understand, and then suddenly realized he must have already seen the marks and bruises left on her body from being pinned under Walker. "One of them grabbed me around the neck, but that was all."

His eyes softened. "It's not your fault if they did anything more, my dear."

Lilah couldn't let him think she was raped, but how else would she explain the other bruises? Thanks to her ability to heal quickly, by now they would be turning yellow-brown, and by tomorrow they would begin to fade. He probably thought she got them days ago. . . . That was it.

"Walker was overseas for a long time," she said, trying to look embarrassed. "While he was there, he was faithful to me. When he got home, well, he was . . . And I was . . . " She stopped and ducked her head shyly. "I do bruise easily, Dr. Jemmet, and we were really happy to see each other again."

Stuttering through the lie made her sound convincing even to her own ears, and no doubt the country doctor interpreted her anxious flush as a sign of her embarrassment. But Lilah had to be sure he was buying her story, and as he pressed two fingers to her wrist and glanced at his watch, she reached out with her mind to see if she could pick up any trace of emotion from his.

Poor young thing. That boy is too big and rough for her, but I can hear the love in her voice. I guess I've mortified her enough for one night.

Lilah began to reply when she realized his lips hadn't moved. She was hearing the man's voice—his thoughts—in her head. It was so unexpected and frightening that she flinched away from him.

Dr. Jemmet frowned and took his hand away. "Marianne?"

"Sorry." She rubbed at her wrist as she tried to grasp what had just occurred. "It's still a little sore from being in those handcuffs." She eyed the door. "Do you think you could get Walker for me?"

"Of course. My son should be finished giving him the third degree by now." The doctor draped her legs with the blanket and stood. "Don't worry, my dear. You're among friends now, and in a few days all of this will seem like nothing but a bad dream."

Or a nightmare, she thought as she returned his smile. "Thank you."

Walker returned almost at once, and as he closed the door behind him, Lilah could hear Paul Jemmet arguing quietly with his son. "The roads are blocked," he said as he came over to the cot. "We won't be able to leave."

Lilah wanted to get as far away from Frenchman's Pass as she could, but at least if they were snowed in, GenHance wouldn't be able to get to them. "Did the sheriff believe you?"

"I don't know," he murmured. "He seems more interested in what happened to our abductors than us." He studied her face. "What is it?"

"The doctor thinks you and I had rough sex a few days ago, when you got back to the States." She touched the blanket where it lay over her side. "That's how I explained the bruises here."

He pulled back the blanket to look at her. "You said I didn't hurt you."

"You didn't, and don't worry, he believed me." She didn't know how much time they would have to speak privately, so she'd have to be blunt about the rest. "I know because I read his mind."

"You said you can't do that with humans."

He was already thinking of people as a different species, Lilah thought. "Maybe I can now." She looked down at their linked hands, and then into his eyes. "Think of something. Your favorite color. Don't," she said as he started to draw his hand away. "I have to know if my ability has changed, and it's safer if I try it on you."

He went still. "You may not like what you see in my head."

"I like everything about you," she chided. "Now, think. Your favorite color. Please."

They sat together in silence, Walker watching her as she tried to reach out to him. She not only couldn't read his thoughts; she couldn't feel any emotion coming from him. It was as if he'd turned into a stone statue.

At last she stopped trying. "It's not working with you anymore."

He stiffened. "You read my mind before this?"

"I felt your emotions, or at least, I thought I did." Her head began to ache miserably. "I guess there's one good thing about it. If I can read the minds of normal people, and the sheriff is planning to arrest us, I'll know in advance."

She tried not to jump as someone knocked and an older woman looked in before entering.

"Evening," she said, carrying several tote bags over to the desk across from the cot. "Sheriff Jemmet asked me to bring over some clothes and food for you folks."

The woman wore a heavy plaid wool coat, which she removed to reveal a flannel shirt and a heavy denim jumper. Her salt-and-pepper hair had been cut into a short, neat bob that flattered her broad features and light blue eyes.

"I'm Annie Peterson, and Ethan tells me you're Mari and Walker." Without waiting for an answer she began unloading the bags. "I've got hot chicken soup, grilled ham sandwiches, and a thermos of coffee. Should warm you up in a jiffy."

"We appreciate the meal, Mrs. Peterson." Lilah tucked the blanket around her before she sat up.

"Since Mr. Peterson high-tailed it out of here twenty years ago, I much prefer Annie." She sized both of them up with a glance before digging into another bag. "What I brought ought to fit you, hon, but I'll have to find some bigger duds for your man."

"Is there a place we can stay in town until the roads are cleared?" Lilah asked.

"You'll be staying with me. I run the B and B here, and I've plenty of rooms." She turned to Walker. "Ethan says you were robbed, so no need to worry about paying. It'll be on the county."

Walker gave her a direct look, and then glanced at Annie.

Of course, he wanted her to test her new ability. Lilah reached out as Annie brought the clothing over to her and touched the woman's hand. At the same time, she opened her mind as she had with Paul Jemmet. "This is very kind of you."

She's near too pretty to look at, and twice as sweet. Annie took a deep breath. *Lord, she's ripe as a harvest moon. No wonder Ethan's back is up.* Out loud she said, "Way you folks have been treated, it's the least the town can do. I'll be back in a bit."

Lilah held on to her hand and reached out to the

other woman's mind, quickly finding her way in. "Okay, Walker, I'm in." To Annie, she said, "I want to ask you some questions. Will you answer them for me?"

Annie's face went slack. "Yes."

"Is there a phone here I can use?"

"None that works. Storm's knocked out all the land-lines," Annie said, her voice going low and rough.

Lilah looked over at Walker. "She's under my control now. It's just like I've done with animals. She'll tell us whatever we want to know."

He circled around the older woman. "How can you be sure you're in complete control?"

"Annie, bend down and touch your toes." Lilah watched as she obeyed. "Now hop on one foot three times. Tell me, why did your husband leave you?"

"I'm barren." Annie lifted one foot and began to hop on the other. "He hated me for it."

"She would never tell a stranger something like that, Walker." Lilah felt awful for forcing the woman to confess such a private, painful secret, but at least it proved her theory.

Walker passed his hand in front of her face, but Annie didn't blink. Once she finished hopping, she simply stood and waited.

"This will be very useful," he said at last.

"Only as a last resort," she warned. "A mind is fragile, especially when it's been taken over by someone else. If I try to control her for too long, I might cause permanent damage." Lilah took her hand away.

Immediately Annie's expression became confused. "Beg your pardon—what was that again?"

"I said, thank you." Lilah forced a smile. "You've been very helpful."

Chapter 12

T he inn by the lake had taken 125 years to acquire its genteel shabbiness, and most of the antique hunters who came to stay in its small rooms considered its squeaking staircases and temperamental plumbing to be part of its charm.

"The girl at the front desk said President Coolidge stayed in this room," Gabriel heard his *sygkenis* say as she disappeared into the bath. "Is that why they haven't cleaned these windows since nineteen thirty?"

He went to the bay windows and looked down at a wedding party being photographed by a small gazebo festooned with tiny white lights. The bride, a petite brunette whose lace and sequined gown surrounded her like a fat, sugarcoated meringue, beamed up at her groom, a reedy boy who tugged with nervous fingers at the confining grip of his black velvet bow tie.

"What's so interesting?" Nicola appeared beside him and peered down. "Oh. Christ. Is that a wedding dress, or a parade float?"

His lover had been making caustic jokes since the flight they had chartered from Scotland had landed in Orlando. Gabriel knew the sarcasm served as a way to manage the stress of their mission. But there was something more to it this time; he could hear a specter of desperation haunting every biting word.

"We can go back," he said, putting his arm around her. "I have only to call the airport, and we can be in Madrid by morning."

"No, we can't. We said we'd do this and we're doing this." She moved away, picking up her suitcase and placing it on the end of the bed. "You'd think they'd at least put one of those minibars in here. I doubt Coolidge's ghost would be offended by the presence of overpriced soda and stale candy bars." She removed the insulated pack that contained several units of human blood. "Did you see an ice machine anywhere in the hall?"

"Nicola."

Her shoulders drooped as she dropped the pack back into the suitcase, and then turned and sat on the end of the bed. "You don't want to have this conversation with me now, baby. Trust me. Just let it go."

"You can say anything to me," he assured her. "You know that."

She eyed him. "I've never killed a vampire. Stupid, right? I've wanted to—I planned to for ten years—but actually doing one? Hasn't happened yet."

He came to sit beside her, and took her hand in his.

"It's weird," she said after a long silence. "Richard's wife slaughtered my parents, turned me into a monster, and completely fucked up my life. If anyone deserves the top spot on the payback list, I think we can all agree it's me."

"You are not a killer, Nicola."

She looked at him. "What about you? The Darkyn knew the holy freaks had snatched you in France. They knew exactly what they were doing to you. And when those bastards told them they'd tortured you to death, they didn't check it out. They bought it. They forgot about you. End of Gabriel, end of story."

"They sent Richard photographs of my decapitated body," he reminded her. "He had no reason to suspect the images had been doctored, or that the Brethren would keep me alive for as long as they did."

"I wish I could be as forgiving as you." She got to her feet and wandered restlessly from one window to another. "When is this guy going to get here?"

As if to answer her, someone knocked on the door.

She went and checked through the peephole, and saw a large, handsome Latino wearing a dark blue uniform. "You expecting FedEx?"

Gabriel stood. "Richard uses them."

She opened the door and smiled at the big courier. "Hi, there."

"Ms. Jones?" When she nodded, he scanned the bar code on a padded mailer before handing it to her. "Have a good evening."

"Thanks." She closed the door and turned the mailer over. "Domestic. Atlanta." She pulled the end tab and removed a neat file containing typed reports, photographs, and a map. Once she skimmed it, she brought it to Gabriel. "Everything but the kitchen sink."

He reviewed the material more carefully. "The Kyndred female rented a house a few miles from here. The last person to see her alive dropped her off there after her car was stolen."

Nick had already pulled on her jacket. "Then that's where we start the hunt."

Knowing his *sygkenis* was more comfortable on two wheels than four, Gabriel had arranged to have a motorcycle delivered to the inn. As he expected, she grinned as soon as she saw it.

"A brand-new Rocket Three Triumph? Oh, honey." She walked around it. "You really shouldn't have."

It took so little to please her. "I know you hate to be parted from your Tiger."

"I don't miss it that much." She crouched down to peer at the engine. "I was reading about this one. They upped the torque fifteen percent with the new exhaust system. Supposed to be real quiet, too." She straddled the bike and started it. "Whoa, man. Listen to that purr." She gave him a mischievous look. "Speed limit in town is twenty-five. How about we go smash it all to hell?"

"No police chases," Gabriel warned as he climbed on and rested his hands on her slim hips. "And no making of donuts on people's lawns."

"You're no fun." She kicked the stand, shifted up, and took off.

A few minutes and several hair-raising turns later, Nicola cruised up the narrow drive to a small cottage-style house and continued around the back, parking the bike in the shadows and shutting off the engine. She looked around at the abandoned houses and empty lots surrounding the property.

"Looks like she had no neighbors." She took out a pocket flashlight and moved the beam over the back of the house. "Anyone home now?"

Gabriel sent out a tendril of his talent, gathering a thousand tiny bits of information at once from the resident insect population. "The house is empty."

Nicola accompanied him to the back door, the frame of which bore recent tool marks around the lock. "Crowbar. These guys were in a hurry." She opened the door.

The air inside the small kitchen smelled of herbs and overripe bananas, the latter emanating from a brown-skinned bunch sitting in an uncovered basket. Gabriel noted the general tidiness as well as the woman's purse sitting on the counter by the coffeemaker.

"One cup, one plate, one set of utensils," Nicola said as she inspected the dish-drying rack. "She lived alone." She checked the calendar hanging next to the fridge. "No appointments, no notes. Probably kept to herself."

They walked out into the sparsely furnished front room, where Nicola immediately went to inspect a dark-screened laptop. When she turned it on, it showed only a password-prompt screen. She frowned. "Not Windows. Hmmm." She tapped a few keys, swore, and then quickly shut off the power.

"Nicola?"

"She's got this thing suicide-encrypted." She blew out a breath. "If I try to force a log-on, it'll fry the hard drive." She reached down and unplugged the laptop, rolling up the cords. "I'll have to spend some quality time with this later."

He glanced through an adjoining door. "Her bedroom is in there."

Nick followed him in, and then stopped to shine the light around the four walls of the room. The light revealed that the two windows had been bricked in, and the inside of the bedroom door had three sturdy locks on it.

"Okay." Nick closed the door and switched on a lamp. "What the hell is all this?"

Gabriel went to one of the windows. "This brickwork is not new. It's been in place for some time."

"Same with the locks. So who makes their bedroom into a fortress?" Nick wondered out loud.

"Someone who was very frightened," he said, trailing his fingers along a line of mortar. He turned and looked at the cup sitting on the bedside table. He went over and picked it up, and saw several dead ants floating on the contents. He sniffed the rim of the cup and detected a powerful chemical. "This is tainted with something."

Nicola joined him and sniffed it. "Diazepam. It's a sedative." She sniffed again, more deeply. "Whoa. There's enough in here to knock out a small elephant."

He arched a brow. "You know this how?"

"Back in the day I knew better than to take on a posse of holy freaks by myself," she said mildly. "So when there were more than two, I drugged them." She heaved a sigh and glanced around. "But why was this chick sedating herself? You think she was a major insomniac?"

"I don't know." He sent out more of his talent, summoning the smallest inhabitants of the house. "But I will ask."

His lover's eyes flashed up as a pebble-size gray spider on a nearly invisible thread of silk descended between them. Others climbed down the thread to cluster with the first. "Spiders. Why does it always have to be spiders?"

He smiled a little. "Because the two roaches nesting in the closet infested the house only last night."

She shuddered. "Okay, spiders are fine."

Gabriel placed a hand under the spinners, who abandoned the web line and landed on his palm. In his mind he both saw them and saw his face through their eyes as his talent expanded.

Arachnids were unique among the millions of other creatures Gabriel thought of as the Many; the carnivorous hunters had evolved to become in a sense the Darkyn of the insect world. They also did not sustain a hive mind as most insects did, but instead tasted the experience-memories of other spiders through minute traces of chemicals they exuded onto their webs. A spider had only to check the web to remember, and any who encountered another's web would be able to read from it the experiences of the former occupant.

The seven spiders on Gabriel's hand were siblings, and had inhabited the woman's home since hatching that summer. Their mother had left behind many memories in her web: the arrival of the human female, her occupancy of the house, and some of the strange things she had done alone at night during the first month.

"She brought the bricks and locks with her, and installed them the first week she was here." Gabriel sifted through the spiders' collective memories, seeing the same one repeating over and over. "She would bring her laptop in here before she locked herself in."

"A homemade safe room," he heard Nicola murmur. "She probably didn't have enough money for an alarm system. Had to be a way out, though." She paced around the room, then bent and lifted the bed skirt. "Now, why would someone put a rug *under* their bed? Watch out, baby."

Once Gabriel had stepped aside, Nicola pushed the bed to one side, exposing a dusty rag rug. She pulled it up, revealing a rectangular section that had been cut out of the hardwood floor and then fitted with hinges and a latch and replaced. She popped the latch, opened it, and used the flashlight to inspect the interior of the space below it.

"Opens down into the crawl space under the house." She sat back on her heels. "This had to be her escape hatch. Why put it under the bed, though?"

Engrossed in chemical memories, Gabriel hardly heard her. He learned that the woman had been aware of the spiders, had never disturbed them. He found one vivid memory trace, of her standing on a chair to inspect one web. Her lips formed words the spider didn't understand, but he did.

You can catch all the mosquitoes you want, little sister.

True to their nature, the spiders remained ever wary of the new tenant, but in time they began cautiously moving in and out of the room when the woman left the door open during the day. That was why they had witnessed other odd incidents: men watching the woman and taking photographs of her through her windows, one picking the lock on the back door and searching the house while she was gone, while in the kitchen a second mixed a packet of white powder in the canister of hot-chocolate mix the woman kept there.

The siblings had also witnessed the men returning

later that night, entering her unlocked bedroom, and taking her limp body from her bed.

"She was drugged by her abductors, and fell unconscious before she could secure herself in here," Gabriel said as he released the spiders and watched them climb up the strand of silk. "These men, they watched her long enough to learn her habits and see her vulnerabilities."

"She was right to be afraid." Nicola eyed the bricks. "I know we can't mess with anything in here, but I really wish I could tear down those damn things."

After years of torture, Gabriel had been crucified alive and left to die in a sealed room. It had been Nicola who had found him, who had used a sledgehammer to break through the bricks of his eternal prison in order to free him. Gabriel's cool detachment, brought on by communing with the spiders, disappeared under the fierce rush of love for his woman.

Forced to become Darkyn against her will, Nicola had had every reason in the world to despise their kind, and yet she had risked everything—even her life—to save him.

He came to stand behind her, his arms encircling her narrow waist. "When was the last time I told you how precious you are to me?"

"It's been a good three, four hours." She rested her hands over his. "I didn't mean to remind you about when we met."

"I have some very fond memories of that night." He brought one hand up to cup her breast, caressing it as he used the other to release the button of her jeans. "One is how soft and giving you were in my arms." He slipped his hand into her panties and parted her with one long finger. "How heavenly you felt when I touched you."

"I was?" She caught her breath as his fingertip pressed in. "Oh, yeah. That's pretty heavenly."

"You didn't know what I wanted to do to you." Gabriel eased her jeans down over her hips, exposing the sweet, tight curves of her pale bottom. "Did you?"

"I was too preoccupied at the time." The scent of juniper rose from her skin with delicious warmth, blending with the fragrance of evergreen radiating from his. She reached behind and opened the front of his trousers, her fingers curling around his stiff shaft. "Stuff like this kept distracting me."

"You felt like wet satin under my hand, just as you do now," he whispered against her ear. "I wanted to be inside you so much."

"Your problem is that you're just too damn polite." Nicola released him, shoving her jeans down to her calves before she bent to brace her hands against the bed. "I remember you wouldn't let me do this."

"No." Gabriel fisted his penis and guided it to her, closing his eyes as he felt the delicate lips of her sex enclose the dry, tight head. "And I swore to myself I would never trespass here."

Her thighs shook as she clenched around him, trying to draw him in and hissing with impatience when he clamped his hands on her hips to hold her in place. "You'd better start trespassing. Right now, pal."

Gabriel smiled as he slid his hands up, stroking her breasts before he followed the tight muscles of her arms down to her hands. As he entwined his fingers with hers, he sank into her, bringing another long, soft sound from her throat. When the curve of her buttocks pressed into his belly, he put his mouth to her ear. "So now you know. This is how I wanted to take you that night. With you beneath me, trembling as you are now. Eager to feel me inside you." He drew back, and then surged into her again. "Needing more." He went deeper. "Wanting more."

"Oh, God." Her hips jerked as he brought her hand and his to feel the slick, hot juncture of their sexes, and pressed the heel of his hand to the swollen, exposed pearl of her clit. "Don't hold back this time." She turned her head, shifting her curls away from her left shoulder. "Gabriel, please."

He kissed the lovely line of her throat, pushing into her as he rubbed her clit and sank his *dents acérées* into her flesh, tasting the cool, spicy nectar of her blood. The twin penetrations brought her over the edge, and he drove into the center of the tight contractions around his penis, fucking her through her pleasure and feeling the dark satisfaction of their bond, of the delight only he could give to her, only he would ever feel her take.

He held himself inside her as he took his mouth from her throat, and used his hands to keep them joined as he turned her onto her back. "I want to see your eyes," he said as he began to work in her again. "I want to see you come for me again."

"You won't have long to wait." Her voice shook as much as her hands as she latched onto his arms. "I love the way you make me feel. I love this." Her eyes went wide as he brought her over again. "Gabriel. I love you."

The words she rarely said slammed into him, smashing through everything he was and making him more than he thought he could ever be. As his body drove into hers, he felt the fire of that love healing him again, erasing more of the hidden wounds he had carried for so long. Never had he dreamed it could be like this, not even on that terrible night when she had found him, and as he pumped his seed into her, he lost himself in all that was Nicola, all that they were together.

She held him for a long time, drawing him onto the bed with her and kissing his mouth with dreamy absorption. "You really should have done that the night we met, you know. You were way too polite."

"Perhaps I was." He nuzzled her throat, and as she turned her head to give him better access, he felt her go still. "Nick?"

"Something's taped under the nightstand." She reached out to the small bedside table, feeling under it until she pulled off a book with strips of tape across the top and bottom of the outer cover. "Well, what do we have here?"

Gabriel reluctantly withdrew from her body and settled her against his side. "A book."

She opened it. "Better than a book. A journal. Hmmm. Starts off like a letter: 'Dear Paracelsus, If anything happens to me, I hope you'll be the one to find this.'" She glanced at him. "Why does that name sound familiar?"

"Paracelsus was a well-known physician and alchemist who died in the sixteenth century," Gabriel told her. "And before you ask, no, he was not made Darkyn."

"Lucky him." She flipped through the handwritten pages, pausing now and then to read. "Okay, it looks like she mostly wrote stuff about her work. Wasn't all dog-catching. Caught a coyote, relocated a gator, rescued a kitten down a well, yada yada yada. Wait, here's something." She read for a few moments, and then blew some air over her lower lip. "Whoever this Paracelsus guy is, it seems like he wasn't around. All she did was work or spend her nights here, alone. Had a hard time coping with the solitude, too."

He felt a twinge of pity. "Perhaps he was someone she met on the Internet?"

"Maybe. She doesn't give too many details on anything. Must have been afraid someone else would find it. Here's the last entry, dated a few days ago." Nicola frowned. "She was planning to move after the first of the year. She was afraid of something. Seriously afraid." She flipped the page over. "Oh, shit."

"What is it?"

"There's another reason she was locking herself in here every night." She handed him the journal.

Chapter 13

Like every building in the town, the small hotel appeared old and well built from the outside. The interior, crowded as it was, kept out the cold and seemed reasonably secure. Lilah openly admired the thousands of objects the townswoman had used as decorations, especially a small red wagon filled with shabby stuffed toys.

"Look at this one, Walker." Lilah pointed to a bear with an eye missing and honey-colored, patchy fur darkened by years of being handled by small, grimy hands. An old metal button stitched inside the tuft of its left ear bore the image of a tiny elephant. To Annie, she said, "Isn't this a Steiff bear?"

"I wouldn't know," the older woman said, her voice gruff. "I just like them. Now, I've got a room on the second floor with a nice view overlooking Main Street—"

"We will stay on the first floor," he told her. When both women stared at him, he added, "Mari is tired and hurt. The stairs will be too much for her."

"Shoot, I didn't think of that. Of course you can stay downstairs. Let me get some clean linens and make up a room for you." Annie hung up her coat and disappeared down a hall.

"I don't think you have to worry about these people," Lilah chided. "I'm sure they believe our story."

"For now." The sheriff had taken an instant dislike to him, and would probably check on their identities as soon as his phones and computer were functioning again. The only way to know what the man was thinking would be to have Lilah read his mind, but he wasn't allowing Ethan Jemmet within ten feet of her. "You must be exhausted."

"After what happened the last time I fell asleep, I don't know if I'll ever close my eyes again." Her smile turned rueful. "I hope Annie's water heater is still working. I'm dying for a long, hot shower."

The image that came into his head made heat surge through him, and he took off his hat and jacket. When he noticed her staring, he went still. "What is it?"

"You can't feel it?" She reached up and ran her fingers over his scalp, which was no longer bare. "It's like black mink. Sometimes mine does that, you know, seems to grow a couple of inches overnight, but yours is . . . " She stopped herself and gave him an apologetic look. "It's okay. I mean, it happens to all of us. Sometimes our fingernails and toenails do the same thing."

He caught her wrist, and then brought her hand to his mouth to kiss her palm. "It's only hair, Lilah. Not snakes."

She stared at his mouth. "Snakes?" she echoed, her voice soft and dreamy.

Annie emerged from the hall, her mouth curling on one side. "You two really *do* need a room. Come on, it's just down here."

The room was large, not as crowded with things, and had an adequate bath adjoining it.

Lilah seemed enchanted, and ran her fingers over the heavy stitching of the old white coverlet on the large bed. "What a gorgeous quilt." She bent closer. "Wow. It's all one piece."

"Whole cloth," Annie said. "I make 'em myself on a

rack in the back room. Helps pass the time when I don't have guests." She gestured toward the bath. "I put some nightclothes in there next to the towels. Before you go to bed, turn the taps on to a trickle. It helps keep the pipes from freezing. If you need anything, I'm right down the hall. Good night."

"Thank you." Lilah waited until the other woman left before she sank down onto the bed. "She's such a nice woman. Everyone here is."

"Yes." They were all a little too welcoming for his taste, but as isolated as the town was, strangers were probably a novelty to them. Once he locked the door and checked the windows, he investigated the size of the bath. The freestanding tub appeared to be large enough for both of them, and the thought of bathing with Lilah made his blood surge. He ran the taps to check the temperature, and then shut them off and walked back out.

"There is no shower, but I think—" He stopped as he saw Lilah using her thumbs to type something on the keypad of a mobile phone. "How did you get that?"

"I swiped it from the doctor." She finished and pressed a button. "There we go." She smiled up at him. "I thought with the storm clearing I'd try to send a text to Samuel's e-mail. Looks like it went through."

The sound of the man's name made something brutal and ugly twist inside him. "What did you tell him?"

"I couldn't risk going into details, so I just gave him the phone number. Hopefully he'll call back soon." She set the phone aside and rose to her feet. "Walker, Samuel was changed when he was a baby, like me. He's my friend; he can help."

"So you think." He turned his back on her. "What if he was one who betrayed you?"

"He'd never do that." She sighed and came up behind him. "I know after what happened to you that you don't want to trust anyone, but there are good people out there." She rested her hand against his back. "Not everyone wants us dead."

"You think death is the worst that can happen to you?" He turned and seized her by the arms.

"I know it isn't," she said quietly.

He saw the frostfire in her eyes, the gentle green of her irises dividing into crystals of molten gold and glacial blue, until he felt sure she could see into the black depths of his soul. And still he couldn't spare her. "How did they find you, Lilah? Who told them your name, and where you lived, and what you are?"

"It wasn't Samuel," she insisted. "He doesn't know my real name, or where I live, or even what I look like. About a month ago I messed up and used my ability in front of some people. They told some reporters about it and the story made the news. We think GenHance monitors the papers and police reports and other things like that so they can identify us. So if you want to blame someone, it was probably me."

Someone knocked loudly on the door, and he released her, striding over to yank it open.

Ethan Jemmet stood outside. "Mr. Kimball, you and I need to have a word."

"Tomorrow." He tried to shut the door, but the sheriff blocked it with one hand. "We're tired, Sheriff."

Ethan glanced over his shoulder at Lilah before averting his gaze. "It won't take long."

He closed the door behind him and followed Ethan into the front reception area. Once there, Ethan produced a clear plastic bag marked with the word EVIDENCE across a red strip. Inside the bag was a torn, bloodied shirtsleeve.

"I went back out to the main road to have a look around. I found your tracks." He held up the bag. "And this."

He kept his expression impassive. "It's not mine."

"Seeing as you still have both arms attached, I gathered as much. I found it sticking out of the snow, a yard away from your tracks." He tucked the bag back into his jacket. "Now you want to tell me what you really saw out there tonight?"

Killing the sheriff would not improve their situation, but it would do wonders for his mood. "When we escaped from the truck, the storm virtually blinded us. My only concern was finding shelter. Someone could have slaughtered an elephant a few inches away, and I doubt we would have seen it."

Ethan regarded him steadily. "I don't believe you, Kimball."

He curled his hands against a burning sensation that shot through his fingers. "I don't care what you believe, Sheriff."

Ethan Jemmet took a step forward, and suddenly the crowded room shrank in on them. With one lunge he saw himself ripping out the other man's throat, and his jaw ached to do just that.

The sheriff's aggressive stance shifted, and his anger faded into astonishment as his mouth moved and shaped a soundless word.

"What?"

Ethan took a step back, shattering the unseen tension between them. "Tomorrow. We'll talk again tomorrow." Without another word he turned and walked out into the night.

Denied an outlet, the rage roiling inside him made going back to the room seem foolish, but he needed to see Lilah, to soak himself in the gentleness of her, the warmth of her. She would bring him back from this, this wildness, this terrible need to chase and attack and kill. And when he walked into the room, and saw her standing by the window, he knew she was watching Ethan Jemmet walk away from the inn. A slight smile curved her lips, as if she was thinking of something that gave her pleasure.

Samuel, or Ethan? Or both of them? The final, frayed strand of his control snapped.

She heard him before he reached her, and turned. "Is everything—"

He pulled her into his arms, sweeping her away from the window as he made her look at him.

"Do you think of him?" he heard his voice snarl. "Do you want him?"

"The sheriff? No. Why would I?"

He filled his hands with her hair as he shifted her backward until he had her pinned against a wall. He lowered his body against hers, flattening her breasts against his chest as he parted her thighs with his knee. "What about this Samuel?"

"Samuel's a friend." Again she didn't cower from him, but looked into his eyes without fear. "Walker, I'm not with anyone. I don't have anyone. I can't be with anyone like that."

"You are with me." He dragged her hand to his mouth and buried his mouth against her palm, catching the mound of her thumb between his teeth before he lifted his head. "Be with me, Lilah. Be with me, or send me away."

She went still, her expression stricken.

He'd gone too far. She didn't want him, and he couldn't spend another moment near her and not have her. He drew back. "I will go."

"No."

Lilah had never in her life thrown herself at a man, but the thought of Walker leaving her sent her into some kind of instinctive frenzy. Before he could say a word, she had her arms around his neck and pulled his head down until her mouth could touch his. As kisses went, hers was clumsy and desperate, so pathetic in fact that he didn't move a muscle.

She made her hands slide down so he could straighten, but she couldn't seem to take them off his chest or look him in the eye. "I shouldn't have done that."

"No," he agreed in a strange voice.

Her head whirled as Walker's hands clamped on her waist and he lifted her off her feet. Three steps later she was flat on her back on the bed, and his hands were tearing at her clothes and his. She felt the air on her thighs just before his hips parted them.

Lilah shifted her legs, widening them as she curled her right leg over the backs of his knees. Her movements inflicted a subtle abrasion over his erection as she positioned herself, opening her body wider to him and caressing him with the small notch of her sex. The soft curls of her body hair tangled with his. Then he was pushing into her.

Walker looked down the length of their bodies, watching his penis sinking into her. His expression was such a sublime blend of frantic desire and blessed relief that Lilah knew he felt as desperate for it as she did.

Despite her need her body was not ready for him; she felt the dry tightness of her flesh dragging painfully at him as his shaft went deep. He must have felt the resistance, too, for he stopped to reach down and squeeze his shaft. She felt the cool silkiness of fluid seeping from his cockhead and softening his passage. He pressed deep until she felt the broad base seat against her folds.

He was almost too much for her, and they both felt it. Lilah clutched at him, her nails digging in as her body spasmed around him and her breasts pressed into his chest. He cupped the back of her head, holding her brow to his shoulder, rubbing his hot face against her hair as he shuddered.

The weight of his body, the aching invasion of his penis,

and the violent way they had come together all dissolved away as she discovered the heat they generated together was more than physical. It went deeper, stirring and revealing some alien clarity inside her that she never knew even existed. It had been hiding, perhaps waiting for him, all this time. Now that he was inside her, it flowered around him, opening her mind as well as her body to his.

I am to be yours, she thought to him.

Yes. He answered without hesitation. *Always.*

Walker held himself inside her without moving, allowing her time to adjust. Feeling the weight and fullness of him brought a rush of tenderness and excitement. The emptiness of her body and her heart vanished, and Walker became the world. Everything made sense now, and she had no idea why. She didn't care, either. The smell of his skin, the force of his strength, the mesh of their bodies, were all that concerned her.

She wrapped her legs around his hips, lifting her lips to kiss him. Her mouth opened under his, drinking in the sounds he made, filling her head with dark hungers. He rolled with her off the bed and onto the floor, pinning her there as he tore open her shirt and bared her to his mouth. For a few moments he played with her, suckling her gently, until she groaned and rolled her hips.

Walker seemed to snap then, for he swore and dragged her over onto her hands and knees, yanking her into position and holding her there with one arm around her torso as he crouched over her. The spike of his cock impaled her again, this time with one furious stroke, and her back arched up, shifting her hair to fall over her face, exposing her nape.

Lilah felt him latch onto the back of her neck with his teeth, sucking at her flesh with his mouth while he drove into her body with pounding strokes. He fucked her without mercy through one orgasm and then another before he came.

The jet of his seed seemed to pump into her for hours, but even that did not mollify him.

He lifted her from the hard floor, carrying her over to the bed, dropping her onto her back before covering her with his body. Lilah could see her face like a pale mote in the blackness of his eyes, a small blurry oval of blue and gold and rose and cream. All she could hear was the slick collision of his flesh to hers, the liquid rhythm of his cock as he worked it into her, and the helpless, needy sounds coming from her own lips.

Darkness closed in on her, shadows greedy to steal her from him, but Walker wrapped her in his arms and instead took her with him. When he spilled himself in her a second time, she felt two sensations from the explosion of her own pleasure creeping up through her womb, like ribbons of ice and flame that had become entwined, gentling each other until they were as cool as a northern breeze, as warm as sunlight on an upturned face.

Walker held himself over her, his eyes watching her as the heat of his fluids pulsed into her. When he had finished, and tried to roll away from her, she went with him, settling atop him and sighing against his open mouth before tucking her face against his neck.

He felt her relax as she fell asleep on top of him, and found himself doing the same. He slept as he never had, mindless and dreamless, and when he next opened his eyes, he felt new strength surging through his limbs.

When he woke in the thin gray light of dawn, she lay entwined with him, her hands resting on his chest and her body still linked to his, soft and giving. She stirred as he did, opening her eyes, drowsy and puzzled.

Walker?

He came back to consciousness with all the force he had used to take her, and he pushed her out of his head, horrified to know what he had done, helpless to take it back. He wrenched himself from her body, staggering back from the bed, unable to bear seeing what he knew would be in her eyes.

Lilah had trusted him. She had brought him back from the brink of death. And in return he had used her, just like all the others before her.

"Walker, don't." She pushed herself upright as he jerked on his clothes. "Please. Don't go."

He ignored her, stopping only when she came to him, and only to avoid her touch. "Stay away from me."

"I can't." She came around him, trying to make him look at her, stumbling on the edges of the sheet she had wrapped around her body. "Walker, I'm all right. You didn't hurt me."

He ripped the sheet from her, forcing himself to look at what he had done. Bruises had bloomed on her knees, as angry as the abrasions on her breasts and the swollen redness of her lips. Thin scratches scored her shoulders and hips. He saw the imprint of his fingers against the sides of her thighs, and turned her, pushing her hair away from the bite-mark-shaped bruise on her nape.

"It's not as bad as it looks," she said quickly.

"Where is it not bad? Where did I not hurt you? The top of your head? The soles of your feet?" He lifted the sheet, swaddling it around her before he set her away.

"Things got a little rough last night," she admitted, "but sometimes they do. I wanted it as much as you did."

"You're lying." He grabbed the jacket Annie had given him and pulled it on. "I won't do this. Not anymore."

"Wait." Lilah ran ahead of him to block the doorway. "I'm not letting you walk out of here."

He glared at her. "You would rather I stay and make use of you again?"

"You didn't use me," she assured him. "You can't do that to me, not when you and I—"

"You have no idea what I can do." He reached past her for the doorknob, and went still as she put her hand over his. He would have to hurt her again, one last time. "Did you think you were the first? I've had other women. I've taken them and left them as soon as I had finished. You're nothing to me."

She straightened her shoulders, her voice going quiet. "I was something last night."

"This town is filled with women." He pulled her hand away from the knob.

"Then they'll all see me running naked after you in the street." She held on to his hand. "Walker, please. You have to listen to me. Don't go like this."

He pushed her away and strode out of the room. Once outside, he eyed the coming dawn, and the emptiness of the street. He could go and find the sheriff, and finish what they had started last night. Or he could spare the other man's life and give himself to what he had become.

Turning, he walked into the drifts at the base of the mountain.

Lilah almost made good on her threat to run naked after Walker, until she tripped over the sheet again and barely avoided falling on her face.

"Wait." She hit the door with her fist before she whirled around and hurried into the bathroom.

Grabbing the first clothes she found, she pulled them on. Annie had given her a pair of loafers to wear, probably her own, but they would do until she caught up with him.

Outside the bitter cold snapped at her face, and it was still too dark to see much. She looked down to see Walker's fresh tracks leading across the porch and down the steps, but then they circled around the side of the inn, disappearing behind it. Lilah followed them until she hit the snowbank at the base of the slope. Walker's trail led straight up into the trees.

He'd gone into the forest?

Lilah gingerly took a few more steps, but quickly began to sink down in snow up to her knees, and finally lost her balance and fell sideways onto her hands. She pushed herself up, and then spotted a much fainter trail running parallel to Walker's. Overnight the older tracks had been reduced to little more than shallow hollows. She waded over to them, and moved so that her shadow didn't fall over them.

The rising sun illuminated the remnants of the tracks, and their oval shape and curving lines at first made her think of stylized blossoms, somewhat flat and indented at the bottom, as if they'd been plucked from their stems. No flower had made these marks, however; the tracks had been left in distinct sets of four: two large and two small. They belonged to an animal that walked on all fours.

Lilah had extensive tracking experience, enough to recognize the distinct alignment of the front two depressions; she could also make out a thorn shape of a claw at the top of each. Those clues alone would have indicated the tracks had been made by a large canine, probably a domestic dog. The problem was the number of depressions; she counted five toe pads on the front- and back-leg tracks. The only creatures that left five-toed tracks were raccoons, weasels, badgers, and skunks.

"A raccoon, right," she muttered, disgusted with herself. "Maybe one the size of a cow."

Lilah brushed away the top layer of soft flakes, and found with further gentle excavation that the depressions were much larger than they appeared—easily as large as bear tracks, but without the elongated heel. She placed her hand next to the uncovered track to make a rough measurement, and figured the track was at least ten inches long. She looked up at the trail, and saw the distance between the tracks widened as they went into the trees. The last sets she could see were almost ten feet apart.

Whatever had left this trail had limbs long and fast enough to cover more than three yards with one stride.

Like that thing that attacked the men at the truck.

Lilah struggled out of the bank, swiping at her clothes until she'd knocked off most of the snow. She wasn't worried that Weirdfoot was hunting Walker; the animal's tracks had been made while it had still been snowing, and from the evidence of how fast it moved, it had to be long gone by now. Walker must have seen the tracks when he walked back here, and followed them into the forest, but why would he want to hunt that thing? He'd seen firsthand how fast and lethal it was, and that it wouldn't even hesitate to attack a human. . . .

Lilah clapped a hand over her mouth. "Oh, God, Walker. No."

Chapter 14

She couldn't go after him dressed as she was; while the sky was clear, the temperature was well below freezing, and the snow had to be at least two, maybe three feet deep.

"Morning," Annie said, smiling as Lilah rushed back inside. "You folks like pancakes and sausage? I've that for breakfast, or . . . " She paused as she saw Lilah's face. "Why, honey, you're white as a sheet."

She didn't bother to lie. "It's Walker. He's gone up on the mountain. I have to go after him."

Annie's eyes widened for an instant before she reached for the phone on the wall. "No, you can't do that; you'll get, ah, lost. I'll call Ethan, and he'll round up some of the men and bring him back down."

Lilah seized her wrist, reaching into her mind as she guided the receiver back onto the base. "You're not going to call Ethan, Annie. You won't tell him or anyone about this."

"Not a soul," Annie agreed, her eyes glazing over instantly.

"I need gloves, boots, snowshoes, and a coat." She guided the other woman around the desk and followed her to a closet, where Annie retrieved the articles. "Are there wolves up there on the mountain?"

"Wolves?" The older woman sighed. "No."

Holding on to Annie's wrist, Lilah walked her back to her room. "I want you to go back to bed for a couple hours. When you wake up, don't bother to check on us. If anyone asks for us, tell them we're sleeping in."

Once Annie had gone inside, Lilah closed the door and finished dressing in the hall before leaving through the back door, stopping long enough to buckle the straps of the snowshoes over her boots before following Walker's trail up into the high drifts.

All around her the snow began to sparkle as the full circle of the sun appeared on the horizon. Lilah focused on using the snowshoes, which she'd expected to feel awkward and cumbersome at first. Once her legs had remembered the way to walk in them, she looked ahead, trying to see the direction of his trail. He had waded through with enough force to push the snow up onto the drifts on either side, carving two narrow, continuous trenches through the dense pack of the snow.

He'd clearly followed the beast's tracks, because his trail never crossed or strayed away from the blossoms in the snow.

Lilah could see how determined he was. Plowing through the drifts as he had would have exhausted an ordinary man, but the trenches cut ahead of her as far as she could see. The trail also angled up with the slope of the mountain.

How could he do this? After last night, after being with her, how could he even *think* of killing himself this way? What was wrong with him?

Her chest burning, Lilah stopped and braced herself against a fir the storm had half buried, dislodging a swatch of white clumps from the branches. Her breath puffed out in harsh, billowing clouds, each one rising and dissipating slowly in the still air. She tried and quickly realized that she couldn't warm herself alone; she needed Walker to generate the heat that had protected them last night. The only way to keep warm was to keep moving at a brisk pace, something the snowshoes made impossible. To chase after him like this was not only foolish; it was dangerous.

I don't care, she thought as she drew herself up and trudged on. She wasn't going to leave him out here like this, not thinking that by making love with her he'd somehow abused her. Why hadn't she been able to stop him? It was as if he hadn't believed a word she'd said.

Maybe he didn't.

Last night Walker had been angry, out of control, and it had startled her, even scared her a little. She didn't understand what had set him off like that, and she always avoided situations that involved anger because they often touched off her own. But at no time had Lilah been afraid that he would hurt her. He'd been rough and wild, almost crazed with lust, but he'd brought the same out in her. Hadn't she jumped on him when he'd tried to leave?

By the time they'd made it to the bed, she'd stopped thinking altogether, and instead immersed herself in that frantic, merciless passion. She'd never felt anything like it, and when she'd woken this morning, she had wanted to cling to him and touch him and kiss him for hours. She was convinced that if he hadn't pushed her away, they would still be in bed now.

"But you didn't do that," she scolded herself. "Did you?"

Instead of telling him what she wanted, and how much she needed him, she'd wasted her words, begging him not to leave her. She should have stopped whining and given him reasons to stay. She could have shoved him onto the bed, climbed on top of him, and shown him what she wanted, what had made her whole for the first time in her life. Now, because she'd been too worried about becoming angry, she might never get the chance.

Why hadn't she done that? *Because I've trained my-self to be nice*, she answered herself. *A nice, polite little wimp. Who Walker thinks he abused.*

Her lungs burned as she tried to move faster, spurred on by the images in her head. He was out here some-where, alone, hurting, maybe even delusional. He could be suffering from post-traumatic stress disorder, she re-alized. Whatever the cause of his behavior, she was the only one who could absolve him of whatever wrongs he imagined he'd done. If he didn't find the beast, he might do something equally desperate, like jumping off a cliff. She had to stop being so timid and useless and tell him how she felt. Whatever the rest of the world had done to him, however confused he was, he was hers, and she was not going to spend another hour apart from him.

Lilah took in a breath so painful that it felt as if she were inhaling a thousand tiny knives, and knew it was only partly due to the cold. Some of the pain came from recognizing that the life GenHance had stolen from her no longer mattered. Even if she could go back to Flor-ida, there was nothing there for her.

She'd spent her entire adult life hovering on the fringe of society, hiding inside her solitude, terrified of being exposed for who and what she was. She'd never thought being kidnapped by people who wanted to dis-sect her like a frog would be liberating, but it had freed her. The moment she'd woken in Walker's arms, she'd stepped out of a prison cell she'd built around herself. She was never going back to that.

Walker's trail came to an abrupt end outside a broad thicket of brush surrounding an old log cabin. So did the other trail, although the tracks had changed over the last fifty yards. All Lilah could see were sets of twin de-pressions, now distorted into longer, broader tracks that sank almost as deeply as Walker's had.

As she looked all around the hidden cabin, she saw

no sign of an attack or a trail leading away from it. She walked up to the brush, and examined it until she found an area of disturbance. From the broken branches and dislodged snow, she could see someone had pushed his way through the overgrowth.

Joy and relief made Lilah's heart flutter madly against her ribs. He'd found shelter. He'd gone inside. He wasn't suicidal. She wanted to shout his name, and jump over the brush, but another, darker emotion made her go still.

Not this time.

She wasn't warning him that she was here, or giving him another chance to dodge her. This time, she'd make him listen. Even if she had to bash him in the head with something.

Icy branches clawed at her face as she navigated her way through the brush, which had grown up to cover two-thirds of the cabin's walls. When she broke through, she stood directly in front of an old string-latched door, and bent to peer into the narrow groove around the string. The inside of the cabin was dark, but she could smell a trace of woodsmoke. Glancing up, she saw a thin tendril of smoke rising from the stone chimney.

Suicidal men didn't build fires.

Lilah tugged on the dry, cracked strip of hide until the door creaked open, and stepped inside. A little sunlight filtered through a filmy square of glass at the back of the cabin, illuminating an old plank floor, a wide dusty table, and a rocking chair with a broken back. Dusty cobwebs hung from sagging rafters, creating a ragged, ghostly canopy. Five pallets, their mattresses split and spilling rotting hay, lined one side of the room, while a hearth with a small fire occupied the center of the opposite wall. The air, thick with dust, smelled of burning pine and oak.

She closed the door behind her and let the wooden latch bar fall into place, not bothering to disguise the sound. Equally silent, Walker emerged from one shadowed corner by the hearth, inspecting her as she moved toward him. Melted snow dripped from his hair, and his pants were soaked to midthigh, but he looked much better than she felt.

He didn't have to ask what she was doing here; his entire body was shouting that question.

"I tracked you. It wasn't difficult. I'm an animal control officer, and you leave a trail like a bulldozer." She bent down to unfasten the straps of the snowshoes. "Is there someplace I can hang this coat to dry?"

He peered at her as if she'd sprouted another head, but still said nothing.

"Yes, it was ridiculous for me to come after you. A lot of stupid things have happened this morning." She took off her coat and shook it off by the door before walking to the table and draping it over one end. "I don't suppose you found a coffeemaker or a stash of doughnuts around here. I didn't even get a chance to brush my teeth."

"Lilah," he said, his voice low. "Go back to town."

"No, I'm not going to do that." She went to the split-log bench in front of the hearth, and gingerly tested it with one hand before she sat down and took off her gloves. "Come over here."

"I don't want you."

Anger, always her enemy, welled up in her, but she let it pass through and out of her. When she felt calm again, she said, "I've spent the last hour in subzero temperatures snowshoeing up a mountain to find you. I don't know where I am. I can't feel my nose or my ears. My lungs feel like I've been snorting snow cones." She held her hands out to the hearth. "So come over here, Walker, and sit down by the fire with me, or I'm going to hurt you."

He approached the bench and sat down as far away from her as he could without falling off. "You shouldn't have come here."

She held up one finger. "You're not going to do any of the talking this time. I am. You're going to sit there and listen to me." When he opened his mouth, she wagged her finger. "I mean it. Not a word. Or I swear to God, there will be pain."

He stared into the fire.

"I've never really talked to anyone much. I always had to be careful not to let anyone get too close—even my friends on the Internet. So I already know I'm not going to be good at this." If she stopped to think about it, she wouldn't be able to continue, so she forced herself to go on. "Last night you and I had sex. It was consensual. I did not fight you off, or ask you to stop, or scream for help. We both had orgasms. You had two. I think I had three. Maybe four. I haven't had that many that I ever needed to count. After the sex was over, we cuddled and fell asleep."

Walker didn't move.

"Look at me." She waited until he turned his head toward her. "None of that—not one second of that—was unwanted or abusive."

His eyes narrowed, and then he shook his head.

Lilah understood. He wasn't going to agree or argue with her. He had pushed her away and now he was shutting down. Which put the full burden squarely back on her.

For him, she would bear it. "I know why you came up here, and it wasn't to move into this place and play mountain man. You thought you'd go after those things that killed our kidnappers. But not for revenge, right? You were hoping they'd do the same to you." She folded her arms. "This death wish of yours is really getting on my

nerves. I've been there, Walker. Getting torn apart by a
starving animal is not the way you want to go. I speak
from personal experience."

His shoulders stiffened.

"Yes, I guess I forgot to mention exactly how I got
my ability. It takes a near-death experience to switch on
our psychic powers, and mine happened to be a wild-
animal attack." She rubbed a hand against her throat.
"Do you know what it's like, to be knocked down, to
feel the fangs tearing into you? The blood doesn't gush.
It sprays. Everywhere. You hear it spraying."

He stared at her, appalled.

"The pain is like the animal: It's big and terrifying
and tries to eat you alive. The only good thing about
it is when you black out, and even then you're thinking, you're wondering, how much of me will be left for
someone to find? If anyone finds me at all." She looked
into the fire, sickened by her own words. "Believe me,
Walker, it's not how you want to go. Anything is better
than that."

He propped his arms against his thighs, his head
bowing.

"I don't know what made you so angry with me last
night, or so upset this morning," she told him. "I have
some theories, but honestly, I don't have to know everything you're thinking. We've both been through hell, but
we got through together. I've never been able to depend
on anyone else like this, and I'm guessing you haven't,
either. Maybe it's new, and scary, but compared to being
drugged and experimented on and kidnapped, I think it
should be a piece of cake."

He rested his head against his palms.

"I told you, I haven't been with a lot of men," she
added. "The truth is that I only dated when I couldn't
stand to spend one more night alone. It wasn't that
often, maybe once or twice a year. Most of the time,

Walker? I didn't even sleep with them. It didn't make me feel better, but while I was with them for a couple of hours, I could pretend that I was like other women. That I was normal. But I know I'm not." She blinked, hard, and cleared her throat. "There are plenty of other women in town, like you said, who are probably better in bed than me. Just keep in mind, none of them were in that truck with you. I was. And while I'm not normal, I have a lot to offer that they don't." She suddenly remembered she'd ordered him to shut up. "You can say something any time now."

He made a strangled sound. "I've taken enough from you."

"It's not something you can take." She shifted closer, and curled her hand around his. "This, I have to give."

She saw the faded bruises on their wrists, remnants of the hours they'd been cuffed together. In another day they would likely be gone, but Lilah thought she would always see a ghost of them there. And now he had dropped his hands and was looking at her, his expression so bleak it tore through her heart, and gave her the strength to tell him the rest.

"I didn't track you just so we could talk about last night," she told him. "I came after you because I'm in love with you."

He didn't move a muscle. "You don't know me."

"I don't know a lot *about* you," she corrected, "but from the way I understand it, you don't fall in love with someone's past, or the mistakes they've made, or whatever they think of themselves. You fall in love with them, and that makes them the most important person in the world. That's who you are to me."

She pressed her lips together until she could control their trembling, but she couldn't do anything about the tears that refused to stop filling her eyes.

"I don't know why or how this happened, but it did."

She had to tell him the rest. "Walker, you're not just the man I love. You're the love of my life. That's why I'm here. If you die on me, if you kill yourself, I'm going to be alone forever, and I can't . . . I won't . . . " Her voice broke.

"Lilah." He hauled her across the bench and onto his lap, and bundled her in his arms. "I won't die."

"Okay. Good." She buried her face against his chest and sobbed.

He let her cry all over him while he held her and stroked her hair. When the tears ebbed, he brought a handkerchief from his pocket and pressed it in her hands. Lilah knew she wasn't a pretty crier, and red splotches probably covered her face, but he didn't look away as she mopped up and blew her nose.

"Thanks." She rested her cheek against his shoulder and released a shuddering breath. "I almost wish we were back on the truck. Things seemed a lot simpler when we were naked and handcuffed together."

"Things will never be simple with me," he said softly, and for the first time she heard the shadow of an accent coloring his words. "There are things about me that you must know. You will find them difficult, if not impossible, to believe."

"I just stole clothes from a woman I put to sleep telepathically," she reminded him. "Trust me, my belief system is wide-open." She remembered the tracks outside. "Were you really going after that thing that killed the men?"

He nodded. "I tracked it here and came inside to see if it was occupying the cabin. From the window I saw more tracks leading away toward the peaks." He glanced around. "Someone from town has been using this place as shelter. The hand pump works, and there is soap and towels. I also found clothes, stacked firewood, and a radio."

"But you didn't find any food," she guessed, thinking of the shape of the tracks at the end of the older trail. "Did you?"

He shook his head.

She thought for a moment. "It hunts out in the open with a group of others like it. They drag off their kills, probably to a place where they can hide them from other predators, or maybe the townspeople. So they'd only need to come here to wash and change."

"Change what?"

"Their bodies," she said. "Walker, that thing wasn't an animal. It's human, or at least it is part of the time."

He regarded her steadily. "How do you know this?"

"I've tracked a lot of animals, and this one has five toes on each foot, weighs maybe two hundred pounds, but can run so fast it doesn't sink into the snow," she said. "It can also walk erect on its hind legs. The cabin says it can take shelter, chop firewood, wash, and use a radio."

His expression grew skeptical. "You cannot believe an animal has been living here."

"No," she agreed. "I think what made those tracks and uses this cabin is a human who can change into an animal. I think you've been hunting a werewolf."

Lilah must have expected to be derided for her werewolf theory, as she hurried into an explanation of the tracks outside the cabin and the reasons they couldn't belong to a dog or any other large, wild predator.

"There are no wolves in Colorado, according to Annie," she added quickly, "and I read an article once about how they were exterminated back in the forties by cattlemen who wrongly blamed them for attacks on their livestock. But whatever is out there is leaving canid and biped tracks, moves like lightning, and is probably the size of a pro wrestler. Since we've only seen it at night, it could be nocturnal. Maybe the shifting process takes place after dark, and then during the day, the werewolf takes human shape. . . . " She made a face. "Feel free to tell me I'm crazy any time now."

"You know these animals better than I." He considered telling her about all the strange things he'd seen during his lifetime, but she would not believe him. That, along with other revelations, would keep for now. "Whatever is using this cabin will not care to find us here. We will return to the inn." When she started to protest, he said, "We are unarmed and certainly outnumbered. Besides, you need food and rest."

Her expression turned stubborn. "I need you. I'm not leaving without you, Walker. Where you go, I go."

She thought herself in love with him, and while he knew that wouldn't last, he couldn't resist basking for a time in the pleasure of it. "Then you are going back to town with me."

Lilah put on her coat, but when she reached for the snowshoes, he took them and tucked them under his arm.

"I need those," she warned.

"Not with me." He held out his hand.

She grumbled as he banked the fire and led her outside. "I can't slog through the snow like you. My legs will turn into icicles and fall off." She frowned as she took a step onto the surface of the drift nearest the door. "I'm not sinking. Why am I not sinking?"

A flicker of movement caught his eye, but before he could catch sight of what made it, Lilah stepped in front of him.

"I know sunlight melts the top layers, and the cold air freezes them again, but not this fast." She tried to push her boot through the snow. "It's not budging."

Instead of walking down the slope, she went around to the back of the cabin, and peered up at the peaks above. As she moved around to get a better view, she stumbled over a pair of planks sticking up out of the snow.

"Look at this." She brushed the snow away from the surface of the crude cross. "Josiah Paul Jemmet. It's a grave marker."

He found three others hidden by snow and brush and read the names from them. "Anna Peterson Jemmet. Daniel Ethan Jemmet. David Nathan Jemmet."

Lilah stood. "Why is everyone in this town named after dead people?"

Chapter 15

"I don't know." He took her arm. "But we'd better go."

Something was watching them from the cover of the trees; he could feel the eyes tracking their movements. There was also something about the watcher that crept inside him and pulled at him, as if trying to lure him away from the woman. He turned his back on it and hustled Lilah around the cabin and down the slope, boosting her over obstacles and steadying her with his arm when she stumbled.

"Your mother should have named you Runner," she grumbled breathlessly as the trees thinned and the back of the inn appeared. "I need a bath, and coffee. Lots of coffee. Maybe a bathtub filled with coffee. Are you a coffee or tea person in the morning?"

"Neither." He glanced up at the mountain. Whatever had been outside the cabin had followed them. He was sure of it.

"Walker?"

He forced himself to look at her. "I will have whatever you like. Come."

Once inside the inn, he helped her put away the things she had borrowed from Annie before he led her back to their room. He secured the door, and then stood beside it listening for any sound.

"Hey." She came to stand beside him. "Don't worry, Annie won't wake up for a couple more hours."

"Good." He pulled off the knit hat from his head, and hair fell into his eyes—hair that was twice as long as it had been last night. He could not be seen like this. "Are there scissors in the bath?"

She nodded, and reached up to brush the black tangle back from his face. "Do we have to cut it?" She rubbed some strands between her fingertips. "I like you with all this Goth hair."

He smiled a little. "Goth?"

"I can't call it coal black; that's too cliché. Tar is too gross." She slid her fingers up to his scalp. "Onyx isn't this silky. Neither is lava rock." She dodged his mouth. "Oh, no, mister. I smell."

"You smell of me. I like it." He pulled her against him. "I want to kiss you."

"You can do that." She tugged him toward the bath. "But you have to scrub my back first."

The same wild, unreasonable desire for her flared inside him, but this time he would show her that he was not a beast. He let her draw him into the bathroom, but when she began unfastening the buttons on his shirt, he stopped her.

"That will wait." He bent to attend to the tub, and once it was filling, he began to undress her.

"A shower would be quicker," she said.

"Not everything must be fast." He took care not to tear at her damp clothes, but drew them off with all the care of a personal valet. From the basket on the counter he took the bow, untying the ribbon and gathering her hair up with it until it spilled from her crown like a fountain of fire. He helped her into the tub, and when she settled down, he quickly stripped off his own clothes and stepped in behind her. The water rose around them as he slid down and cradled her between his legs.

"You don't really have to scrub my back, you know," she said, sighing with pleasure as she nestled against him. "We could just soak for a couple days."

"We could." He picked up a bar of scented soap and worked it between his wet hands until they were white and slick with lather. "But the water would grow cold, and the innkeeper suspicious." He placed his hands on her shoulders, smoothing them down her arms and back up to cup her throat. He had never taken a moment to appreciate how lovely and soft her skin was, delicately smooth but firm and resilient.

Her bottom wriggled against him as he lifted one of her arms from the water and soaped it down to her hand, covering her palm with his and then bringing her hand to her breast. He pushed his fingers through the backs of hers, and used them together to encircle the fullness, brushing her nipple with the inner pads until the plump peak contracted into a tight, pebbly bead.

Lilah made a low sound, but when she tried to turn, he held her in place. "Not yet."

He attended to her other breast, and then took up the soap again. He shifted her up so he could rub the sweet curve of her belly, and slide his hand over the twin bows of her hip bones. Her head fell back against his shoulder as he massaged her thighs beneath the water, and stroked the sensitive creases behind her knees.

"I see what you're doing," she said, her words rushing with her breath. "This isn't a bath. It's revenge."

He lifted her so that his erection slid between her buttocks, but he left it to rest there while he stroked the inside of her thigh. "This is for you, my heart. Not for me."

She took in a sharp breath as his fingers drifted up and toyed with the curls over her mound. "Can I make a request?"

He brushed his lips over her ear. "Anything."

"I want to feel you inside me." She went still as he pressed two fingers between her folds, finding her and slowly filling her. "Could you . . . ?" She broke off, her breasts arching as her hips rolled. "Walker, please."

As hard as he wanted to thrust his cock inside her, he held back. He had done little more than ravage her; now he would show her that he could also give her the tenderness and care she deserved.

Water slopped over the side of the tub as he turned her to face him, pulling her legs around his waist and perching her against his hips. He looked down to see the head of his penis protruding from her curls, and worked it in slow strokes against her.

Her eyelids drooped and her lips parted as she rubbed back. "Oh, that's . . . just . . . oh." She shivered as his ridge rode her clit, and clamped her hands on his shoulders. "You feel so good."

He'd never held himself back like this, intent only on pleasing his lover, and now he understood how much he had denied himself. For him the act had never been much more than ridding his body of an uncomfortable need and finding a few hours of oblivion.

Watching Lilah finding her pleasure sank through the fortress around his cold heart, soothing the old wounds that had never healed, fading the shadows of despair and loneliness that had dwelled there for so long. It was an exquisite pain, this melting of the ice of his soul, but it could no longer withstand the force of her fire.

She bent her head to put her lips to his, and he brought her up, sliding against her until he felt the ellipse of tight, soft heat that melted over him like warm honey. Sliding into her body with tongue and cock made him groan, his body bunching under hers as he fought for his control.

Lilah's breath painted his mouth as she writhed, working him deeper. The ribbon he'd tied in her hair slipped down and her hair spilled over her wet shoulders and curtained their faces.

He cupped the back of her head and put his mouth to her ear, grazing the rim with his teeth before he kissed it. He had never been a man trained for anything but war and death, but he wished he was more for her. He wanted to adorn her with poetry and gray pearls, drape her in love songs and lilac satin. More than that, he wanted to hear her say them again, those words no woman had ever spoken to him.

"Tell me," he said before he could stop himself. "Tell me again what you feel for me."

"You know it." She looked down at his face and smiled, her eyes clear, her expression pure joy. "You're all over me, inside me, in my bones and my blood and my heart. You're part of my skin and my breath and my secrets. You're my love, my lover, my beloved, the sun in my dreams, and the stars in my soul." She closed her eyes as she reached the brink, and then opened them wide as he pushed deep and brought her over. "I love you."

She fell against him, boneless and trembling, and he released the chains, falling into the tide of her passion as he poured himself into her, until they were lost together in that nameless place where two were made one.

As the door to the small suburban house opened, and the short, silver-haired woman behind it stared up at him, Samuel Taske put on his most benign smile.

"Mrs. Kimball? I'm Samuel Taske." When she didn't move, he gently added, "We spoke last night on the phone."

"Yes, of course. I wasn't expecting . . . " She trailed off and stepped back. "I'm sorry. I'm not quite awake yet. Please, come in."

He followed her through the hall to a family room,

where she asked him to sit and offered him coffee. "I'm fine, thank you." He braced himself with his cane as he lowered himself carefully onto what appeared to be the sturdiest piece of furniture, the end corner of a brown suede sectional sofa. She hovered, her hands twisting together. "I apologize for dropping in so unexpectedly, but as I told you last night, you may know something that can help me find my brother."

Martha Kimball had readily accepted his lie about a younger brother who had served in the same region of Afghanistan as her son, and who like Walker Kimball had gone missing. "I don't know that I can do that, Mr. Taske. They never told us what Walker was doing over there; it was all classified. You'd probably get more information from the Marine Corps."

He'd already acquired Walker Kimball's service records from a civilian data clerk who would now be retiring from her civilian job much sooner than she had anticipated. "Did Walker send a letter to you before he went on that last mission?"

"His unit wasn't allowed to write home. No letters, no e-mail, not even a video at Christmas." She drifted around the room, shifting things slightly here and there when she could find nothing to tidy. "I thought that was wrong. Walker would never say or do anything to compromise the mission. We only wanted to know that he was all right. You must have felt the same about your brother."

"Yes." Taske's self-disgust rose another notch. "How did he keep in touch?"

"He would call us when he could, always at strange times. Every time the phone rings, I still run for it." Martha Kimball stopped in front of him. "The counselor from the base, he said I should begin preparing myself, but I can't."

She bent down, picking up a wooden box inlaid with

slivers of brass. "His commander sent this to me after my son was declared missing. Until they find his . . . him, it's all I have." She held it out to him.

Taske took it and carefully opened the lid. Inside lay an envelope filled with photos of what he assumed was the Kimball family, a compass, and a water-resistant watch with a broken nylon black band. No, not broken, he saw as he examined it, but sliced through, as if someone had been too impatient to unfasten the clasp and had instead cut it off.

Taske palmed the watch before he closed the lid and placed it back on the table. He was able to place the watch in his suit jacket pocket when he reached for his wallet, from which he took one of his business cards.

"If you do hear any news, or there is anything I can do for you, please call me," he said as he stood and handed her the card. She smiled. "You're very kind, Mr. Taske. I hope you find your brother soon."

Taske couldn't get out of the Kimball house fast enough. To Findley, who was waiting by the car, he said, "James, I am a complete and utter bastard."

"I can't agree, sir." Findley helped him into the car before going around to slide in behind the wheel. "Shall I take you on to the hotel?"

"Yes, please." He took out the watch he had stolen from Walker Kimball's grieving mother, holding it between his gloves as he tried to clear his mind. He had stolen one of the few, pitiful artifacts Martha possessed to remind her of her only child's noble sacrifice. It was one of the most unforgivable things he had ever done.

But as miserable as the guilt that gnawed inside him was, it was nothing compared with the barbed snake coiled around his spine. His doctors had been very clear about the rapid deterioration of his condition. In six months he would be in a wheelchair; in twelve he would be bedridden. The thought of spending the rest of his life staring at a ceiling gave him the strength to strip off his gloves.

Taske closed his eyes, and opened his mind, flinching as the barrage of psychic imagery began, starting on the other side of the world in the Kyoto factory where the watch had been manufactured. Flashes of the same type of wholly impersonal handling and transport followed, until the watch was shelved at a department store in Denver by a middle-aged woman, who showed it to five different customers before selling it to Martha Kimball.

It's a birthday gift for my son, she told the clerk. *He's going overseas and he needs a good watch.*

Watching Walker Kimball unwrap his gift and kiss his mother was too much for Taske to bear, and he rushed past them, catching only brief glimpses of the marine on a plane as he changed the time on the watch. Through the face of the watch he saw Walker being deployed, crossing the desert, showering in a tent, smearing his face with black camouflage paint, crawling through brush, firing a weapon into the night.

He slowed his pace, carefully examining each image that came now. Walker crouching down to fill a canteen from a stream and add a white pill before capping it and shaking it. Walker dropping an armful of dead, broken branches onto a small campfire. Other men, dressed in desert camouflage, passing around a pack of field rations. Walker talking to a man dressed in black fitted garments; from the hood covering his face, Taske guessed him to be a local informer.

An explosion roared through Taske's head, shattering his concentration and dragging him into the middle of a vicious battle between the marines and a small group of bearded, screaming men. One of them slashed at Walker with a short sword as broad as a machete, cutting almost clean through the watch strap as they struggled. The marine fought back hard and, in the process of disarming him, dislocated his attacker's shoulder. The hooded man returned in another image at the campfire, coming to crouch beside Walker as the last thread holding the watch to his arm unraveled. Before the watch hit the ground, the hooded man reached out and—

Taske dropped the watch in his lap, clapping his hands over his eyes as golden light speared through his mind, splintering the images like so much cheap glass. When he could speak, he said, "Findley, don't go to the hotel. Drive to the veterans' hospital."

His driver glanced at him through the rearview mirror. "I think the only VA hospital in Denver closed back in the nineties, Mr. Taske."

"It's not closed anymore." He rubbed at the side of his head. "Please take me there."

Chain-link fencing surrounded the grounds of the old veterans' hospital, and from the outside the darkened windows and chained doors did make it appear as if it had not been in operation for some time.

"Go around the back," Taske said as he pulled on his gloves. "Drive through the open gate and park behind the ambulances."

Findley delivered him to the back of the old hospital, and helped him out of the car. "Do you need me to come along?"

"Yes." He leaned on his driver's arm for a moment until the dizziness passed. He fumbled in his jacket until he took out a pair of sunglasses and covered his eyes with them. "For the next twenty minutes, I'm General Sullivan Perry, here to visit one of my men."

"I assume the general is retired," Findley said as he guided Taske around the ambulance, "and reclusive."

"That he is." He gritted his teeth as the new pain in his head met the old snake of agony throttling the life out of his spine. "He's also quite fond of antique pistols, which he keeps in a locked display case, unlike his credentials."

The two MPs that came out of the back of the defunct emergency room were armed and dressed for recall. Both leveled flashlights and weapons at Taske and Findley.

"Hands up where I can see them," the senior MP barked. "Identify yourselves."

Taske held out his identification folder, turning it so that the beam illuminated the counterfeit credentials.

The MP plucked the folder from his hand, holding it beside Taske's face to compare them. "Stand down," he said to his partner as he handed the folder back to Taske. "I apologize, General. We weren't notified that you would be making a visit."

"I prefer to stay under the radar, Corporal." Taske nodded toward the doors behind the MPs. "You have a patient arrived today from Walter Reed. I need to see him immediately."

The MP looked uneasy. "Sir, the only soldier admitted today is in intensive care, and not expected to survive the night."

"That's why the general needs to see him," Findley said in a clear, hard-edged voice. "Pronto."

"Yes, sir." The MP stepped back. "Right this way."

The guards led them through the dark halls of the emergency, through a second checkpoint, and into the busy lobby. Taske noted the black spray paint on the interior window surfaces, the racks of biohazard suits, and another dozen armed MPs stationed at strategic points.

The men who had been brought to this covert facility for treatment were not here for ordinary wounds; that much was obvious.

As they approached an elevator, Taske leaned in to say to Findley, "This situation is far more hazardous than I thought. You should go back to the car and wait."

"I should," his driver agreed, "but I'd rather not, General."

Taske lurched along with Findley into the elevator, and when the MP would have joined them, he shook his head. "What floor?"

"Seven, sir."

"That will be all, Corporal." He reached out and pressed the button. As soon as the doors closed, he slumped against the wall. "We only have a minute or two. I'll need you to run interference for me."

"Focus on him," Findley said, and took out a penknife. He flipped open the blade and carefully made a short cut on the front of his scalp, letting the blood from the wound flow down his face. "I'll keep the military busy."

As soon as they stepped off the elevator onto the seventh floor, Findley clapped a hand over his self-inflicted wound and staggered forward toward the nurses' station, calling out for help. Taske hobbled in the opposite direction, taking cover behind a tall supply cart until the nurses had ushered his driver into a treatment room.

There were six soldiers on the floor, but Taske followed his instincts blindly, knowing the rapidly dimming thread of light in his mind would lead him to the man who was about to die. That took him to the second unit, and in to stand beside the bed of a battered body swathed in bandages.

Taske peeled back the adhesive tape over the intravenous needle in the back of the soldier's hand, and then gently withdrew the needle from his vein, which stopped the flow of the medication, a lethal dose that the ICU nurse had just administered from a mislabeled bottle. Beneath the gauze swaddling his scalp, the soldier's swollen lids parted, revealing twin slivers of his bloodshot eyes.

"I'm sorry to disturb you," Taske said, "but someone made a mistake with your medication. Everything will be all right now."

"Thanks," the soldier murmured. "Where am I?"

"Denver. You were flown in today from Walter Reed." Taske pulled a chair over to the side of the bed and sat down. "Do you remember what happened to you?"

"Yes, sir. We were embedded in the Kunar Valley, near the Pakistani border, working ETT with our guys there. My team received intel on a major infiltration unit coming across the border, and we were ordered to turn them around or bring them in for interrogation. When we got to the coordinates, it didn't feel right to me— border jumpers like room to run and plenty of cover, and this was a bottleneck between two ridges. We stopped to confirm the intel with camp, and that's when I saw that the only way out was through a couple of poppy fields."

"Fields that are controlled by the terrorists."

The soldier nodded. "They were waiting on top of the ridges for us, and began firing. When we tried to move into flanking positions, we discovered they'd mined the fields. They brought reinforcements in behind us, cutting off our retreat. We were trapped. No." The soldier closed his eyes. "We were dead and we knew it."

Taske glanced out at the still-empty nursing station. "Someone must have helped you escape."

"A mercenary came through the mines. I don't know how he did it, but he got to us and said he could get us out if we followed him in twos," the soldier said. "And he did. I covered them from the rear, until I was the last one left and he came for me. That's when they tossed five grenades at us. We couldn't run through the mines— we'd have set them off. So we found three, and threw them back, but ... "

"The last two went off," Taske guessed.

"He threw himself on top of them. Son of a bitch used himself as a blast shield for me." The soldier took in a hitching breath. "When they went off, they blew us both clear of the mines, but he was ... the merc didn't make it." He paused for a long moment. "I knew they'd come, so I crawled into the brush to hide. I watched them drag his body away." He cleared his throat. "I don't remember much after that. They said the medics didn't find me for a week."

Taske leaned forward. "What was this man's name?"

"Mercs never use real names," the soldier said. "A couple of the friendlies knew him. They called him Guide." He stared at Taske. "How did you know someone screwed up my meds?"

"I delivered the shipment, and noticed some of the bottles were incorrectly labeled," Taske lied. Given the length of time he had spent with the soldier, he couldn't risk staying more than a few more seconds. He rose stiffly from the chair and put his hand over the soldier's wrist. "Rest now, ah . . . " He broke off into a chuckle. "I was in such a hurry to get here that I never asked for your name."

The soldier told him.

Feeling battered all over again, Taske reached into his jacket and placed the watch with the broken band in the soldier's hand.

Bruised fingers felt the split in the band. "Where did you find this?"

"I didn't find it." In reparation for what he had done, Taske could tell him one fragment of truth. "I stole it from your mother, Sergeant Kimball."

PART FOUR

Wolf Moon

Chapter 16

October 4, 2009
Kunar Valley, Afghanistan

"Tell him I need completely intact bodies," George Parker snapped as he used his hat to fan the flies away from his face. "Arms, legs, heads, nuts, the works. And they gotta still be attached."

The Afghani translator relayed his demands in his native language to the professional scavenger, who scowled and shook his head as he rattled off a lengthy reply.

"He say, Americans, they come after the bombs go off." The interpreter moved his hands in a universal gesture of helplessness. "They take all the bodies to choppers, fly them away to American hospital. He only find feet, hands, legs."

"Like I thought, a waste of time." Parker jammed his helmet over his head. "Come on, we might as well move to the north."

A boy in a stained robe came running out of one of the hovels in the village, waving and screeching at the interpreter. Parker reached into his pocket for some of the candy and coins he tossed to the kiddies, but the interpreter put his hand on his arm.

"This boy, he say his uncle has a good body in his

field," the interpreter said. "He will let you have it extra cheap."

"Now, why would he do that?" Parker asked, and tossed the kid a Tootsie Roll. "Not out of the kindness of his American-hating heart."

"The GIs, they burn his poppies, so he need money." The Afghan asked the boy something, and then chortled. "He say his uncle scared of it. Say it watches him. That's why you get it half price."

Parker heaved a sigh. "How far away is the uncle?"

"Two miles north." The interpreter looked hopeful. "On our way, boss."

He scowled at the boy. "This body better have all its parts, boy, or I'm coming back here to personally whup your ass." He nudged his driver with the butt of his rifle, and pulled his bandanna up over his mouth and nose to keep the dust out as the jeep rattled over the dirt roads.

Parker wasn't especially fond of being this close to the Pakistani border, where skirmishes between the U.S. and Al-Qaeda regularly turned into all-out massacres, but the demands for suitable cadavers had tripled since the project had moved into its last phase. Besides, he only had to retrieve the bodies and send them up the line; that was a lot better than marching them out in the jungle where they knew what was going to happen the minute they looked into the bottom of the pit. Dead men didn't try to up and run for their lives.

The farm turned out to be little more than a shack sitting in the midst of five acres of scorched ground, and the boy's uncle was a weathered rail of an old man, the type Parker's father had often called a Moses-through-a-reed.

The interpreter exchanged greetings, and after he explained what had brought them to the farm, the old man pointed to a bundle of rags hanging from a crude cross.

"He says we go out, boss, look first," the interpreter said.

"Damn straight we are." Parker wasn't buying a bunch of bones wrapped in rotten meat.

The body was male, long and lean, and still dressed in close-fitted pants and an undershirt. Long black hair hung over the man's face, covering it completely.

"Not American." Parker covered his mouth and nose again before stepping close enough to lift the head and check to see that the birds hadn't been at the eyes or nose.

The man's skin was burnt black, but his eyes were only faintly milky, and his nose and lips were still in place. Parker groped the rest of the corpse's limp, cold flesh until he was satisfied.

"All right," he told the interpreter. "Cut him down. We'll take him."

The farmer accepted the money, but refused to go near the jeep as the driver and the interpreter were loading the cadaver in the back. He kept his face turned, and made several finger gestures in the direction of the corpse as he chattered on in a low, disgusted voice.

"Why's he getting all worked up?" Parker demanded.

The interpreter came over and asked the old farmer, who snapped something at Parker before he retreated into his shack.

"He say, dead man worse when guerrillas dump him in the field. Guerrillas not want long-haired man; he not American. They say dead man fall on grenades and . . ." The interpreter mimicked the sound of an explosion, and flung out his arms. "Now he look better."

"Worse? Better?" Parker scratched his cheek. "Shit, he's dead. This is as good as it gets."

The interpreter shrugged.

"Why was he pointing his fingers at him like that?" Parker asked.

"Keep-away-evil fingers." The interpreter grinned and imitated the gestures. "Demon no take my land, demon no take my life, demon no take my children, demon you have my wife."

Parker chuckled. "I know that one."

That night, as Parker arrived at the private airstrip with the five bodies he'd managed to collect, he stopped to have a smoke while the corpses were wrapped and loaded onto the contract cargo plane. Genaro ran a sweet scam with his special-delivery planes, which brought over tons of church donations, packages from home, and other morale boosters for the troops every month. Genaro's generosity was such that no one ever bothered to check where the planes went once they'd dropped their precious cargo, or what exactly was in the planes when they made the trip back to the States.

"Hey, George." The pilot, who had finished his pre-flight, stopped to bum a cigarette. "How's the grave-robbing business?"

"Shit, Judd, they weren't in no graves," he chided. "Found one this week hanging from a cross in the middle of a burned-out opium farm."

"What a friend we have in Jesus." Judd snickered. "You run 'em through the metal detector?"

"Don't I always?" Parker spit on the ground. He'd learned the hard way that the guerrillas liked to leave bodies booby-trapped so they could relieve the U.S. military of a few medics without even having to be there. "Just watch out for the long-haired one. Old fart that sold him to me says he watches you like a hawk."

The pilot leaned in, pulling the plastic shrouds away from the ruined faces until he found the one covered with black hair. "You mean, this old boy?"

Parker grinned as he looked over, and then the butt between his lips drooped. Two black eyes, open, clear, and bright, stared back at him.

"Yeah." He turned his back on the dead man watching him. "That's him." He trotted off, and didn't puke until he was out of the pilot's sight.

October 4, 1999
Scarvaville, Oregon

Waking up didn't seem right to Elle, not after dying. She'd expected the darkness, but not the light. Then there was the place she woke up to. Evelyn had always promised that if she was a good girl, she would end up in heaven, which was decorated by the angels. According to her mother, it was supposed to be a place of pure light and eternal peace.

So why was she on a bunk in a camper? And why was she so thirsty?

The thick layer of gauze over the front of her throat kept her from moving too much, but when Elle worked up the courage to touch it, it felt wrong, too. When you died and went to heaven, you were supposed to become an angel. She'd never seen a picture of one wrapped in bandages.

Carefully she poked a finger under the lowest edge, expecting to feel stitches and pain. The only thing beneath the bandages was her skin. It was tender, the way it felt after she sunburned and peeled, but she couldn't feel any tears or repairs.

Finally she worked up the nerve to pull at the dressing, wincing as the adhesive tape holding it in place peeled away from her skin. Dark red-brown streaks of dried blood stained the inside of the bandages, but she couldn't feel so much as a scratch on her throat.

She checked the rest of her body, what she could see of it. Her clothes were gone, and all she wore was a large man's flannel shirt. She was virtually naked, she'd been attacked by a cougar, and there wasn't a mark on her.

Be a good girl, Lillian, and you'll get your reward.

But she hadn't been a good girl. She'd run away. She'd never done anything so bad as that. What would her mother say now?

The camper shook a little as someone walked back toward her, and she sat up to see a grim, familiar face. "Mr. Huntley?" Her voice came out in a dry, straining rasp that sounded nothing like her.

"Lillian, you're awake. That's good. No, don't try to get up just yet." He picked up a glass of water from a little table and brought it to her. "Drink," he said as he held it to her lips. "It'll help."

She drank until she had emptied the glass, and then cleared her throat. "Thank you." Her voice still sounded wrong, but there were more important things she had to know. "Where am I? What happened to me?"

"You're safe." He put the glass aside and drew a little camp chair up by the side of the bunk. "How much do you remember?"

Why wasn't he just telling her what had happened? "I was up in the hills with Dancer, and something spooked him. He took off." The scratchiness in her throat came back, making her swallow. "Then something knocked me to the ground, and it . . . my throat . . . it was a cougar, right?"

He didn't answer her, but hunched over to look at the floor of the camper.

When it became obvious that he wasn't going to answer her, she asked, "Why am I here, Mr. Huntley? Shouldn't I be in the hospital?"

"I couldn't risk taking you to a doctor." His head came up. "The thing that attacked you only looked like a cougar. It's a man, or at least, it was a long time ago. I was sent here to put it out of its misery, but I never got close enough. It's still human enough to outthink me. I think the only reason it went after you was because it tracked me back to your mother's land. It must have been waiting up there for me."

"Mr. Huntley, maybe you should take me home now," she said carefully. "My mother is going to be really worried about me."

"Evelyn left California the day after you disappeared. I can't say for sure, but I don't think she'll be coming back." He sighed. "I know you think I'm crazy right now, girl, but I'm not, and I promise, I won't hurt you. As soon as I saw how fast you healed, I knew you were special. I don't understand what you are just yet, but we'll figure it out together."

What she was. Elle touched her throat.

He stood. "I've got a fire going outside. I'll bring you some clothes, and we'll get you up and around a bit."

Neil Huntley did talk like a crazy man, but he brought her some clothes and left the camper so she could dress in private. As soon as Elle stood, the weak and trembling condition of her body made it plain that she would not be able to run away from the stable manager. She'd have to talk her way out of this, or try to get help from someone else.

Elle realized her second idea wasn't going to work as soon as she climbed out of the camper. She didn't recognize the empty hills around the campsite, which was deserted except for the camper hitched to Huntley's truck. The strange mountains on the horizon didn't look right, either.

"We're in Oregon," Huntley said as he dropped some dry wood onto the stone-encircled campfire.

"Okay." Elle wrapped her arms around her waist as she cautiously approached him. "Why are we in Oregon? Do you live around here?"

"It's outside the search area." He brought over a pair of lawn chairs from the back of his truck. "Come and sit down, Lillian. I'll tell you as much as I can."

After scanning the area and finding no sign of anyone who would hear her scream, Elle went to the fire and sat down.

"Don't want you to catch a chill." Huntley covered her with a dark wool blanket, tucking it in around her but taking his hands away when he felt her stiffen. "I am your friend. Don't be afraid of me, girl."

"How can I not be?" she asked without thinking. Then she quickly added, "Mr. Huntley, this is kidnapping. They'll put you in jail. But if you take me back right now, I won't say anything to the police. I promise."

"You can't go back." He sat down and held his head in his hands for a minute before he straightened. "My name isn't Neil Huntley, and I'm not American." The country accent disappeared from his voice, replaced by a soft, liquid accent. "I was sent here by the men I work for to hunt down this creature, the one that attacked you. It's in a kind of eternal torment, and it can't stop itself anymore. The only way to end its suffering is to kill it."

He was genuinely, deeply nuts. "You could tell the police about it," she suggested. "They'd help you find it."

"They wouldn't believe me, and even if they did, I could never let them near it. It would kill them all before they could even hurt it." He stared at the tiny sparks rising up with the smoke from the fire. "It remembers women from when it was a man. It loved many women. I think that's why it didn't kill you." He sighed. "Or maybe it was hoping to use you to lure me up there."

Elle's instincts told her to agree with him, to go along with anything he said so that he would feel she wasn't the enemy. The shock had faded, however, and she suddenly felt a terrible anger. Who was this man to snatch her like this, to take her away from Evelyn and keep her like some stray dog? She didn't know what he'd done to her throat wound to make it disappear, but it wasn't right. She could have died. She should be dead, no thanks to him.

"I want you to take me home, Mr. Huntley," she told him. "I'll tell the police you found me, as long as you swear that you'll never do this to anyone again."

He stared at her. "Haven't you been listening? You were dead when I found you, Lillian. The monster tore out your throat. I was carrying your body to my horse when you began coughing up blood." He pointed at her neck. "I watched your wounds close up and vanish, as if they'd never been. The only thing on this earth that can do that isn't human. You're not human."

Anger suffused her, spiking through her head and making her hair stand on end. It lifted her up, taking away the soreness in her back and the lingering dryness in her throat.

"Lillian?"

She rose up out of the chair. "Take me back," she said, her ruined voice sounding low and rough, her entire body shaking. "Now."

Huntley stood, his eyes wide. *"Lillian."*

After it happened, Elle was terrified. She dragged Neil Huntley's body back inside the camper, and only after she had hefted him onto the bunk did she realize how strong she had become.

He has to weigh two hundred pounds. I can't lift two hundred pounds. But she had, and her arms weren't aching even a little. *It's adrenaline. It'll go away.*

Huntley moaned.

"Oh, God." She turned around, looking desperately for something to put over his chest and stanch the bleeding. Her head pounded as she began frantically searching through the cabinets, crying out in relief as she found a large first-aid kit. She knelt on the floor, grabbing at packages of gauze and tearing them open, making a pile of patches until she thought she might have enough. Then she got up and bent over Huntley, pushing aside the torn ribbons of what had been his shirt to expose the wound.

Four huge gashes ran across his chest, and when she blotted the welling blood from them, she saw that they went so deep the inner tissues bulged out like raw meat.

"I don't know what to do, Mr. Huntley." She piled the gauze over the wound and tried to tape it down, but the adhesive tape wouldn't stick to his bloody chest, and oh, God, she was going to kill him; she knew she was—

"Lillian." Huntley's voice, like the whisper of a ghost, hummed in her ears. "I'm all right. You have to clean it. Stitch it."

She stared down at the slits of his eyes. "Mr. Huntley, I'm not a doctor. I can't do this."

"You can. You watch Doc with the horses. Same thing." The side of his mouth curled up. "Good ... practice ... "

He'd fallen unconscious again.

Be a good girl, Lillian.

Elle turned her back on him and took several deep breaths. *I can do this. I can save him.*

She thought back to the time she had worked with Dr. Devereaux to treat an open wound on the side of one of the stock horses who had run afoul of some barbed wire.

Infection is the biggest problem, the vet had told her. *We'll give him a shot after we're done, but you can start out right by making sure everything is clean: your hands, what you use on the wound, the wound, everything.*

She used the tiny sink to wash her hands with the bar of soap in the little dish beside it, and wiped them dry with a paper towel. From the first-aid kit she took a bottle of rubbing alcohol and a small suture pack, and began putting together the same kind of setup the vet had arranged, so that everything she needed would be at hand.

Are you ready to fix up this big guy? the vet asked in her head.

"I'm ready."

Neil Huntley opened his eyes, and touched the bandages wrapped around his chest.

"Don't try to move, Mr. Huntley." Elle came over to the bunk with a glass of water. She placed a straw in the glass and brought the end to his lips. "I wish I had something for the pain, but all you have in your kit is some aspirin, and I'm afraid that will make you start bleeding again."

"Mauled?"

She nodded. "It's my fault. If I hadn't lost my temper, if I'd just listened to you ... " When he shook his head, she took his limp hand in hers. "I've never hurt anyone in my life, Mr. Huntley. I would never have done this to you if I'd known. I'm so sorry."

He tucked in his chin and looked at the bandage on his chest. She had run out of gauze after the second dressing change, and had started using his white undershirts.

"You remembered what to do," he said. "You could have run away and left me here to bleed to death. But you stayed, and you lived up to the responsibility of your actions. It was very hard, wasn't it?"

"I was so scared." She covered her face and sobbed.

His hand came to rest on the top of her head. "You are a good child, Lillian."

It took another week for Neil Huntley to heal enough to be able to drive. During those seven days, they discussed everything that had happened, and everything that mattered. Huntley couldn't tell her a great deal about his life before coming to America, or anything about the men who had sent him there.

"We are born to this life, and take vows, like priests," he explained when she pressed him for details. "As did my father, and his father, and his father before him. Thirty-two generations of my family have served. It is not the vows I took as much as the trust that I have been given along with my name. All of those who came before me made the same sacrifice. That is why I cannot break my vows, Lillian. Not even for you."

They picked up supplies from a small town, and from there Huntley drove to Seattle, where he rented a small apartment for them. Elle, who had cut her hair and dyed it brown to match his, posed as his daughter. He stayed with her until he finished recovering from his injuries, at the same time teaching her how to cope with the terrible gift she had been given.

"Are you going to tell them about me?" she asked the night before he left for California.

He fell silent for a long time. "No, Lillian. I believe you can control yourself now."

"But if I don't, you'll come after me," she guessed.

"I hunt monsters, my dear. You are not a monster. You are the victim of one." He gave her a troubled look. "But you are also dangerous, and if you are to make a place for yourself in this world, you must never forget that."

"It won't happen again," she assured him. "I'll be careful."

"You have to do more than control yourself. You must not let anyone discover who and what you are. No doctors, no hospitals. You cannot confide in anyone." He frowned, thinking. "You should not remain here in Seattle for too long. No more than a year, I think."

"But I like it here," she protested. "I've got a good job at the café, and I'm making friends."

"You can't stay here," he told her. "You can't stay anywhere. If you do, people will discover what you are." He studied her face. "You're still thinking of contacting your mother, after everything that's happened?"

"I'm not a monster." Ashamed, she ducked her head. "I wasn't going to tell her where I am. I just want her to know I'm okay."

"She will want to see you, Lillian, and in your loneliness you won't be able to refuse her." He sighed. "How long do you think you can control it? A week? A month? What happens when you lose your temper, or you simply have a bad dream? Does anyone deserve to die like that? Could you live with yourself, knowing you could have stayed away and spared her life?"

Before he left, he paid the rent on the apartment for a year, and gave her the rest of the cash that he had. "I will tell my masters that I was robbed," he said when she tried to refuse. "They are very wealthy. They will send more."

She walked him out to his truck, and on impulse hugged him. "Thank you for everything." She drew back. "I can't believe you're leaving. Will I ever see you again?"

"This is my last field assignment. After I finish my work, I am going home to be a teacher." He took a scrap of paper from his pocket and wrote a long number on it. "If you are in trouble, call this number and leave a message for me. I will try to do what I can for you."

She folded the paper and put it in her pocket. "I don't even know your name."

He smiled sadly and kissed her brow. "Ask for Brother Tomaseo."

Chapter 17

" . . . e non c'e' nessuno, che mi può cambiare, che mi può staccare da lei . . ."[1]

Through the telephoto lens of her camera, Valori Trovatella murmured another chorus of the old, sad song as she watched Teresina Segreta help a tall, groggy man from the back of the limousine. Tracking the private car from Denver International Airport to a newly constructed facility outside the city had required a simple game; she had walked down the row of cars in the executive pickup area, punched in VINs on her BlackBerry, which illegally accessed the state's registration database. When she'd found the car registered to GenHance, Inc., she went over to the driver's window and tapped on it with the end of an unlit cigarette.

"Those mean security people took my matches away at the gate," she told the driver as she bent down, putting her breasts at his eye level. She allowed a bit more Texas twang to color her voice as she asked, "Any chance you can light me up here, cowboy?"

The poor, muscle-bound dolt had produced a lighter, but the proximity of her chest had distracted him so much it took him three attempts to light her cigarette. That gave her ample time to drop the tracer in his pocket,

---

[1] "Quando M'innamoro," music and Italian lyrics by Mario Panzeri, Roberto Livraghi, Daniele Pace, and Alfonso Alpin.

although she probably could have tucked a small bomb between his legs and he wouldn't have noticed.

The policeman would have, Tomaseo chided from inside her head.

"He was a sheriff," she corrected her dead mentor, using the Cigarette Slut's accent. She wrinkled her nose as she realized she still smelled faintly of tobacco. "He would also be suspicious that my brain had shrunk to the size of a walnut while my breasts had doubled in size."

Breasts that were half padding and now itching unbearably, thanks to the spirit gum she'd used to hold the edges of the flesh-toned plastic falsies in place under her body makeup. She took one hand from the camera to reach into her blouse and pull the augmentations off her body, dropping them into the open tote on the floor.

You should not have dallied with him, Valori.

"It was one night of very good sex," she pointed out, this time in her Snobby Blue Blood tone, "not a dalliance."

You know what I mean. He is nothing to you.

"Perhaps." If she hadn't enjoyed Ethan Jemmet so much, she would have agreed. "But I was something to him," she told Tomaseo in Lori's voice.

Valori had rarely used the sweet, shy girl-next-door persona she had shown that night to the lonely lawman. "Lori" worked only on a narrow range of men with specific issues, such as the grieving father of a lost daughter, or a nervous, virginal postadolescent who feared aggressive women. But she'd instinctively brought out Lori as soon as she'd looked into Ethan Jemmet's stern, handsome face, sensing an innocent charmer would be the woman to whom he would respond with the most kindness. In the end she had been gratified to know that Lori had been the perfect fit for the sheriff.

Just like our bodies.

Recalling the sex with Ethan, like hunger, exhaustion, and all her other personal needs, would have to wait for now. As soon as Teresina and the tired man disappeared into the back entrance of the building, Valori switched off the camera and checked her watch. Knowing Teresina, she would hand off the man and get straight to business; she had only a few hours before she would have to meet the men she'd hired to steal the bodies from Jonah Genaro.

You must stop her, alunna.

She started the engine. Her conversations with Tomaseo's ghost were strictly products of loneliness and her own imagination, but that didn't mean he was wrong. "I'm trying, *mentore*."

Valori drove from her vantage point to a fenced-in cluster of electrical boxes, small satellite dishes, and other equipment that fed power and communications to the remote facility. While she suspected she would need a small army of operatives to break into GenHance's new lab, they had yet to secure their perimeter. The only thing separating her from their data systems was a padlock on the fence gate.

Before she got out of the unmarked van she had stolen, Valori rolled her curls tight against the back of her head and used a slide clip to hold them in place. She then changed her silk blouse for a utility-company uniform shirt and clipped on a laminated ID tag with a smiling photo of her own face and the name of a real female district field inspector. A yellow hard hat, a company jacket, and a tool bag completed the illusion.

She checked her face in the visor mirror, pausing to wipe off a lingering trace of Cigarette Slut's red lip paint. "I'm Inspector Pat Drysen," she said in a colorless, no-nonsense voice. "Denver Power and Light. I am joyless but excellent at my job. I have an apartment, a cat, and no life. I hate men. No," she corrected herself.

"I envy men their superior salaries, which I don't think they deserve simply for possessing a penis. I do not like being touched. I carry pepper spray in my purse. I am a Democrat and a Methodist. I eat microwave dinners. I watch television crime dramas obsessively."

Until she dropped the persona or changed to another, she would be Pat Drysen, uptight and unforgiving career woman working in a man's field.

It had not always been so. After discovering Valori had a natural affinity with electronics and machines, her many masters of childhood had taught her how to identify and infiltrate any security system. Unlike the other children at the Temple, she had not been born into service, but had been brought in from the streets where her unknown mother had dumped her. If Valori had been sickly, troublesome, or limited, she would have been promptly turned over to the Italian authorities, but she had been a healthy, placid infant who had grown into a quiet, highly intelligent toddler. She'd begun her training as soon as she could walk.

The council had originally designated her to serve as a servant or secretary, the most invisible member of any important household or business. It wasn't until she matured that her other talent had come to their notice, and abruptly changed the nature of her tutelage.

Tomaseo had been the one to explain it to her, and he'd done so with as much kindness as he could. "You will be the butterfly now, *alunna*. Everyone who sees you will think, 'Ah, how beautiful.' They do not think this of the moth in the closet."

She had been dutiful and devoted, still a child in many ways. Part of her dreaded this change in her duties, but for Tomaseo's sake she hadn't protested. She also knew her place. Only those born to service were treasured, her masters had taught her early on. A nameless bastard like her could only be of service to those who served.

They expected only that she fulfill the traditional obligation, that of giving one year of her life for every year they had cared for her.

That she would spend eighteen years as a butterfly instead of a moth had not seemed so terrible in the beginning, not to a child of sixteen.

Valori was sent to Milan for initiation, and then on to Paris for polishing, and reported back to Napoli some two years later. She'd expected to be assigned as a monitor to one household, but after testing her abilities, the council revealed other, important plans for her. Her secret, fragile hope of finding happiness and belonging had finally died that day.

Tomaseo had kept her from descending completely into despair. To the council he had been her handler, but to Valori he had been her friend and confidant. He'd recognized the hopelessness and sadness beneath her many butterfly masks, and he'd promised to intercede on her behalf with the council when her term of service was concluded. That he had died before he could free her didn't matter; his intentions had been genuine. But losing the man she considered a brother as well as a mentor had torn something out of her. After that, it had been easy to strike the bargain with the council.

"I will go and resolve the issue in America," she had said before the grim faces of the fourteen *padrones*. "If I return, I wish to be freed of all further obligations and released from service."

She owed them four more years, and they had no one as effective as she had been in the field, so for them the bargain had been costly. At the same time they didn't expect the American issue to end well, and Valori had always been disposable to them. She hadn't been surprised at all when they had agreed to her terms.

Surviving this final task would be next to impossible, but Valori didn't fear death as much as losing what was left of her soul. She was glad she had given in to the impulse to spend the night with the handsome young sheriff.

It was a sin, Tomaseo said as he watched her work. *An act of selfishness. A mistake.*

"Yes," she agreed readily in Pat's dry voice, "and every moment of it was much better than having two glasses of wine and twenty minutes with the vibrator in my nightstand."

Poor Pat was like too many women in the world; she simply needed to be tied up and pleasured by a slow, thorough lover.

Valori reached to remove her bracelet before she accessed the electrical panel, but felt only bare skin. She took it off only when she worked near high voltage, and her flawless memory raced backward in time to the last time she had seen it. She had been paying the waitress at the diner after leaving Ethan. It had jangled on her wrist as she handed over the money. The clasp had been old and worn; she had meant to have it replaced. . . .

She discarded Pat, shifting her thoughts back into Lori, and then flipped open her phone. After calling information for the number to the diner, she dialed it.

A tired voice answered, "Mel's. What can I get for you?"

"Hi," she said, adjusting her voice to Lori's hesitant, partially apologetic tone. "I was wondering if anyone found a charm bracelet there? I think I might have dropped it when I stopped in for some coffee the other day."

"Oh, yes, we did find it, honey," the waitress said. "I gave it to your boyfriend when he came in later. He said he'd make sure to get it back to you."

"My boyfriend, Ethan, the sheriff, has my bracelet?" Valori asked, just to be sure.

"Uh-huh. It's safe and sound with him. I have to say,

sweetheart, he wasn't too happy about you leaving before him. But you know men." The older woman sighed. "If they could keep us on a short leash, we'd all be wearing collars."

"That we would," Valori agreed. "Thanks for your help." She ended the call.

So Ethan Jemmet had her bracelet, did he? Another man would keep it as a trophy of an easy conquest, perhaps, but not the sheriff. He had enjoyed their night together as much as she had, but her abrupt departure likely hurt his pride. No, she suspected Ethan would use the bracelet to try to find her, and while she could easily avoid that, any serious inquiries he might make could alert the council and otherwise interfere with her business.

His curiosity could cost you your life, Valori.

"Peace, *mentore*," she murmured. "I don't need the Evil Eye looking for me on this trip. Which, as we both know, will probably be the death of me."

You must forget about him.

She nodded absently. "As soon as I get back my bracelet."

As she remotely accessed GenHance's security system, Valori opened a second window and ran a search on Ethan Jemmet. She already knew he was a Larimer County sheriff from the emblem she had seen on his truck. Within a few seconds she discovered that he lived and worked in a tiny mountain town west of Denver, and she then ran a MapQuest on Frenchman's Pass. While that loaded, she used her primary window to bring up the feed from the facility's security cameras covering the back platforms, all of which were empty.

The absence of the truck told her that Teresina had ignored her advice. She was going through with her plans to cheat her employers and fake her own death, and frame another for both crimes. Before being turned out by the council, Teresina had undergone years of training similar to Valori's, and she had gone even further developing skills on her own. The odds of success weighed heavily in her favor.

Under the circumstances, stealing Teresina's victory from her seemed almost obscene, but Valori could not allow her sympathy for Tomaseo's wayward sister to compromise her own mission. Teresina would despise having to return to Italy and accept the protection of the council, but she was the last of her line; if she cooperated, she would be well treated, even pampered and indulged.

If she didn't, she would spend the rest of her life imprisoned and at the mercy of the council anyway.

Valori checked the records for the missing truck, and discovered it carried a GPS unit. She accessed the satellite tracking network for the popular brand and pulled up the last twenty-four hours of activity, comparing the readings with her map of the region. The truck had taken an abrupt exit from the freeway and had traveled west of Denver up into the mountains. She frowned as she traced the path across the map with her fingertip; from that road there were no junctions that led to any cities or towns. Her second window blinked as the map to Frenchman's Pass finished loading, and she glanced at it. The purple line indicating the route she would have to drive to reach Ethan Jemmet was identical to the path of the missing truck.

It's not a coincidence. Evil forces are gathering, Valori, and you will be caught between them.

She needed to retrieve her bracelet and the bodies Teresina had stolen from GenHance. Now she could do both with one trip, and for once smiled her own smile, and answered Tomaseo with her own voice. "Not if I get there first, *mentore*."

*   *   *

The sun's long descent toward the horizon poured golden light through the frosted glass, and roused Lilah from a delicious, dreamless sleep. It had been so long since she had slept in a room with normal windows that at first she didn't understand the glow bathing her and Walker. Then she smiled, snuggling back against her lover and turning her face toward the warmth.

I don't have to be alone anymore, and neither does he. We belong together. As long as we have each other, we're safe.

You can't stay here. Another voice, one from long ago, echoed in her memory. *You can't stay anywhere. If you do, people will discover what you are.*

She answered the voice the same way she had ten years ago. *I'm not a monster.*

How long do you think you can control it? A week? A month? What happens when you lose your temper, or you simply have a bad dream? Does anyone deserve to die like that?

Carefully Lilah shifted out from under Walker's arm, and silently rose from the bed to dress. Ten years ago she had made a promise to the man who had saved her life. She had never broken her word to him, not once. Not until she went up the mountain after Walker. Then she had discarded the most solemn vow of her life without a moment of hesitation.

I'm stronger now. I can control it. I can be with him.

She smelled coffee and followed it out of the room, and found Annie yawning over a steaming mug in the back kitchen. "Can you spare a cup or twelve of that?"

"I was just thinking I'd need a pot or two myself today," the innkeeper confessed as she rose, smothering another yawn. "I never sleep in past dawn, but here it is one o'clock and I'm just now dragging myself out of bed." She brought a clean mug to the table and filled it. "You take cream or sugar?"

"Only when someone doesn't ask me." She took a sip of the strong brew and sighed. "Which makes this perfect. Thanks for letting us sleep in."

"Oh, I wasn't going to bother you folks until sometime tomorrow," Annie said, giving her a wink.

Lilah cringed a little inside, but also realized this was an opportunity to discover just how powerful her new ability was. "I thought I heard you walking around earlier," she said carefully. "It was still pretty dark outside."

The older woman shook her head. "I was out cold from the minute I lay my head on my pillow. The noise was probably the siding creaking. Sometimes the wind makes this place remember how old it is. Don't let it spook you, honey." She frowned as the front door to the inn opened and closed. "Excuse me, Mari."

Annie left the kitchen, only to return a few moments later with Sheriff Jemmet. "Seems Ethan's got nothing better to do than bedevil people today." She turned to the sheriff. "Why don't you sit down and have a cup of coffee like a civilized man before you ride herd on these young folks?"

"Thank you, Annie, but not now." Ethan eyed Lilah. "Ms. Gordon, I need to speak to you and Mr. Kimball over at my office."

"My boyfriend is—" Lilah broke off as she saw Walker appear in the doorway. "Right behind you," she finished.

The sheriff turned around, staring at Walker for a long moment before he repeated his request.

"We just woke up," Walker said softly. "Lilah needs to rest. Perhaps we could stop by your office later."

"I need to settle this now," Ethan told him. "I'll wait while you get your coats."

Walker met Lilah's worried gaze before he said, "Very well. Give us five minutes, Sheriff."

Lilah edged past Ethan and took Walker's hand, trying to keep her pace slow as they walked down the hall toward their room. As soon as they were out of earshot, she glanced over her shoulder. "What do you think he wants?"

"Me, locked in a cell," he said bluntly. "You, naked in his bed."

"Not going to happen." She slipped into the room and took their coats from the closet. "Don't jump to conclusions, Walker. He may just want to question us again."

"He could do that here," Walker said as he helped her into her coat. "He knows something."

"If he tries to lock us up, don't fight him," she warned. "All I have to do is touch him and I can alter his memory."

He gave her an odd look. "Can you change mine?"

"Nope." She moved in, putting her hands inside his coat and hugging his waist. "If I could, I'd definitely make you forget every other woman you've ever known."

He took her hand and brought it to his lips. "You've already done that, my heart."

When they emerged, Lilah saw Ethan standing at the end of the hall and watching the door to their room. As before, his eyes shifted to her first. For his benefit she produced a benign smile and clasped Walker's hand as they walked toward him.

"Annie will bring over some breakfast for you," Ethan said. The scowl on his face suggested he'd gotten an earful from the innkeeper about marching them over to his office before they'd had the chance to eat.

"That's very kind of her," Lilah said.

Outside the inn, the street was still somewhat deserted, although Lilah spotted a few shopkeepers shoveling off their doorways and steps. No one looked directly at them or Ethan Jemmet, but she got the distinct impression everyone watched them as they followed the sheriff into his office.

Something else bothered Lilah, something that had

to do with the people and the stillness, but she couldn't quite decide what it was.

Two chairs were sitting in front of Ethan's desk, and Lilah saw an unlabeled folder on his blotter from which a fax protruded. She also noted his computer monitor, which was switched on and displayed an opening screen for Internet Explorer.

"Have a seat," the sheriff said, not bothering to remove his coat or ask them for theirs as he went around the desk. He didn't sit, but picked up the folder and opened it.

Lilah sat down by Walker, who was watching Ethan with unblinking intensity. She squeezed his hand, shaking her head a little when he glanced at her.

"The weather up here cuts off the pass from the outside world for most of the winter," Ethan said, "but it seems this blizzard shifted earlier than expected, and didn't have time to do its worst. I was able to run some background checks when I came in this morning."

"On us," Walker said.

"Yeah. I like to know who comes into my town." He closed the folder and tossed it onto his desk. "According to the Marine Corps, Sergeant Kimball, you're on active duty. You also went missing in Afghanistan nine weeks ago. Since you're here and not there, that makes you AWOL."

Chapter 18

Ethan waited for Walker to say something, and when he didn't, he turned to Lilah.

"You, Miss Gordon, aren't in near as much trouble as your boyfriend." He put a hand on the desk and leaned over to emphasize his next words. "Seems you up and walked out on your job and your landlord in Huntsville about a year ago. When your landlord reported it to the police, they ran their own background check, and discovered you actually died sixty-seven years ago."

"Obviously there's been a terrible mix-up," Lilah said. "As you can see, I'm alive, and Walker isn't AWOL—he's home on leave."

Before the sheriff could reply, a man came through the door and slammed it behind him.

Ethan's mouth became a thin, white line. "I'm busy here, Nathan."

"Indeed." The man pulled back the fur-lined hood of his jacket, revealing a mirror image of Ethan Jemmet's face, cracked across the left side in four places by thin vertical scars. "This them?"

"I said—"

"Shut up." Nathan strode forward, and Lilah found herself being jerked up and shoved behind Walker.

"*Nathan.*" The sheriff's voice stopped him in his

tracks. "This is my ground. You take yourself back up the mountain. Now."

Nathan ignored him, staring at Lilah in the same strange, riveted fashion that his brother had. He also muttered a single word in a guttural language she didn't recognize.

"You must be the sheriff's brother." She stepped out from behind Walker and held out her hand. "I'm Marianne Gordon, and this is my boyfriend, Walker Kimball."

Nathan shuffled back, jerking his head toward Ethan as if his neck didn't want to cooperate. "If you don't cage her, I will."

"I am the criminal here," Walker said suddenly. "Lock me up, but leave her alone."

Nathan uttered a sharp laugh. "Not likely, soldier."

"This is what's going to happen," Ethan said flatly. "Nate, you're leaving. Kimball, sit down. Miss Gordon, you can go back to the inn for now."

"You stupid bastard," Nathan sneered. "Can't you smell her? She's all over him, and he can't keep his hands off her. He won't let her out of his sight. Put them both in the cage. Then you can jerk off while you watch. Hell, brother, you can sell tickets to every man in town."

The sheriff lowered his head, and a heartbeat later lunged at his brother, knocking him down. The two men were punching each other before they hit the floor.

Walker pushed Lilah toward the door. "Run."

She refused to budge, and saw the door opening again. "We have to stop this."

The woman who entered the station wore a black leather coat and a white crocheted scarf over gleaming golden brown curls. Her lively hair framed an equally pretty, animated face. She halted as soon as she saw the brothers fighting, and put a white-gloved hand to her throat. "Ethan? What on earth are you doing?"

"Squabbling." Walker stepped over the men, grabbing Nathan's parka and using it to pull him off the sheriff. When Ethan tried to throw himself at his brother again, Walker planted his boot against his chest and shoved him back. "Enough of this," he snarled. "Control yourselves. There are women here."

The pretty girl gave Lilah a wry look. "There goes a hundred years of liberation, right out the window." She moved carefully around Walker to stand over the sheriff.

The sheriff wiped the back of his hand across his bleeding mouth, and then looked up and froze. "Lori?"

"Hello, Ethan. Cozy little town you have up here. A bit like Currier and Ives on crack." She offered him a hand up, and as soon as he stood, she glanced over at Nathan, who had propped himself against the wall. "Oh, dear. Either that's your doppelgänger or an evil twin brother."

"A groupie." Nathan wiped the blood that was trickling from his nose. "How cute."

The sheriff put his hands on Lori's shoulders, gripping them as if he expected her to run out. "What are you doing here?"

"I wanted to see you again." She smiled brightly. "So, Ethan, how have you been? Where's my bracelet?"

"How did you get up here?" Ethan countered. "And how the hell did you find me?"

"Well, first I Googled you," she replied easily. "Then I followed a map and a snowplow." She eyed Nathan. "By the way, evil twin brother, I'm not a groupie. I'm a one-night stand."

Nathan pinched the bridge of his swollen nose. "Same thing." He looked up at Lilah, breathed in deeply, and some of the harsh lines around his nose and mouth eased. "I was wrong. It's done. You can't keep them locked up—it won't do any good. Let them stay."

"After all this bullshit, you want me to offer them sanctuary?" Ethan demanded.

"Yeah." Nathan gave Walker a narrow look. "You'll live longer."

The sheriff rubbed a hand over his face. "Kimball, take your girlfriend back to the inn. Get something to eat. We'll talk later." He turned on Lori. "I woke up and you were gone. Why did you run out on me?"

Walker hustled Lilah out through the door, closing it carefully before he looked down either side of the street.

"Why did he let us go?" she asked, still not sure of what had just transpired. Most of what Ethan and Nathan Jemmet had said to each other had gone right over her head.

"He didn't," he told her. "He'll come for us after he deals with the woman and the brother."

"So will GenHance, now that the sheriff has done a background check on you." She huddled in her coat. "They'll be monitoring police communications. The roads are clear, so there's nothing to stop them from getting to us."

"Agreed." He peered in the window of the Land Rover parked at the curb. "The keys are still in the ignition." He tried the passenger door, which opened. "Get in."

"So, this is Frenchman's Pass," Nick said as she climbed out of the truck. "He must have been pretty damn skinny. I've seen bigger turnstiles."

Gabriel spent more time examining the dark, empty street, moonlight gilding the stark beauty of his features as he took in every detail.

"This place is old." He glanced up at the peaks around the town. "Much older than it looks."

"Well, it looks like a set from *Bonanza*. No lights

in the windows. Doesn't look like anyone's up watching Letterman." Nick felt someone approaching and turned casually to face the man walking up behind them. "Hello." Her gaze dropped to the badge on his breast pocket. "Sheriff."

"You folks lost?"

"No, but we're trying to find some people who might be." As Gabriel came to stand beside her, Nick noted the way the sheriff's stance changed, his knees and elbows loosening, his hands coming out of his pockets to poise ready by his sides. *Expecting a fight, are you?* "A man and a woman. They were abducted in Florida by a couple of thugs in an unmarked truck." She gave him general descriptions, keeping her tone friendly and light, but he didn't relax. If anything, his tension ratcheted up several notches.

That made his bland response even more of a surprise. "Sorry, but they're not here. We haven't had any strangers in town since the storm hit. You might try asking around in Chamberlain."

"Chamberlain is thirty miles away," Gabriel said.

Nick hid a grin as her lover deliberately shed his scent, and a warm waft of evergreen enveloped them.

Again the sheriff astonished her, this time by showing one of the most powerful pheromones on the planet didn't faze him in the slightest. "Right by the entrance to the interstate," he told Gabriel. "Head due west and you can't miss it." He nodded to Nick and strode past them, disappearing into one of the quaint old buildings.

"So much for the warmth and friendliness of small-town America." Nick glanced sideways. "Either we're losing our mojo, or *l'attrait* doesn't work this high above sea level. He didn't even stutter."

"Cold dampens the senses, and some humans are capable of resisting us," he reminded her.

"Well, I think that human doesn't like us too much."

She closed her eyes and breathed in. "The rogue was here. So was someone, maybe the woman. Do you smell that?"

He nodded. "It's Lilah Devereaux, but something has altered her scent."

Nick ran through the short mental list of what she knew could change the scent of a human being. "Oh, shit," she muttered as she realized what it was. "He didn't. That son of a bitch." She stalked across the street.

Her lover caught up to her. "Nicola, wait. It may not have been voluntary."

"Right. She was asking for it." She stopped in front of a bed-and-breakfast, where her sense of the rogue abruptly changed directions. "They were here, too, but . . . " What her talent was telling her confused her. "He took her up on the mountain." There was only one reason a Darkyn wanted alone time with a human. "If I find this girl enraptured or dead up there, I'm ripping off the bastard's head and stuffing it down his throat. Just FYI." She stalked around the inn.

Gabriel followed her and examined the ground all around the back of the inn. "He left a trail, there. Nicola, you can't confront him directly. He'll attack you."

"Here's hoping." She drew out her dagger as she followed the trenches up to the tree line. She saw one faint trail, and a duplicate with fresher tracks. "He wasn't the only one hiking up here." She crouched beside the tracks and glanced up at him. "What made these? Hunting dogs?"

He ran his fingertips over the rounded, flowery marks in the snow, and then peered ahead. "I don't know."

Nick's jaw dropped. "I beg your pardon?"

"I've never seen anything like this."

"Baby, you've been a tracker for seven hundred years. You know things about hunting that even God's forgotten. And you're telling me you *don't know* what made these tracks?"

"I know it was an animal. A large one. Four-legged." He followed the tracks a little farther into the forest and stopped. "Wait." He turned around. "There should be blood."

"And *why* should there be blood?"

"The tracks end here, where the human's begin. A hunter intercepted the creature, perhaps." He pointed to a distinct pattern of footprints, frowning again. "No boots."

Nick saw the shape of the toes and heel, too. "What kind of hunter tramps around in the snow barefoot?"

"One who cannot be harmed by it." He straightened and looked up the slope. "He went up there."

Nick's hands itched for her baseball bat, her weapon of choice in any conflict, but instead drew the copper dagger she carried on her belt. "Let's go change his smell again."

Ever protective, Gabriel insisted on going ahead of her, but for once Nick didn't mind. The stillness of the forest and the strange vibe she was getting from the mountain grew stronger with every step she took. By the time they reached a cabin buried in brush, her skin crawled with nerves.

"Gabriel." She couldn't stop him from entering the cabin, and swore as she shoved her way through the branches to go after him.

Inside she found her lover standing in front of a fireplace and staring at an old bench. Other than some furnishings that looked like they belonged in a museum, the rest of the cabin was empty.

"They are not here," he said absently.

"Oh, you think?" She sheathed her dagger. "I hope *you're* not feeling suicidal again. 'Cause I'll go and get the baseball bat out of the truck."

"I am well." He sat down in the middle of the bench, pressing his hands to the rough surface on either side of him. "She wept. I can still taste her tears in the air." He breathed in. "He did not. He was filled with rage, regret. And . . . " He got up slowly, his expression filled with disbelief as he stared at Nick. "Love. Nicola, he loves this woman."

"That is highly unlikely, Lord Seran."

Nick's dagger was in her hand before she saw the human female leaning against the cabin door and bending over to remove snowshoes. "Who invited you to the party?"

"The *tresoran* council, my lady." The woman bobbed at her and then Gabriel. "I am Valori Trovatella, at your service. Forgive me for not introducing myself in town, but I thought I should deal with the sheriff first."

"And how did you do that?" Nick asked.

"Discreetly. Sheriff Jemmet will wake in a few hours with a mild headache. If I may?" When Gabriel inclined his head, she stepped forward, holding out her hand.

He took it and examined the charm bracelet she wore. "You're an infiltrator."

"You can tell that from her jewelry?" Nick asked.

"It is how they identify their operatives, like the black cameos our *tresori* wear." Gabriel released her hand. "Miss Trovatella's bracelet indicates that she is a very experienced field operative."

That didn't make much sense to Nick. "The Vampire King know about this?"

Valori looked puzzled. "My lady?"

"She means the high lord," Gabriel said. To Nick, he said, "The *tresoran* council would have notified Richard when they sent Ms. Trovatella to America. In matters such as these, he prefers to have alternative measures in place."

"So you're Plan B." Nick studied the other woman. "I

don't want to insult you, second string, but how, exactly, does a cute little spy take out a rogue?"

"I was first trained as a dispatcher, my lady. Since I am very familiar with America, I was happy to volunteer my services." Her tone turned brisk. "The rogue has assumed the identity of a human soldier. Before I could deal with him, he and the female stole my vehicle and stranded me here. They are presently en route to Denver."

Swearing wouldn't bring them back, but Nick muttered a few choice words anyway.

"Why Denver?" Gabriel asked.

"The sheriff has been conducting a discreet investigation. It seems the woman stole a mobile phone from the local doctor. According to the records from the service provider, which the sheriff obtained this morning, she used it to contact a wealthy antique dealer. He could be anything to her. A friend, a lover, or an accomplice." She shrugged. "We won't know until we catch up with them."

Nick's brows rose. "What's this 'we'?"

"*We* are here for the same reason," the other woman reminded her. "Your chances of successfully locating and eliminating the rogue are better if you allow me to accompany you and Lord Gabriel."

The subtle change in the female's scent told Nick that she wasn't being entirely truthful. "What's in it for you? And don't bother lying—we can tell."

"The GenHance employee who arranged the transport of the rogue to the States and the abduction of Lilah Devereaux is a *tresora* named Teresina Segreta," Valori said. "She is now trying to recover them, and if she reaches them first, she will kill them both, and quite possibly expose the existence of the Darkyn to the human world."

"A *tresora* who works for a biotech company, who

would betray us?" Gabriel sounded as dubious as Nick felt.

"A former *tresora*, my lord. She was cast out many years ago for betraying her line, and now it seems she is set on taking revenge for that." For the first time Valori's mask slipped and Nick saw a glimmer of real grief. "Her brother was my mentor, and through him I knew her very well. I believe I can stop her before it is too late. I would appreciate the chance to at least try."

"We could use some backup," Nick said to Gabriel. "Especially if things go down during the day."

"Very well, Miss Trovatella. You may join the hunt with us." When she would have thanked him, he held up one hand. "We cannot permit this outcast *tresora* to endanger the Darkyn."

"Once the rogue has been dispatched, I will take her back to Italy and turn her over to the council myself," Valori promised. When she saw Nick's face, she frowned. "My lady?"

"I didn't get the whole dispatcher-dispatching thing, but now I do. You're not a spy—you're an assassin." She glanced at Gabriel. "Any reason no one has ever mentioned to me that the *tresoran* council trains humans to kill Darkyn?"

"We do not dispatch those Darkyn who are loyal to the high lord, my lady," Valori said quickly. "We are sent after only those who have chosen to betray or turn their backs on their lords."

"It is considered a kindness, Nicola," Gabriel said quietly. "Such rogues recognize and attack other Kyn. Often a dispatcher can get close without alarming their target."

"We are trained to assure those we dispatch do not suffer, my lady," Valori added.

"Why don't you just call it what it is? Execution." She realized she was practically defending the rogue. "In case I haven't mentioned it in the last fifteen minutes, I hate being a vampire."

"But, my lady, you are not ... " Valori trailed off as she saw Gabriel shake his head.

"It's okay, sweetie. Whatever you want to call the fangs, I didn't ask for them." She thought for a minute. "There's a civilian mixed up in this, and she probably thinks she's in love with the demented bastard. So when we find them, Valori, your job is to get her out of the way, sit on her, and keep her alive while Gabriel and I finish the job. Are we clear?"

"I will see to it that she is not harmed, my lady."

"Good. That's all I care about." Nick headed for the door. "Come on, let's get out of here."

Nathan moved away from the cabin's back window, and gave a hand signal to the other men surrounding it. They moved as one, dispersing into the shadows as soundlessly as they'd emerged from them.

He'd nearly jumped the smiling little slut in town after he caught her coming out of the sheriff's office with Ethan's blood on her. But the mild ache in his head that had jolted him out of bed told him she hadn't killed his brother, but had simply knocked him unconscious.

She was a resourceful and determined bitch, judging by the ease with which she'd helped herself to a pair of snowshoes on Annie's porch, and the quick pace she'd used to follow the two new arrivals up the mountain. Their scent infuriated him almost as much as Valori's, calling for the Fury, but years of painful lessons had taught him to wait before unleashing the mountain's wrath on anyone.

Now after listening in on the conversation between Valori and the two strangers, he was glad he'd held back. They were leaving the pass, and that was better than killing them in it. As much as he still ached for the promise of the woman, it was not to be. In a way he was glad. He'd never admit it to Ethan, but his brother was right: The best way to handle trouble was to run it out of town.

Nathan waited until they were out of sight, and then climbed higher up the slope, past the trees, and into the deep snows surrounding the caves. Smoke rose from one of the vent holes, telling him they were waiting for him.

He entered the main cave, glad that for once he had some good news to deliver.

Chapter 19

The Land Rover they'd stolen must have belonged to Ethan's girlfriend, Lori, Lilah decided as she looked around the tidy vehicle. She could smell the other woman's perfume, a light, sweet floral that seemed to be coming from the glove compartment. She opened it, retrieving a small spray bottle of fragrance and a zipped black vinyl case. When she opened the case, she found a folded bundle of twenties, four passports, and a long, thin knife with a sharp, dark-colored blade.

Walker glanced over, scowling as soon as he saw the dagger in Lilah's hand. "She's an assassin."

"Or she's a woman traveling alone who doesn't like guns." Lilah slipped the dagger back into the case and examined each of the passports. "Lori Baker. Laura Parker. Valerie Teller. Larry Barker?" She chuckled. "I can't believe it. She dresses up and poses as a man, too."

"The best killers can be anyone." He picked up one of the passports, flipped it open, and then handed it back to her. "Are the rest stamped by Italian customs?"

"Italian, French, British, Swedish . . . " She reeled off a few more nations. "This girl really gets around." She put the passports back in the case and counted the twenties. "Whew. She also carries a thousand dollars in cash."

"There will be more hidden away."

Lilah replaced everything in the glove compartment and sat back. "Did you know that woman?"

"No, but I know who sent her." He slowed as they joined a long line of cars at a ramp, waiting to merge onto the highway. "This wealthy friend of yours that you called—Samuel—do you trust him?"

At this point Samuel was the only person besides Walker whom she trusted. "Completely."

"We will need his help," he said, as if he hated admitting it. "New identities, transport out of the state, and a place where we can stay for several weeks without attracting notice."

"I'm sure he can take care of it." She studied his face. "But before we contact him, we should stop for the night, get something to eat and a room somewhere."

He smiled a little. "Yes. I would like that."

So would she, his tone implied. But now that they weren't in danger of being dissected, locked up, or torn to pieces by werewolves, there were other matters they had to settle. "We should also talk about a few things, like what we're going to tell people about you."

"Such as?"

This was going to be harder than she thought. "Your name, for one thing. It's too dangerous for you to keep using Walker Kimball. And we also have to stop telling people that you're from Denver."

He looked at her, frowning. "Why?"

"Because you're not from Denver. I'm guessing that you're not even American." She hesitated before she added, "And you're not Walker Kimball."

He didn't say anything, but a muscle along his jaw ticked.

"It's okay." She put her hand on his arm. "I've known for a while now."

"When did you realize?"

"I knew when you told me what you saw in the parking lot of that truck stop," she admitted. "I didn't think about what you said at the time, but it kept bothering me, and then later I figured out why. Someone from Denver would have instantly recognized Colorado license plates."

He nodded. "Why didn't you ask me before now?"

"A lot has happened since we jumped off that truck." She tried to gauge his mood, but all she could feel was despair. He didn't want her to know who he was, and yet she also felt sure that was the key to everything about him. "How did you end up with Walker Kimball's dog tags?"

"We met in Afghanistan. Kimball and his men were ambushed, and I went in to bring them out. Everyone got out alive but us." The muscles of his arm bulged under her fingers as he tightened his grip on the wheel. "Grenades were falling all around us. The chain around Kimball's neck became snagged on a tree branch and snapped, but I caught it before it could fall to the ground. I remember holding his tags in my fist, and trying to shield him from the explosions. They must have found them on me when they recovered my body."

"Is Walker Kimball dead?"

"I don't know," he admitted. "After the final explosion, I remember nothing until I woke up in the truck."

"So what country were you fighting for?"

"I have no country." His tone hardened. "No home, no family, no friends. I went to war as a mercenary, intent only on joining the battle where and when I could. No." He sighed. "I went to Afghanistan to die, Lilah."

The harsh words made her heart constrict. "But you rescued those soldiers, and you tried to save Walker Kimball. People who want to kill themselves are selfish; they only think of themselves and the pain they feel. You risked your life to keep those men alive."

His mouth hitched. "Most of those men were little

more than inexperienced boys." He glanced at her. "You're not angry with me."

"You're not the only one with a secret." She wanted to tell him—if they were going to be together, she had to—but the words just weren't there. It wasn't something she wanted to tell him while they were in a car; she'd wait until they were someplace safe, with four sturdy walls around them. "My name isn't Lilah Devereaux. It's Lillian Emerson."

"Lillian." He said it slowly, drawing out the syllables. "It is a lovely name, but I think prefer Lilah."

"Me, too. Lillian seemed so old-fashioned and dreary to me when I was a girl. Everyone but my mother called me Elle." She thought of Evelyn, and what a disappointment she'd been to her, and what a relief it had been to shed Lillian Emerson. Maybe her lover felt the same. "I'm not trying to push you into telling me your real name, by the way."

"I want to tell you everything," he said slowly. "But some knowledge is dangerous, especially if we are captured again. For now, it is better that you not know who I was."

"Not a problem," she assured him. "Samuel and my Takyn friends know me as Delilah, and I'll probably use that until we're out of here. We just need a new name for you."

"Yes." He thought for a moment. "I know." He smiled. "Samson."

Lilah laughed. "Oh, that's terrible." The phone in her pocket rang, and she was still chuckling as she took it out. "Uh-oh. Please don't be a lady in labor looking for Dr. Jemmet." She flipped it open and read the screen. "It's Samuel."

When she answered the call, a man with a deep, smooth voice said, "Del? Are you all right? Where are you?"

"We're fine. We, ah, borrowed a car and we should be in Denver in a couple of hours."

"I was so worried when I received your text," Samuel said. "You said 'we.' Who is with you?"

"A new friend." She really did have to come up with a new name for her love, and fast. "We were both kidnapped by GenHance, but he and I were able to escape together. In fact, I wouldn't be talking to you if it weren't for him."

"Then I'll be very glad to meet him and shake his hand," Samuel said. "Now, what can I do to help?" •

"We were just talking about that. We should really leave Colorado before GenHance or the law catches up with us." She gave him a brief explanation of what had happened without going into the stranger details about Frenchman's Pass or the werewolves who had helped free them from their kidnappers. "I don't know if we have enough money for plane tickets," she added. "Could you wire us some funds?"

"I arrived in Denver last night," he said, startling her. "I can pick you up myself."

Lilah felt uneasy. The only information she had sent to Samuel in the text was the number to Dr. Jemmet's phone. "How did you know we were here?"

"I had my people trace the text message back to the cell tower from where it originated." He sighed. "I know, Del, it's against the rules for us to track each other, but frankly all I could think about was getting to you before GenHance did."

She felt instantly ashamed of her suspicions. "I won't tell anyone if you don't. We need to get cleaned up and rest, so we're going to stop and get a room. Why don't we meet sometime tomorrow?"

"Of course. There is a park in the southwest part of the city." He gave her the address, and then said, "The botanical gardens have some of Henry Moore's sculptures on exhibit; you can pick up a guide at the entrance on York Street. I will meet you and your friend by the reclining mother and child at three."

"We'll see you there tomorrow, then. Thank you so much, Samuel." She switched off the phone, closing it and running her thumb idly over the hinges. "I was wrong when I said that I have no friends. I have some great friends." She glanced over at the man beside her. "But don't worry, that's all he'll ever be."

"I am not worried." He picked up her hand and held it. "Now choose a name for me so that you can introduce us."

"Right." She studied him. "It's a shame we can't use Walker; it suits you. You're not a Tom or a Joe or a George. My grandfather's name was Robert."

He shook his head. "Not Robert."

"You're right, that doesn't fit. We need a Takyn nickname for you, the kind we use online. You'd be something like Hunter, or Hawkeye, or . . . " She recalled the dream she'd had, the night she'd been taken. "I know. Guide."

He gave her a strange look.

"Come on," she chided. "It's not that bad. Certainly not as tacky as Samson." Her stomach rumbled, and she pressed a hand against it. "All right. Until you can think up something better, we'll keep using Walker. Now, please find a place we can stop and eat, because if I don't eat something soon, I'm going to start nibbling on you."

He took the next exit and, after consulting with her on her preferences, parked outside a country diner. Lilah happily ordered an enormous breakfast and a pot of coffee, and vetoed Walker's ridiculous request for a glass of water.

"You have to eat something," she scolded him after telling the waitress to bring a duplicate of her order for him. "You didn't touch that food Annie brought for us. In fact, you haven't eaten a thing since you woke up."

He glanced at an older couple dining at the next table, and looked away. "I am not hungry."

"That's from not eating. You're so hungry it's killed your appetite." She reached across the table for his hand. "Just go slow. Like you're pregnant."

"I have been many things," he told her, "but never that."

"I mean, eat like a pregnant lady." When his expression didn't change, she peered at him. "You've never been around a pregnant woman?"

He shrugged. "Not since I was a boy."

"Okay, here's the crash course: Start with dry toast. Take small bites, chew it up well, and don't drink until you know it's doing to stay down." She thought of poor Sadie, whose last pregnancy had upset her stomach so often she had practically lived on crackers and water. "Also, if you feel sick, stop eating and take deep, slow breaths until the feeling passes."

Their meals arrived a few minutes later, and Lilah couldn't help attacking the food. Breakfast was her favorite meal, and the diner's cook had scrambled her eggs exactly the way she liked them.

She glanced over and saw Walker had taken her advice, and was testing a triangle of toast. At first he chewed as if his mouth were full of cardboard, and then swallowed with effort. He put down the toast and waited, his brow furrowed.

"Do you want some butter or jelly?" she asked gently. "That might make it taste better."

"No." He picked up the toast and tried another bite, and suddenly wolfed down the entire piece. His eyes shifted after he swallowed, and then he looked up, his expression filled with wonder. "This is good."

"These little country places usually are." She didn't know why he was staring at his plate, as if he hadn't seen food in years. . . . Of course, the last time he'd eaten had been in Afghanistan. "I guess you didn't have anything like this over there, huh?"

"It has been a long time." He picked up his fork and cautiously sampled everything on his plate. "What is this?" he asked her, pointing with his fork.

"Hash browns."

He grinned at her. "I like hash browns."

Walker went to work then, and ate so fast Lilah was convinced he'd be sick. He only cleared his plate, downing three cups of coffee in between bites, before gesturing for the waitress.

"I would like another," he told her.

She took the pencil stub from behind her ear and held it over her check pad. "Another what, hon?"

"Another breakfast." He gestured to his empty plate. "The same as the first. Please."

"Coming right up." The waitress removed his plate, ogled his chest briefly, sighed, and went back to the kitchen.

Lilah couldn't believe it. "Just how long has it been since you had something to eat?"

"Seven . . . days," he said, filling her coffee cup before pouring the last of the pot into his own. He noticed she had almost finished, and frowned. "I should have asked. Do you want another breakfast?"

She laughed. "No, I think one's enough."

Lilah's breath fogged the Land Rover's window as she watched Walker disappear into the motel's tiny office. Above it, a cracked neon sign blinked: MOTHER ODE MOT L VACA CIES. Only two other cars occupied the guest parking lot, and none of the windows in the blocks of rooms on either side of the office were lit from within. Hopefully the shower was hot, the bed didn't sag too much, and the door had a good dead bolt on it.

Walker came back a few minutes later and climbed in to start the engine. "We have a room at the back of the building, but we should leave before dawn."

"I was hoping we'd sleep in till at least noon," she teased.

He smiled a little. "When we reach safety, I plan to keep you in bed for several weeks."

Walker drove around the back, parking in reverse so that the rear of the Land Rover faced the building.

"The woman may have reported her car stolen," he explained. "This way, a patrol car cannot see the license plate."

Lilah still felt guilty for stealing Lori's car and using her money stash for the motel room, but they'd had no choice, and she felt sure Ethan Jemmet would look after her. "We'll park it somewhere they can find it easily when we go to meet Samuel tomorrow."

Walker looked around carefully before leading her into the room. A single full-size bed covered with a burnt orange chenille spread occupied most of the small space, which smelled of lemon-scented disinfectant and carpet cleaner. The dark blue commercial carpet had been recently cleaned, and still looked damp in the corners. Under the front windows, the room's heating unit rattled faintly as it tried and failed to heat the cold air they'd let in. The bathroom proved to be little more than a sad, closet-size study in distressed tile and cracked porcelain.

Still, Lilah thought, it was better than trying to sleep in the car.

"I wish I had some clean clothes," she said as she sat down on the edge of the bed and turned on the television. "Do you want to use the shower first?"

"Wait." Walker went out and brought back a suitcase,

placing it on the bed beside her. "This was in the back-seat." He popped the locks and opened it.

Lilah reached for a neatly folded swatch of black lace lying on the top of the clothes inside, which turned out to be a scanty lace and silk camisole. "I like her taste in underwear."

Walker plucked a matching thong from a side pocket. "So do I."

"Sure, because you don't have to wear it. Men never realize how uncomfortable this stuff is." She took the thong from him and stretched it out. "Yes, I might be able to fit this around my big toe." She tossed it aside and searched through the rest of the clothes. "Look at this stuff. She dresses like a preppy princess on the out-side and a Playboy Bunny underneath." She shook out a bra made of satin straps with flower-shaped openings in the center of each cup, and found a matching pair of crotchless panties. "Or maybe a working girl."

"Perhaps that is how she knows the sheriff. He ar-rested her." Walker took the racy lingerie from her and set it aside. "You do not need this. I would rather sleep with you naked."

She lifted her brows. "Oh, really? Are you going to keep me warm?" She laughed as he pounced on her, pinning her on her back. "Okay, I see you are."

He brushed the hair back from her face, and his ex-pression sobered. "I would do anything for you. I would die for you."

Chapter 20

Abruptly he rolled away and flung an arm over his face. "I should not have said that."

He was still struggling with how he felt, and fighting some inner demon she didn't understand. She had to let him know that she wasn't afraid of that or him.

She turned on her side and propped her head on her hand. "You know, my mother never married. She was attractive and intelligent and very wealthy, and could have had almost anyone she wanted. But she didn't believe in love; she said it was a fairy tale men told women so they could get in bed with them."

He made a low sound. "Sometimes it is."

"She made me go to an all-girls school and she wouldn't let me date or go to parties or do anything where I might meet some boys." The old resentment, which had burned in her for years, seemed tired and rather pathetic now. "When I got my period, she sent one of the servants to explain what was happening to me because she thought it was vulgar and disgusting. I thought she was cold because of the way she was brought up, or maybe from having her heart broken, but now I know it was because she never really loved anyone. Not her parents, not me, not even herself."

He dropped his arm and turned his head to look at her. "Perhaps she was too afraid."

"I don't know. She never told me." Lilah plucked at the burnt orange fuzz of the bedspread. "We never talked very much at all. She made me feel as if I were her possession. Sometimes I thought she took me in only because I made her look good, like a new purse, or a pretty pair of shoes. But now I think I know the real reason she adopted me. She refused to love me or anyone else, but she didn't want to die alone. And in the end, that's exactly what happened to her."

He reached out to touch her face. "It is not your fault, Lilah."

"I know that, but it still hurts. It always will, because no matter how she felt about me, I loved her." She rubbed her cheek against his palm. "It's not a fairy tale, Walker. It doesn't always end in happily ever after. Sometimes we love people who can't love us back. It doesn't make it wrong. Neither does being afraid of getting hurt." She put her hand on his chest, and drew a spiral with her finger over his heart. "The only tragedy is when we shut down our hearts for good. If my mother taught me anything, it's that a life devoid of love is simply not worth living."

He sat up, turning his back to her. "Do you believe that I am like your mother?"

"No," she said simply. "But you do."

His broad shoulders rounded as he buried his face in his hands. Lilah sat up, but before she could touch him, he stood and strode out of the room.

It tore at her not to go after him, but she knew it was wiser to wait. She couldn't force him to tell her what she wanted to hear. Loving her had to be his choice.

She went into the bathroom, stripped, and took a long shower. Lori's toiletries were as pleasantly scented as her perfume, and Lilah felt much better once she was clean.

After she towel-dried her hair, she put on the one

nightgown that fit her from the suitcase, a peach satin gown that barely contained her breasts but fell around her legs in soft, swaying folds. She came out to see the room was still empty, which hurt, but she went around and shut off all the lights, leaving the television on. Once she got into bed, she huddled under the chenille coverlet until her body warmed the cold sheets.

He'll come back when he's ready, she told her aching heart, closing her eyes and hoping she hadn't just made the biggest mistake of her life.

Lilah drifted in and out of sleep, unable to stop listening for him. Then the door to the room opened, and she felt a shadow looming over her.

She didn't open her eyes, and he retreated into the bathroom. She heard the shower turn on, the sounds of him washing, and then the water shutting off. Imagining him naked was not helping; her body tingled all over in anticipation.

He came out a short time later, and climbed into bed, his body warm and slightly damp against hers.

"You are not naked," he murmured as he pulled her back against him.

She turned around to snuggle against him, so relieved she could have wept. "You weren't here to keep me warm."

"I was not always as I am now." The words came out of him as if he had to drag each one. "My mother was like yours, a cold woman who refused to open her heart. She married my father only for his wealth. Growing up in such a house, I suppose I was destined to be the same, but then I did fall in love. I fell in love at first sight. It was as complete and hopeless as the poets say, except that I was my mother's son, and I was determined to have her. So I pursued her, and I schemed and manipulated and used my father's wealth and position, and in the end, I married her."

Lilah heard the pain in his voice. "Walker, you don't have to tell me this."

"I want you to know." He kissed the top of her head. "Our marriage was a disaster. She didn't love me or want me, and left me as soon as she could. I never saw her again. After that, love was a curse. I couldn't be with another woman and not think of her. At least, until I found you."

When Lilah felt his mouth against her hair, she lifted her face and stole a kiss. He took it back, slowly and with great care, his hand against her face, his fingers tracing over her features, as if he'd never touched a woman before her.

"I don't know what this is between us," he said, "but I have never known anyone or anything like you in my life."

Lilah understood. They were in unmapped territory now, both of them.

The satin of the nightgown grew damp between the press of their bodies, and clung to her skin when he gathered his hand in it and tugged it up over her hips. Lilah couldn't keep her hands away from his body; she wanted to stroke every inch of him and then start all over again. He was so big and hard and there, right there, hers to tease and caress and taste. His mouth scored over hers as he mirrored her movements, following where she led, lifting her to sweep away the satin and bring her swollen breasts to his face, his hand cupping her, his tongue stroking over the ache.

She curled her leg over his thigh, opening herself to the probe of his straining penis. He pressed up, gliding into her with one smooth stroke, his hand at the back of her head, his mouth catching her gasps.

Dimly Lilah remembered the first time she had held him in her arms, when he had been a stranger in a nightmare, when he had fought so hard not to hurt her. That had been the moment she had fallen in love with him, she realized, and every time they came together like this, she was going to remember it.

Her arms trembled as she linked them around his neck, and rode the long, deep strokes he was giving her. It was such a simple thing, the push and pull of his shaft, the clasp and release of her sheath, and the delicious heat they created for each other, in each other. Time had no meaning, and the world was gone. She thought it could be forever, and then it was, her body shaking, her muscles tightening as she shattered, coming all over him, taking him with her as he groaned and stiffened. As he filled her with the thick gush of his seed, she bathed him in her own liquid heat.

He held her close, their bodies still enmeshed, his arms cradling her as if she were the most precious thing in the world. She wanted to tell him that he didn't have to die for her, that he had to live, but she was already slipping away into a dream.

"Sleep," she heard him whisper, and she did.

He woke with the dawn, and for the first time didn't feel the disorienting oddness of sleeping through the night. Lilah lay draped atop him, limp as only a thoroughly satisfied woman could be, and he spent a few moments enjoying that new sensation as well. Their room was woefully inadequate, a shabby and anonymous box, and yet he felt as if he occupied a corner of heaven.

"Mmm," he heard her murmur, and watched her beautiful eyes blink open. She rested her chin against his sternum. "Hello. You make a great box spring."

"While you are a very fine coverlet." He shifted her up so he could kiss her pretty mouth. "Are you hungry?"

"Yes. But I can't decide if I want breakfast, or you." She pretended to think. "Can I have both?"

"If I can play coverlet, yes." He rolled with her, bracing himself over her as he pushed between her thighs and sank deep. Feeling how soft and wet she was for him made his thoughts dwindle and turned his body into a pistoning engine, and he fucked her thoroughly and steadily, bringing her to a wrenching, gushing climax.

Another, less enjoyable pounding intruded on his pleasure, and he brought up his head as he heard a muffled voice from behind the wall, against which the bed had been rhythmically moving along with him.

"Come on, man," the disgruntled voice yelled. "It's six a.m. Give it a rest."

"Uh-oh. We're bothering the neighbors." Lilah giggled like a girl. "He must not be a morning person."

"He can get another room," he said as he rolled over onto his back with her. He frowned as she lifted herself from him. "I am not finished with you."

"That's my line." She trailed a line of kisses down his body, settling between his legs.

He bit back a groan as he felt her breath against the slick dome of his cock, and then the sweet enclosure of her lips.

Lilah suckled him slowly, laving him with languid absorption, taking him in with torturous care. His hand found her head, and tangled in her hair as he fought the urge to push deeper, and then he pulled her back.

She lifted her mouth from him, painting him with her breath. Her hair lay disheveled around her face; her sleepy eyes gleamed as sensuously as her lips. "Let me do this."

"I want my mouth on you while you suck me." He sat up, taking her by the waist and moving her body so that she was on her side. He pushed her thighs apart and put his mouth to her mound, parting her folds with his tongue and groaning as he felt her lips slide over his straining cockhead. He tasted her sweetness mingled with his own salt, and worked his tongue into her, stroking the fluttering tightness until he felt her belly tighten and her thighs tense. The soft sounds she made hummed along his shaft, and he drew his tongue back and forth over the little bulge of her clit, his cock swelling in her mouth as she sucked him deeper.

He couldn't stop the jet of his seed, but it brought her with him as she came apart under his mouth, her hips rolling as his jerked, her fingernails scoring his hips as his hands clamped around her soft bottom.

Lilah was still shaking as he lifted her and gathered her close. "That was. I never. You just." She buried her face against his neck. "God."

He closed his eyes.

Lilah had never spent an entire day in bed, but after eight hours of making love and sleeping and eating takeout with Walker, she decided she had been seriously deprived. They couldn't get enough of each other, and if they hadn't agreed to meet Samuel, she suspected they would have stayed in the room until they ran through all of Lori's money.

"I'm becoming a sex addict," she said after they went to take a shower together and ended up having to take a second one. "You're turning me into a nymphomaniac, you bad man."

"You asked me to help you wash," he reminded her, looking annoyingly satisfied. "You did not say with what."

"All right, I guess I like how you wash me." When he reached for her towel, she darted away. "Oh, no. Don't start again. I won't be able to walk. You'll have to carry me to meet Samuel."

"Come here, my heart." Helpless to resist, she went to him, and he bent and kissed the top of her head. "I will not touch you again."

"Wait a minute," she said. "I have to take some of that back."

He pressed a finger against her lips. "Not until we are alone again."

She considered that. "Maybe this meeting won't take that long."

They left the motel and stopped at the diner, where Lilah watched Walker wolf down three more breakfasts. She was so hungry she ordered an extra meal of her own.

"If we keep having these mutual eating marathons, I'm going to end up weighing five hundred pounds," she complained as they left a generous tip for the incredulous waitress. "Then you'll be sorry." She glanced down at her curves. "If you're not already."

"Your body is perfect for me," he assured her. "I do not like skinny women."

She *hmph*ed. "Everyone likes skinny women."

"They are bony and weak, and tire easily." He picked her up, holding her dangling above the ground as he brought her mouth to his. "You are luscious and strong." His eyes darkened. "And delightfully insatiable."

She put her arms around his neck. "I could call Samuel. Put this off until tomorrow."

"There is nothing I would like better." He placed her back on her feet. "But every hour we linger puts us both at risk. I will not let them take you again."

"The same goes for you." When he glanced away, she grabbed the front of his jacket. "I mean it, Walker. There is no more you or me. There's only us."

He pulled her close. "I don't think I could let you go anyway."

Under the frosty blue sky, they drove from the diner south toward the park Samuel had specified.

"According the map, it's just around the corner." Lilah looked through the windshield and spotted a sign by the entrance to an empty parking lot. "There," she said, pointing. "Denver Botanic Gardens. This is it."

Walker drove past the lot and parked the Land Rover at the next curb. He got out and came around to her door before she could do the same. "If anything seems amiss, I want you to give me a signal."

"You can trust Samuel." She tucked her hair out of sight under her cap, saw his face, and sighed. "Okay. If I think something's going wrong, I'll say, 'I'm a big fan of the Broncos.'"

He frowned. "How is that a signal?"

"Because I'm not," she reminded him.

They paid the ticket booth attendant and were reminded to stay on the garden paths.

"Do you have a brochure for the Henry Moore exhibit?" Lilah asked, and thanked him when he handed one over. She looked through it, checking the map on the back, and then pointed past the gift shop. "It's down that way."

Except for some employees emptying waste cans and sweeping the walks, the park was deserted. He put his hands in his pocket, the right hand bulging. Lilah knew he was gripping the hilt of the dagger he had taken from Lori's cache, but she kept quiet. He had been through war and God knew what else; of course he wouldn't like walking unarmed into the unknown.

He just doesn't know how well armed he is with me. Lilah spotted the flowing bronze sculpture of the reclining mother and child, and two men standing a short distance away from it. One wore a standard chauffeur's uniform, and looked ordinary, but the blond, bearded man towering over him could only be called a hulking giant.

"There they are. Samuel." She lifted a hand, and smiled as the big man returned the gesture with one black glove. She glanced at Walker. "Looks like we're home free."

He slowed his pace, scanning the area around the men before he said, "So it seems."

Lilah was startled to see that Samuel dragged one of his legs, and had to use a cane to make his way toward them. His driver also walked with a hand under Samuel's arm, providing additional support.

"Delilah." Samuel's exotic black eyes took in her face as his silky blond beard framed a pirate's grin. "I'm very happy to see you."

"Hello, Samuel." Facing the man she'd spent so many hours chatting with online made her feel a little shy, and she shifted closer to Walker. "Thanks for rescuing us."

"My pleasure." The smile dimmed a notch as he turned and held out his gloved hand. "I'm Samuel Taske."

As soon as Walker took his hand, Samuel's driver released his arm and grabbed Lilah. She fought but couldn't break free of his hold, and then went still as she saw Samuel pressing a gun under Walker's chin. "Samuel, what are you doing?"

"I'm saving your life, sweetheart. Don't even think about it," he said to Walker. "The gun is loaded with copper rounds. Ten of them." He changed the angle of the gun. "But from what I've been told, one through the spinal cord should be enough."

"No, Samuel, no." She lunged again, but the driver laced his arms through the backs of hers. "Listen to me. Don't shoot him. He's one of us."

"He's been lying to you, sweetheart. The real Walker Kimball is here in Denver, but he's in an intensive care unit recovering from serious injuries sustained in the Middle East." Samuel tilted his head. "I thought this impostor was merely a thug for hire who stole his identity to get to you. But you're much more than that, aren't you, vampire?"

Lilah wanted to scream. "For God's sake, Samuel, have you lost your mind? He's not a vampire. Stop it."

"Release her," Walker said, his voice thickening to a growl.

Samuel's mouth flattened. "Findley, take her to the car."

Lilah saw Walker's face moving, bulging and constricting beneath the skin, as if his rage was reshaping it. His black hair rose like a halo, bristling and extending, the ends paling into a glittering silver. His lips darkened and thinned, peeling back from his white teeth, which narrowed and lengthened into rows of pointed fangs.

Unnerved by the transformation, Samuel shuffled back, almost stumbling before he tightened his grip on the gun. "James, get her out of here. Now."

When the driver tried to drag her away, Lilah stomped on his instep as hard as she could and jerked free, almost falling over as she ran back to Walker. The man she loved had become almost unrecognizable, his body swelling and tearing the seams of his clothes, thick, silver black fur pelting the backs of his hands and the wide muzzle that had once been his face. As she reached him, he pushed her behind him, and she saw five huge talons stretching out of his clublike fingers.

Samuel lowered the gun. "Del, get away from him. Run." He hobbled forward, shouting, "Hey," as he lifted his cane above his head.

Walker swept out his arm, knocking Samuel away with one blow. The big man flew twenty feet before he landed and collapsed.

Lilah ran in front of her lover, barring his path to Samuel. "Walker." She met his furious gaze, and reached into him, searching through the nightmare of images in his mind until she found the remnant of the man she loved. *I'm here. I'm not hurt. You don't have to kill him.*

He seized her by the arms, his talons cutting through her coat and into her flesh. The beast inside him wanted only to kill, to tear Samuel apart, to drink his blood and gnaw on his bones.

You are not a monster, Lilah told him. *You are a man. You can control the beast.*

He bared his fangs, lowering his head and releasing a low, ugly growl.

Lilah's hands shook as she pressed them to his monstrous face. *Walker, please. You have to fight it or you'll kill someone. You'll kill me.*

The beast peered at her, and loosened its grip. He lowered his shaggy head and sniffed at the rents in her sleeves.

"Yes," she whispered, pulling his head close and feeling his flesh shifting against her cheek. "It's all right. It's over now."

"I've never been much of a dog lover," a cool voice said from behind them. "I think it's the hair. It gets on everything."

Chapter 21

Lilah felt something stab into the base of her neck, and clapped her hand over a chambered dart. She spun around to see a slim brunette dressed in an impeccable business suit, who stood flanked on either side by four men with automatic weapons.

Lilah's head began to spin, and she felt Walker's arms wrapping around her.

"Leave us alone," he said, his voice still distorted.

"It talks, too." The woman shifted the tranquilizer gun in her hand, aiming for Walker's chest. "That should convince my buyer to add a few more zeros to my check."

Something swung at the brunette—a baseball bat—and knocked the gun out of her hand.

A tall woman with white hair parked the bat on her shoulder. "I wouldn't cash it just yet, sweetie." She turned as one of the brunette's men fired at her, but instead of falling to the ground, she merely glared. "Hey, dumbass. You're making holes in my favorite jacket."

The gunman aimed for her head, and then froze and looked down as thousands of grubs erupted around his feet and began inching up his legs. He screamed and danced, dropping his gun to beat at them with his hands.

As Walker swept Lilah up in his arms, she heard shots being fired, and someone shouting furiously in French.

Then he was running, the park blurring around them as he dodged around trees and leapt over obstacles.

She hung on to him with desperate hands, fighting to stay conscious as the powerful drugs began to paralyze her limbs. A huge truck roared to a stop in front of them, and through blurry eyes she saw Ethan Jemmet jump out and fire a shotgun at something past them. The back door flung open, and Nathan leaned out.

"Get in," he shouted at Walker as the sheriff continued to fire.

Lilah's vision fogged as Walker handed her in to Nathan, who slid over and supported her head with his arm.

"Ethan, I've got them." Nathan looked down at Lilah. "Is she wounded?"

She tried to say no, but his scars distracted her, and she marveled at how they glowed, like streaks of molten silver in the moonlight. Then she was in Walker's arms, and he was shaking her and saying her name.

The last thing she heard was Ethan telling them to hold on, and then there was nothing.

Gabriel returned from pursuing the rogue to find Nicola helping a large human male to his feet.

"Easy." She handed the man a cane, which he used to brace himself, and checked the gash in his side. "This looks painful, but it's not too deep. You probably won't need stitches." She glanced at Gabriel. "They got away?"

"Yes, and they had help." He saw Valori hurrying toward them. "The others?"

"They took off after them." Nick scowled up at the human. "Now, how did you get mixed up in this, Sasquatch?"

"I was walking in the gardens and I heard a woman scream," he said, grimacing as he leaned heavily on his cane. "I thought I could assist her."

"So you're just a Good Samaritan in the wrong place

at the wrong time." She shook her head and said to Gabriel, "This one is lying, so we'll assume he's in cahoots with Little Miss Turncoat and her happy band of shooters." She bent down, retrieved a gun, and checked the chambers. "Copper rounds. Goddamn it." She dumped them out onto the grass before snapping the chamber back into place. "Someone knows we're here." She brought the gun to her nose, and then glared at the human male. "This is yours."

"I didn't shoot anyone. But you, you were shot five times." The bearded man reached out and touched one of the bullet holes in her jacket. "You're not even bleeding." He gave her a wide-eyed look. "You're one of the old ones."

"Old?" She made a rude sound. "I'm only twenty-seven, pal."

Valori joined them and made her breathless report. "Teresina escaped. I think she's gone after them."

Gabriel put his hand on the human male's shoulder, and the air became suffused with the scent of evergreen. "Tell us exactly what happened here, monsieur."

"I'd be delighted to," the human male said steadily, "as soon as you tell me who you are, and why you're here."

"Another one we can't control. Terrific." Nicola lifted her arms and dropped them. "Is there something in the city water, or what?"

"I cannot say." Gabriel grew thoughtful. "Why would the sheriff stage a rescue?"

"The rogue may have him under his influence," Valori suggested. "Like the female is."

"Lilah Devereaux didn't have that I'll-do-anything zombie look on her face," Nicola said. "And we already know the sheriff can't be bespelled."

"Let him go," a man ordered, and Gabriel looked

over to see a chauffeur appear behind Valori, putting an arm around her throat and a gun to her head. "Now, or she dies."

"Go ahead and shoot," Valori wheezed out. "My life means nothing to them."

"Shut up, Valori." Nicola drew her dagger as she eyed the chauffeur. "Why don't you put that away and go polish a headlight or something?"

"Findley, let her go. No, it's all right." When the driver released Valori, the bearded man gave Gabriel a wary look. "My name is Samuel. I came here to meet my friend Lilah Devereaux. She was abducted from Florida, and now is under the control of one of your people."

Gabriel lifted his brows. "My people?"

"The dark kyn." He didn't wait for an acknowledgment. "Some of this situation is my fault. I've been searching for my young friend for quite some time, but unfortunately I employed Ms. Segreta to assist me. Apparently she has been following her own agenda."

"You just figured this out now?" Nicola folded her arms. "Brilliant. Who else works for you? Bernie Madoff?"

"My point is, I am only concerned with Lilah and her safety," he said. "I have no interest in you or this rogue you're hunting."

"That doesn't mean we're going to build a campfire together and sing 'Kumbaya,' pal," Nicola advised him. "And since we can't wipe your memory, you've just made yourself a huge liability."

"How so? I am an injured cripple, and my driver alone can't capture you or harm you. If I were to go to the police and tell them about you, they would have me carted off to a psychiatric ward. Even the tabloids would suggest I add some aliens to make my tale more realistic for their readers." He limped over to a bench and sat down. "So you may safely put away your dagger, madam. I am no danger to you."

"I guess I can't kill you for being a pain in my ass." She sheathed the blade. "So, who told you about the Darkyn?"

"History, my dear. I am an antiquities dealer, and I collect letters and journals that date back to the Sumerians. Your kind have been the stuff of many dark legends over the centuries." He winced, clutching at his side. "I believe I need the first-aid kit, Findley, if you'd be so good to fetch it from the car."

As the driver hurried off, Gabriel went to the injured man and helped him take off his coat. Although the wound in his side was shallow, he was sweating profusely and his face was ashen with pain. "You should be in a hospital."

Taske took out a handkerchief and wiped the sweat from his face. "I'm afraid my discomfort comes from chronic inflammation of the spine. It will pass in a few minutes."

Nicola joined them. "Gabriel, his driver will look after him. We have to go."

"You'll need some bait to draw out Ms. Segreta," Samuel said. "Since I've behaved no better than a worm, I would like to volunteer my services."

Nicola sighed. "No offense, Sasquatch, but the only thing you should be dangling from is a traction rig."

"Tina is only interested in money, something that she knows I have in rather obscene abundance. I have the number to the mobile she is carrying at this moment. And as I was facedown in the dirt when she arrived, she is completely unaware that I was here and witnessed everything. Thus she will never suspect that I am in 'cahoots' with you." His smile faded. "Please. Let me do this. It is the only way I can atone for my part in what's happened to my friend."

Gabriel felt a pang of sympathy for the man. "We all make mistakes, monsieur."

"And penance is overrated." Nicola still didn't sound convinced. "What exactly is your plan?"

He took out a mobile phone. "I will call and arrange an exchange with her. All I ask is that you allow me to take Lilah away when it is over."

Gabriel frowned. Involving the human was a risk, but if the outcast *tresora* had already captured the rogue . . . "Very well, Mr. Taske. You can set the trap, and be our bait."

"She should be waking up soon," Paul Jemmet said as he closed his case. "I can send Annie over to sit with her."

Ethan didn't move from the chair. "I'll stay."

His father's hand rested against his shoulder. "This is not your doing, son. Neither is what happens from here."

"I know that." He rubbed his tired eyes. "But I have to be the one to tell her."

"Call me if you need me." Paul slipped out of the jail cell and locked the door behind him.

Ethan knew his father would be going to the caves; it was where he could best treat the wounded. The women would be there, too, rolling bandages and making up cots. Nathan and the rest of the men in town were probably finished blocking the entrance to the pass. It wouldn't keep them out forever, but it would buy them some time. All they needed to do was hold them off until sunset.

The woman stirred, and he picked up her hand, half of him wishing she would open her eyes and the other half hoping that they stayed closed. Her fingers clutched at his as she murmured something.

The waiting, as it always did, became intolerable. "Marianne." When she didn't respond, he tried the name her man had shouted. "Lilah."

Slowly her eyes opened, her pupils dilating as she focused on his face. "Sheriff?"

He smiled. "I think you can call me Ethan now."

"We were in Denver." She put her hand to her head. "Something hit me."

"You were attacked in a park," he told her. "My brother and I got you out of there and brought you back to Frenchman's Pass. My father gave you a shot to neutralize the drug they used on you." He decided not to tell her that Paul had injected her with Ethan's own blood. "You're safe now."

"Walker." She turned her head. "Where is he?"

"He's with my father. Lilah, I need you to listen to me. We didn't know when you first came here what had happened to you. The things that were done to you. But the blood sample my father took from you, the first night you were here, it made things clear." He paused, wishing the words would come easier. "These men who abducted you and Walker, they infected you with something. Both of you were exposed to a kind of blood that isn't human. The blood is the problem, not you."

She tried to sit up. "I need to go to him."

"You can't right now, honey." He tried to take her hand again, but she cringed away. "You wouldn't want to see him the way he is. It's the blood they used on you. It doesn't have the same effect on everyone, and in a few cases"—his mouth curled bitterly—"it doesn't do much at all. On Walker, well, it's worked real fast."

"What are you talking about?" she demanded, her voice stronger, her eyes clearer. "I don't care about this. I want Walker. Where is he? What's happened to him?"

He couldn't bring himself to describe it. "The blood you two were given is changing you from human to something else. Right now it's changing you on the inside, and when that's done, it'll do the same thing on the outside. You'll be sick for a couple days, and scared, but we'll take care of you." He hesitated. "The same way we're looking after Walker now."

She sat up, holding the blanket to her chest, and looked around. "I'm in jail?" She gave him an incredulous look. "You put me in jail?"

"Until we know how fast it's gonna be for you," he said, "we have to keep you here. It's for your own good."

She stared at him, and then she reached out and grabbed his wrist. Something powerful rushed through his head, scalding and freezing at the same time, and then her voice spoke from behind his eyes. *You are not keeping me here. You're going to take me to him.*

Of course, she was right. "I'm not going to keep you here," he agreed, and stood. "I'll take you to him right now."

I need clothes. When he started to unbutton his shirt, she said, *Not yours. I need my own.*

"Your clothes." He nodded, and took out the key to the cell. He found the stack of garments his father had removed from her, and handed them to her.

Don't move. She pushed him around to face the wall.

Ethan smiled at the wall as he listened to her dress, perfectly content not to move a muscle until she needed him again. Just as he felt her voice seeping out of his head, she took hold of his wrist and brought it back.

Now take me to him.

Lilah followed Ethan out to the street, keeping a firm grip on him as he led her across to Annie's inn and then past it to the snowbank at the bottom of the slope. Someone had used a mini-plow to clear a path up the mountain, and Ethan followed it, slowing his stride only when she started falling behind.

She expected him to take her into the cabin, but he went past it and all the others, climbing higher, putting his arm around her when she struggled against the steep angle of the ground.

"We're almost there," he said, his mouth slack and his eyes blank.

We have to hurry, she told him, afraid more of losing control over his mind than of inflicting any damage. Whatever Ethan and the people of the town had done to Walker, they were going to suffer for it.

The sheriff boosted her up onto a narrow plateau outside a series of caves in the side of the mountain peak. Smoke rose from several vent holes, and Lilah could see light flickering from deep inside.

"He's in there," Ethan told her, pointing to the center cave.

She wanted nothing more than to march right in there with the sheriff in tow, but she didn't know who was waiting, or what they might do to Walker when they saw her.

She led Ethan over to the brush growing at the edge of the plateau. *Take a nap here. Don't wake up until I come back.*

He yawned. "I am tired." He dropped down to stretch out on his side, pillowing his head with his arm as he closed his eyes. A moment later he was asleep.

Lilah left him and headed for the center cave, entering silently and moving along the wall where the shadows best concealed her. The cave turned out to be a tunnel that led straight back to the source of the light, a large fire burning in a natural pitlike depression in the floor of the cave.

Annie and dozens of other women were gathered around the fire, some laying out medical supplies on cloth-covered trays, while others tucked blankets around short-legged cots with thin mattresses suspended by ropes.

"Annie, make sure there's a scalpel and tongs on every tray," Paul Jemmet said as he emerged from another tunnel. "I'll be digging a lot of slugs out of them, and I don't want to have to hunt for instruments while I'm doing it."

Lilah stayed in the shadows, scanning the interior of the small cave for Walker. A terrible sound came through the air, like a wounded animal screaming, and Paul Jemmet shook his head.

"Can't you knock him out for a few hours?" Annie asked.

"I wish I could," the doctor said. "None of the drugs I've tried have any effect on him."

They were talking about Walker, Lilah thought. But what was making him scream like this?

"Doc, do you think he'll change back?" one of the other women asked.

"I hope so, Hannah, but we won't know until it's over and done with."

Lilah edged around the cave, moving slowly and carefully toward the sound, which seemed to be coming from one of the back tunnels. When she reached it, she slipped around the corner and hurried toward the back, where another, smaller fire burned.

A much smaller cave lay at the end of the tunnel, one not much larger than the jail cell Ethan Jemmet had been holding her in. A wall of thick iron bars divided the cave in half, with only a locked gate panel allowing access to the other side. Behind the bars crouched a huge beast covered in silver-tipped black fur.

Walker.

Lilah rushed to the bars, and as soon as he saw her, the beast reared up and howled. She saw a ring of old-fashioned keys hanging from a hook driven into the stone, and took them down, fumbling as she unlocked the gate and wrenched it open.

The beast snatched her into his arms, his fur receding as his body straightened, and she heard the popping of joints and the grinding of bones. She held on to him until his talons sank back into his fingers, and the thick layer of fur around his neck became smooth, hot skin.

"Lilah." His rough voice shook as he ran his hands over her. "Are you hurt? What did they do to you?"

"I'm fine." She lifted her face and tried to smile. "We're going to be okay."

"The sheriff. His brother." His jaw set. "They took you from me. I tried to fight them, but then there were others." He touched his face. "Others like me. They can summon these beasts."

"They are not beasts," Paul Jemmet said quietly. Lilah turned her head and saw him standing outside the cell. "They are the children of the mountain. They are its guardians." He studied their faces. "You are not what I thought. I was wrong about you."

"You were *wrong*?" Lilah demanded, striding out of the cell to shove him back. "How could you do this? How could you put us in cages? How dare you?"

"As I said, I was wrong about you." The doctor glanced at Walker. "The people who attacked you in the city are coming up the mountain after you. Our scouts estimate they'll be here in an hour."

"We are leaving." Walker came and took her hand. "Now."

"You're not going anywhere, brother," Nathan said as he stepped into the cave. "We've blocked off the road, Dad. Everyone is in position. Ethan's outside, unconscious. Annie can't seem to wake him up." He turned to study Walker. "Shit. When did he shift back?"

"As soon as the woman touched him." His father

dragged a hand through his hair. "My conclusions were flawed. I don't know what to think now."

Lilah glared. "Stop talking about us like we're invisible." To Nathan, she said, "Why are you blocking off the road? You don't want us here. Why not just hand us over to them?"

He scowled back. "I'm starting to think that's a damn good idea, Red."

Chapter 22

Convincing Eliot Kirchner to authorize and send two dozen operatives to assist Tina in recovering the acquisitions had taken too much time; it would have been quicker to go to the facility, slit the doctor's scrawny throat, and gather the teams herself.

"You should have reported this to me as soon as the truck went missing," Kirchner had snapped over the phone. "Thanks to you, they could be in Venezuela by now."

"I know I was irresponsible, sir, but we've confirmed the most recent sighting." She had always been good at simpering, but it took all her patience to keep from screaming at him. "I know exactly where they are. All I need are the men to help me bring them back."

"You will make a full report to Mr. Genaro as soon as you've recovered them," he warned her. "He will not be pleased, I assure you."

"I will do that, sir." Before she left for the Caymans, she might stop by the lab and kill him anyway. "Thank you, sir."

She rendezvoused with the recovery teams at a rest stop near the exit to the mountain road, and handed out maps.

"We've traced the missing shipment to a town called Frenchman's Pass, which is situated just off the main road, here." She pointed to her copy of the map. "Local law enforcement consists of a sheriff and a couple of deputies, and we'll try to use them as long as we can. If they offer any resistance whatsoever, terminate them."

"Only one road in." One of the team leaders, a grim-faced mercenary who had spent much of his career in the Congo, examined the layout on the map. "We can use the trees for cover on approach, but we'll have to come in from behind the buildings, maybe put some snipers on the rooftops to cover our asses."

He might be Genaro's best killer, but his cushy job kidnapping civilians had made him sloppy. He had no idea that she had planted pipe bombs in the equipment bags she had directed him to load into the recovery team's vehicles, or that she planned to detonate them once they'd finished the mission.

"I want the male target taken alive." No way was she passing up the chance to sell a shape-shifter. "You can shoot the female on sight."

Halfway up the mountain, Tina's phone rang, and when she saw the number, she smirked. "Mr. Taske," she answered. "I was just thinking about you. I should be able to deliver your merchandise tonight."

"I'm very glad to hear that," he said in his cool voice. "I arrived in Denver last night, but circumstances have changed, and I need to take possession as quickly as possible."

"Well, I'm on my way to pick up the shipment now, and it will be eight hours before I return," she told him, "so it's really not feasible to move the delivery time."

"It would be faster if I came to you, once you've taken possession, of course," Taske said. "I would also be happy to compensate you for the inconvenience. Shall we say an additional one million dollars?"

Tina would never have agreed to a face-to-face meeting, but by the time Taske reached Frenchman's Pass, all he would find would be bodies and burning vehicles. "I think that's acceptable." She gave him directions, and added, "I'll meet you at the turnoff outside town at sunset."

"Thank you, Ms. Segreta."

Nathan's threat taunted the beast inside him, but he knew it was an empty one. "You would not have blocked off the road if you meant to hand us over to our enemies."

The scarred man gave him an ugly look. "We wouldn't be in this mess if you'd stayed put in the first place."

Lilah wasn't finished with the doctor. "Why are you protecting these werewolves? We saw them kill the men who kidnapped us. Whatever you think they are, they hunt people. They eat people. They're a danger to everyone in this town."

"Werewolves. Eating people." Nathan uttered a bitter laugh. "Try talking your way out of this one, Dad." He stalked out of the cave.

"I'd like to explain everything to you, my dear," Paul said, his voice sad. "But as my son said, we can't afford the exposure. Until such time as you are both willing to trust us, and agree to stay with us, we must keep our secrets."

"We're not staying here," he told him.

"I'm afraid you have no choice, Mr. Kimball," Paul said. "I don't understand exactly what you are yet, but you're too dangerous for us to allow you to roam freely among the population. And there are other matters to consider." He turned to Lilah. "Matters that concern you."

He used the momentary distraction to grab the doctor, pulling the gun from his side holster before he thrust him into the cell. He slammed the door shut, pocketed the keys, and handed the gun to Lilah.

"You can't leave," Paul said. "Listen to me. It's not what you're thinking. We are not the enemy."

"Shut up." To Lilah, he said, "If he makes another sound, shoot him."

He strode out to the end of the tunnel, and glanced around the corner. He saw the townswomen around the fire, but Nathan and the other men were nowhere in sight. He trotted back to see Lilah backing away from the cell, her hand lowering the gun, her face pale.

"No," she was saying, shaking her head in disbelief. "I don't believe you."

He took the gun from her. "We have to go, now."

"Lilah, wait." Paul wrapped his hands around the bars. "We are not your enemy. We can help each other."

The doctor continued to call after them as he hustled Lilah down the tunnel. "What did he say to you?"

"He said I'm . . . " She stopped and shook her head. "It's nothing."

Annie was waiting for them at the entrance to the larger cave, and held up her hands as soon as she saw his face. "I'm not going to fight you, boy. I just want to know if Paul's all right."

"He's in the cage." He considered taking the inn-keeper with them as collateral, but she would probably fight him every step of the way, and he needed to move quickly. "Where is Nathan?"

"He's at the barricade, keeping watch with the others." She gave him a speculative look. "They won't let you drive out of here, and if you try to walk, you'll freeze before you get halfway to Chamberlain." She took out a key ring and held it out. "My snowmobile's in the shed. There's gas in the can next to it. Best fill up the tank first."

"Why are you helping us?" Lilah asked.

"I tried keeping Mr. Peterson here when he didn't

want to stay." She shrugged. "After years of fighting and sulking and hating, he left me anyway. So this time, I figure I'll save everyone the misery."

He took the keys. "Thank you."

Annie nodded. "Go down the west side of the slope, and follow the creek out. They won't be watching that."

"Wait a second." Lilah went over to Ethan, who lay on a pallet by the fire, and bent down to touch his wrist. When she returned, she said, "I couldn't leave him that way." She glanced at Annie. "He'll wake up in a few minutes."

The older woman smiled. "You've got a good heart, girl. You folks ever reconsider your place in the world, I hope you'll come back to us."

Lilah followed him out of the caves, where he stopped and listened, breathing in deeply to test the air.

"None of them are here," he heard her say. "Walker, that woman in the park who shot me, who was she?"

"I don't know," he admitted. He had a vague memory of other faces that he had recognized, but the transformation had distorted his mind, making it hard to know what had been real. "Can you make it down to the inn?"

She nodded, and took his hand. "I'm sorry about Samuel. I thought he was my friend."

"It doesn't matter. Nothing matters but us now." He pulled her into his arms and held her tightly. "Come. We have to hurry."

She tried to keep up, but the effects of the drug lingered and made her clumsy, and halfway down the slope he picked her up and carried her the rest of the way. He found he could run as fast as the beasts, and slowed only when Lilah made a sound of protest.

"You'll slip," she predicted, breathless from the quick descent.

"No, I don't think I will." A part of him seemed confident that he was now as sure-footed as the werewolves. "And I will not let you fall."

When they reached Annie's shed, he put Lilah down and checked the street first before opening the door and dragging out the snowmobile.

"You've gotten a lot stronger, too," Lilah said as she retrieved the gas can. She handed it to him, and wrapped her arms around her waist. "Walker, when I was alone with Paul, he told me something."

"Paul is a liar." He filled the snowmobile's tank and tossed aside the empty can. "Can you drive this?"

She nodded and climbed on, scooting forward to make room for him on the seat. "These things go pretty fast," she told him as she started the engine. In a louder voice she said, "Don't let go of me."

He encircled her with his arms. "Never," he promised.

She drove the snowmobile down the snowbank and back into the woods, following a well-worn path to a frozen ribbon of water.

"This is the creek." She steered the snowmobile to the top of the bank, and then turned toward the main road. "They might hear us, so be prepared for a sudden change of direction."

The creek made a meandering path along the base of the pass, close enough to town for him to see the back of each building, but far enough away for the trees to give them cover. Lilah drove to the point where the creek ended in a small dam, and stopped, idling the engine as she looked down at the main road.

"The incline's too steep," she told him. "We'll roll if we try to go down this way." She glanced back. "We've got to go down to the turnoff. I think I can get around them."

He took out the gun. "I will make sure that we do."

*   *   *

Taske removed a bottle of whiskey from the liquor cabinet in the back of the car and regarded the two immortals sitting across from him. "I'd invite you to share in a drink, but I fear my meaning would be misconstrued."

"We're good, Sasquatch," Nick said, squinting against the glare of the afternoon light. "Sunglasses, on the other hand, would be greatly appreciated."

As Taske dug into his pocket, Valori plucked the whiskey bottle from his hand. "I could use a belt." She opened it and took a long swallow, sighing before she handed it back to him. *"Grazie."*

"Prego." He took a sip, grimacing as his movements pulled at the gashes under the makeshift dressing Findley had applied over them. "Tell me, since I was assaulted by this rogue while he was unfortunately indisposed, do you think I'll turn into the same sort of rampaging creature the next time the full moon rises?"

"A changeling cannot infect a human," Gabriel told him. "They cannot even drink your blood without becoming ill."

"I don't think he's a changeling, baby," Nick muttered. To Taske, she said, "We have a doctor on staff. If things start to go hairy, she can probably help, although she only makes house calls at night."

"Indeed." *A vampire doctor.* Taske was impressed. "Why isn't she helping your rogue?"

"That," Gabriel said before Nick could reply, "is private Kyn business, Samuel."

"I see." Taske took out a glass, poured two fingers of whiskey into it, and offered it to Valori, who shook her head. "You're not at all what I've always imagined. From the way humans have written about you, I was expecting something quite different. Anne Rice decadence combined with Bram Stoker moodiness, I suppose."

"Oh, we have dress-up parties now and then," Nick

assured him. "We'd invite you to one, but someone
would probably mistake you for the hors d'oeuvres."

He chuckled. "Heaven forbid it."

Findley eased the car off onto the shoulder and
parked before lowering the privacy screen. "The turnoff
is a quarter mile ahead, sir."

"This is where we get out." Nick turned to Valori.
"You could stay in the car, you know. Gabriel and I have
this covered."

Valori took out the gun she'd retrieved in the park. "I
would rather have your back, my lady."

"All right. Samuel, when she comes to meet you, don't
get too close to her or the rogue. Leave us room, and get
out of the way when we close in. When we're finished,
I'll bring Lilah to the car." Nick patted his shoulder, and
then climbed out.

Gabriel followed, but Valori lingered for a moment.

"I have Findley," he told her. "As you know, he is very
protective, and very quick."

"Don't turn your back on Teresina, signore," she advised, "or she will put a quick end to your pain."

Lilah surveyed the barricade the townspeople had
constructed across the entrance to the pass. They had
parked every vehicle in the town across the gap, and
piled barrels, crates, and even some furnishings on top
of the cars. "No one's driving through that."

"There." Walker leaned forward and pointed to the
west end of the barricade, where a small strip of snow
ran between the front end of an old pickup and the
trees. "Can you make it through there?"

"I think so. Just don't stick out your elbows." She
shifted into drive, and started down toward the barricade.

The sound of the snowmobile brought heads popping
up from the town side of the barricade, and Lilah saw
Nathan wave both arms over his head. He stopped wav-

ing, but then pushed his hands toward her in a shoving motion, over and over.

"Sorry, we'll have to do the hokey pokey some other time." As men came running toward them, she made a hard right turn and accelerated, speeding toward the gap.

"Lilah," Walker said sharply, clutching her waist.

She saw the black SUVs converging on the other side of the barricade, and quickly changed direction, speeding toward the trees. She heard metallic pings and felt the snowmobile rock under her as men began shooting at them from the open windows of the SUVs. A bullet pierced the calf of her left leg, sending an arrow of white-hot pain up into her thigh.

Walker was torn away from her, and she braked, frantically steering around to see him lying on his back, blood spreading over his chest.

"Oh, no. Walker."

Two men from the SUVs ran to him, grabbing his arms and dragging him away. Before she could reach them, they fired at her again, the bullets peppering the snowmobile and causing a black cloud of smoke to billow out from the engine. Lilah jumped off into the snow, hitting her shoulder and rolling into the trunk of a tree. An explosion sent a wave of hot air over her, and she realized the gas tank had erupted when the snowmobile smashed into one of the SUVs. As she rolled over, she saw the huge cloud of smoke and fuel raining fire down on the roof and hood of one of the SUVs.

Her right arm wouldn't move, and hung at an odd angle, and she had to shove herself up with her left. She got her feet under her and clutched her arm as she staggered toward the blood in the snow.

Has to be alive. Has to be.

The woman from the park appeared in front of her, and this time pointed a real gun at Lilah. "I don't need the extra baggage, thanks." She fired.

Lilah felt the bullet slam into her head, and the world revolved slowly until her back crashed into the ground. She couldn't move, she couldn't breathe, and all she could feel was a warm wetness as it seeped down her scalp and dripped onto her neck.

Be a good girl, Lillian, Evelyn Emerson whispered from the grave, *and you'll get your reward.*

Gunshots crackled in her ears as she closed her eyes, and then they fell silent as the heat coalesced in her heart. She had promised, she had sworn, she had gone without, she had been good. She had been so very good for so long.

And now, this was her reward.

Lilah's head pulsed with heat as the holes in the front and back of her skull abruptly filled in and closed. The blood matting her hair dried instantly, and all around her body, the snow began to melt.

Lilah took her useless arm and held it out, barely feeling the wave of pain as the bones shifted back into place. Then she rose, planting her feet, and looked down to see a flattened slug pop out of the side of her bloodied calf. All the pain went away, consumed by the fire burning inside her.

Smoke hazed the air around her as she walked forward, and she felt her hair begin to rise all around her head. The strands that floated in front of her eyes glowed brighter and hotter than the fiery wreckage of the snowmobile.

She didn't have to look over her shoulder at what came down from the trees to follow her. They came, alone and in pairs and in packs. The bears moved slowly, still drowsy from their long winter sleep, but their lumbering movements gradually picked up speed. The cougars padded across the snow, their heads erect and their large eyes unblinking. The winter white fur of the foxes and bobcats made them almost invisible, but the large pack of wild dogs had fur in a dozen colors, thanks to their complex ancestry of innumerable lost, abandoned, and runaway pets. Feral cats, some still wearing the ragged remains of collars, wove in and out of the legs of the larger predators, their jewellike eyes glittering with malice.

Lilah breathed in, feeling the minds her anger had summoned emptying of all thoughts as they absorbed hers. Two cougars came to crouch in the snow by her feet; one lifted its head against her hand as the other licked the blood from her leg. She stroked the big cat's head as she waited for the rest to emerge from the forest.

"Lilah." Nathan stopped just short of her, his eyes widening as he saw the cougars. "What is this? What are you doing?"

"You have your guardians." She smiled as she reached into him. "I have mine."

Nathan grabbed his head before he fell to the ground, writhing.

Lilah watched as her ability swept out over him and the other men of the town, and when the beasts came to her, their minds blank and their claws ready, she added them to the ranks.

With her army surrounding her, she started walking toward the entrance to the pass.

Chapter 23

The last rays of sunlight illuminated a long, dark limousine sitting just outside the pass, and as soon as she saw it, Tina ordered the driver to stop.

"Wait here," she told the men, and glanced at Walker, who was still unconscious. "Get a dressing on that chest wound. I need this one alive."

She checked the front of her jacket and composed her expression before she got out. Taske's size mildly surprised her, as did his hobbling gait, but she kept her smile cool and impersonal.

"Samuel, you're early." She weighed one million dollars against the gun she was holding ready inside her jacket, and reluctantly slid the gun into her shoulder holster. "I was just about to call you."

He stopped several yards away and looked past her. "That's odd. I was under the distinct impression that you were fleeing the scene." He lifted the briefcase he was carrying. "For convenience's sake I bought the additional payment with me. Where is Lilah Devereaux?"

"She's waiting for you just inside the pass." She gestured toward the town. "I'm afraid we encountered some resistance from the locals, and had to retreat. Since she's your friend, I'm sure you'll have no trouble convincing her to go with you." She closed the gap between them, stopping only when Taske removed his gloves. "What are you doing?"

"You've done an excellent job. I congratulate you." He held out his hand.

She wasn't removing her gloves, but saw no reason not to shake with the man who was about to make her a million dollars richer. "I'm glad it all worked out."

Taske's face whitened as his hand clenched over hers and then dropped it like a snake. "You shot her."

"Yes, Samuel, I confess, I did." She yanked the briefcase out of his hand and drew her gun. "Unfortunately, now I have to do the same to you."

"That didn't work out so well for you the last time," a woman drawled, and Tina turned her head to see the bitch from the park, taking practice swings with her battered bat. When she fired at her, she only smiled. "And oh, dear, you still haven't a fucking clue. Maybe you need a poem to help you remember: Sticks and stones won't break her bones, and bullets will never hurt her."

The fair-haired man from the park strode past Tina, knocking aside her men as he went to the SUV and looked inside. "He's not in here."

The white-haired woman gave her an annoyed look. "What did you do with him?"

"What?" Tina turned around in time to see the black streak of motion coming at her, and then it was on top of her, its claws tearing into her shoulders, its fangs an inch from her face.

She screamed.

"Nicola!"

"I got this." Nick swung her bat, knocking the rogue off the woman and stepping over her cringing form as she reversed the swing and smashed it into his snarling face.

Putting all her Darkyn strength behind the bat threw

the beast thirty feet away, but when it landed, it only scrambled to its feet and started limping toward Nick again.

"Huh. Maybe there's something to the sword approach." She drew her dagger, and then almost dropped it as a cougar and a bear joined the rogue. "What the hell?" She turned her head to see Gabriel fighting off a pair of wild dogs.

Taske's driver grabbed her from behind. "In the car, miss. Please." He hauled her over to the limo, shoved her in the front seat, and climbed in behind her. As soon as he closed the door, a bear slammed headfirst into it.

"Get to Gabriel," Nick told the driver, and pointed through the chaos. Findley stepped on the gas as she held on to the door handle, flinging it open as soon as the limo reached him. A small herd of hissing house cats landed on the hood of the limo as she pulled Gabriel in, and reached past him to slam the door shut. "Go, James, go."

"Turn off into the pass," Taske said from the backseat.

Nick turned around. "You know anything about this *Wild Kingdom* stuff, Sasquatch?"

"No. At least, I don't think she could . . . " He broke off as he saw something. "Lilah. There she is. James, do you see her?"

"Got her, sir." Findley spun the wheel and headed for a woman standing in the center of a mass of animals.

None of the critters were attacking the woman, Nick noticed, and in fact all of them seemed to be holding protective positions, as if they were guarding her. "Gabriel, is there a Kyn who can do your thing but with animals?"

Gabriel's eyes glowed briefly. "She is not Kyn." He grimaced, rubbing his temple. "She is also not human."

"How do you know that?" Taske demanded.

"My talent allows me to command the insect world,"

Gabriel said. "These animals all carry some parasites on or inside their bodies. They are trapped now, unable to free their hosts from her command."

"She's doing this?" Nick whistled. "Sasquatch, I don't think I'd try an apology. You might just want to run. Far, far away."

Gabriel touched her arm. "Look."

Nick saw another SUV screech to a stop in front of a group of huge predators. They spread out, surrounding the car as the woman walked toward the front of it. She glanced around, and the beasts collectively attacked the vehicle, ripping off doors and jerking out men, tossing them aside like rag dolls.

Findley slowed to a stop as the woman turned around and saw them, and the beasts gathered around her.

"Oh, shit," Nick murmured. "You might want to put it in reverse now, James. Hey." She saw Taske climbing out of the back, and swore. "That idiot, what is he doing?"

Before she could go after him, one of the beasts leapt at Samuel, swiping at him with its claws and tearing through his coat. Nick jumped out and ran, shoving the beast off Samuel and protecting him with her body.

"Nicola." Gabriel came to her, holding off the beast with his sword, and then turned his head as another figure staggered toward Lilah Devereaux. "*Mon Dieu.* It's him."

He ignored the violence all around him as he kept his eyes locked on the glowing blaze of Lilah's hair. As he came closer, he could see her eyes had turned a glacial blue, as if all the fire had been extinguished by the ice of her anger.

If he understood anything, it was the rage.

Someone called his name, the name he had almost forgotten, and it sounded so strange to his ears that he stopped and sought out the source.

"Guy of Guisbourne," Gabriel Seran repeated. "Stay where you are."

He glanced at Lilah, who looked back at him, her cold eyes filled with confusion. "I will not fight you, Seran. Only give me leave to bid my lady farewell."

"Oh, so *now* he goes noble," Seran's white-haired companion muttered.

Gabriel looked from Guy to his woman, and nodded.

"Walker?" Lilah moved toward him as if in a dream, and then she was running, her hair streaming behind her like scarlet silk ribbons, and when he caught her, she uttered a raw, terrible sound, the sound of a heart breaking, the sound of a wounded animal. "You're alive."

"Hush." He held her close, kissing her brow, her hair, every part of her face he could reach. "Lilah, I love you. I have loved you from the moment I looked into your eyes, and all I regret is that I was too much of a coward to tell you."

Bewildered animals began to mill around them, slinking off into the trees, followed by the equally confused werebeasts.

"I knew you did. I could feel it." She smiled up at him. "Took you long enough to tell me, though."

"I would like nothing more than to spend the rest of my life telling you," he assured her, "but I must leave you now."

"Leave me?"

"My people have laws," he said softly. "Laws I have broken too often. Now the time has come that I must pay for my crimes. I am not afraid of death, Lilah. I am only sorry that I must leave you like this."

"But you can't." Tears filled her eyes. "Walker—Guy—don't you remember? Where you go, I go."

"I will be waiting for you, my heart. I swear it." He kissed her brow, and then turned to look at Gabriel. "My lord, please let her be taken away now."

Ethan and Nathan Jemmet joined them, and Nathan picked up Samuel as if he weighed nothing. "I'll take him to Dad," he told his brother.

Ethan nodded and, after exchanging a glance with Guy, put his arm around Lilah. "Come on, honey. Let's go back to town."

Guy kissed her one last time, and then walked over and knelt in front of Gabriel.

When Gabriel drew his sword from the sheath on his back, Guy heard a scuffle, and glanced back to see Ethan sprawled on the ground and Lilah marching toward him. She knelt on the ground beside him, seizing his hand and snapping Ethan's handcuffs around his wrist. Before he could stop her, she snapped the other side around her own.

"You have to kill me, too," she said, brushing her hair back from her neck.

"Mademoiselle, you are not Kyn," Gabriel said kindly. "I am not permitted to kill humans."

"Then you might want to see this, lover." Gabriel's *sygkenis* tore open Guy's shirt, revealing the chest wound that was still bleeding. To Guy, she said, "Open your mouth." When he did, she angled his head back and made a *tsk*ing sound. "His wounds are open and his palate is closed." She sniffed him. "He smells nice, but he's not Kyn."

Gabriel lowered his sword. "Nicola, we both know this is Guy of Guisbourne."

"Do we? He looks a little like him around the eyes, but Guy was nowhere near this big." She gave his shoulder a friendly slap. "I'd say he has a good fifty, sixty pounds on Guy. Add that to the still-bleeding wound and the lack of fangs, and I think you get a human, right?"

"Miss Jefferson." Guy wasn't sure what to say. "I am not a coward."

"See, that proves it." Nick wagged her finger at him.

"Everyone knows what a horrible, selfish, cowardly coldhearted bastard Guisbourne was. You, you're kissing a girl and telling her you love her and spouting all kinds of mushy stuff. You're crawling with human cooties." She turned to Gabriel. "Well, my lover? What do you think?"

"I think you may be right," Gabriel said, and frowned at Guy. "What did you say your name was, human?"

"It's Devereaux," Lilah said quickly. "First name, ah, to be decided at a later date."

Guy turned to her. "You would give me your name?"

"Why not?" She grinned, lifting their arms and rattling the chain between their handcuffs. "I am very attached to you."

Still not completely convinced of his reprieve, Guy looked at the Darkyn lord and his lady. "What will you tell Richard?"

"The truth," Nicola said. "Guy of Guisbourne is dead, the weather in Denver sucks, and small-town America is a lot livelier than I expected." She glanced at the men lying in the road. "Now let's see how many survivors we're going to have to brainwash before we get out of here."

Guy stood, and took Lilah in his arms. "I owe you my life."

She kissed him. "Then spend the rest of it with me."

Ethan and the townspeople began the cleanup almost immediately, but when Guy and Lilah came to help, the sheriff sent them to his office.

"Just to be on the safe side, you two should stay out of sight," he said as he handed off one of the injured to his brother. "These people might have backup coming to see what's taking them so long." He nodded toward several burned bodies. "We'll tell them that you were caught in the fire."

Guy knew Lilah had questions, but when they

reached the sheriff's office, she simply led him into the back room and sat down with him on the cot there, wrapping her arms around him and resting against him as if that was all that mattered.

Hopefully it was, he thought as he set her away. "I wanted to tell you who I was before this. I should have told you, that first night."

"I kept things from you, too," she reminded him. "The past doesn't matter to me. I know who you are."

"You may change your mind." He took her hand in his. "There is no place for secrets between us anymore."

She nodded. "Then tell me everything."

In the beginning telling her of his life as Guy of Guisbourne made him feel as if he were skinning himself alive. He forced out the story of his human life in England, and how he had fallen in love at first sight with Marian, the serenely beautiful daughter of one of his father's allies. He told her of his cousin, Robin of Locksley, Marian's childhood friend, and how violently he had reacted when he had learned of the betrothal Guy had forced on her.

"We both loved her, perhaps beyond reason, but in her heart there was room only for her devotion to Christ." After centuries of denying it, he could say it now. "I refused to release her, so Robin stole her away on our wedding night, and I went mad."

He described the frantic months he had spent searching for Marian, and the vengeance he had taken on Robin. Then the dull, gray years he had spent alone, bitter and uncaring, the plague that had taken him and transformed him into one of the dark kyn, and how his mother had used it to imprison him.

"She stole my birthright from me and gave it to my half brother," he said. "I spent years in the dungeons, feeding on my mother's enemies, while he took my place in the world. When I escaped, I fled to Italy, and there plotted to take back what belonged to me. But before I could return to England, my half brother instigated a war among the Kyn. When it was over, everyone who had fought with him—my entire family, all of my men and their kin—were put to death as traitors. Once more I lost everything that mattered to me."

He didn't spare her any of the details, admitting to the callous manner in which he had recruited Saracens from the Middle East, surrounding himself with men who had been the worst of the Kyn's mortal enemies. He told her of the duality of his existence, wavering between meaningless depravity and equally empty violence. How often his anger had driven him out into the world, looking for any mortal battles to join, and how little fighting in those wars had meant to him. He described how he and his men had at last been driven from Italy to America, where he met Jayr, Robin's daughter by Marian who had been changed to Kyn as well, and how the old, ugly jealousy had compelled him into an alliance with a madwoman bent on destroying the Kyn by wiping out humanity itself.

"In the end we had to strike a truce between us in order to stop her," he admitted. "Robin nearly died in the attempt, and I was obliged to help save him. After that, I went to Marian's grave to say good-bye, and found it empty. I had thought she might have survived, that she might have been changed like her daughter, but no. Her bones had been removed by her family and reburied under a church in England. When I finally found them, I knew there was nothing left for me to live for. And so I went to war one final time, in the hope that I would be killed in battle."

"Which brought you here, to me," she murmured.

"Yes." Telling her of his past was as if he had crawled out from under a terrible, crushing weight, but he doubted that Lilah felt the same. "I have never been a good man, Lilah. I deserve to die many times over for the things I have done. Nicola and Gabriel may have spared me for your sake, but they do you no favor."

"If you were still Guy of Guisbourne, maybe I'd agree," she said slowly. "But that man died in Afghanistan. He died the moment you tried to save Walker Kimball's life."

He caressed her cheek. "Do you truly believe I wished to save him?"

"I know you did." She turned her face and pressed her lips to his palm. "Because you saved my life, too."

Tina crawled around the SUV to the driver's side, and watched until no one was looking in her direction. Then she stood and opened the door.

"Sister, wait."

She turned and saw Valori standing behind her. "Don't you dare try anything."

"I can take you back to Italy, and speak for you," Valori said, as if she hadn't spoken. "I will explain things to the council. They will forgive you, and protect you, as long as you take your vows again. You can have your life back, Teresina."

"I have a life, and I'd rather cut my own throat, thanks." She opened the door to the SUV, but before she could get in, Valori seized and pulled her back, turning her and giving her a tight embrace. She pushed against her. "Get off me, you stupid bitch."

"Only I can save you," she whispered, and then staggered away as Tina struck her in the face. "Teresina, don't go. Tomaseo loved you. He wanted you to live."

"Tomaseo is dead, and you can go to hell." She got in behind the wheel, started the engine, and drove off.

Valori watched until the vehicle was out of sight, and then switched on the remote she had slipped out of Teresina's pocket. She glanced back to assure no one else was near the other SUVs, and then she pressed the remote's single button.

The explosions rocked the ground beneath her feet, but she stood and watched as the smoke rose from around the curve of the mountain, a mile away.

Valori walked back to where the others were staring at the ruins of the vehicles. Before she reached them, she dropped the remote and crushed it under her boot.

Nick gave her a narrow look. "Mission accomplished?"

"Yes, my lady." She helped Samuel's driver onto his feet. "My work is finished."

Chapter 24

Lilah and Guy came out of the sheriff's office as the townspeople began to straggle back in from the pass. Those who couldn't walk were brought back in a pickup driven by Annie, who parked in front of the inn and began helping the injured inside.

"Can we do anything?" Lilah asked when they joined her.

"We're using the rooms in my place for the outsiders." She handed off a man with a bloody leg to Guy. "If you can get them inside, I'll take the others to their families."

Paul Jemmet arrived a few minutes later to treat the injured, and soon the inn was transformed into a temporary hospital. The most seriously injured survivor was Samuel Taske, who had multiple lacerations and had lost a great deal of blood.

"Findley will take me to a hospital in Denver," Samuel told Paul. "I'd just like a moment to speak with Lilah."

Guy didn't want to leave her alone with Samuel, but she assured him she wouldn't stay long. When they were alone, she went to stand beside his bed, and listened as he told her what he had done, from sending private investigators out to search for her to hiring Tina Segreta to abduct her.

The final straw was when he asked her to forgive him.

"Do you understand what you did? You pretended to be my friend. You had me drugged and kidnapped. That woman who worked for you, she attacked us. She tried to kill me. And for what? Why?"

"I'm dying, Lilah," he said. "Not from these wounds, but from the abilities I was given. If I do survive my injuries, I'll be dead in less than a year. I researched every possible treatment, and I believed the only thing that could save me was you."

He told her about the visions he had had about her, and what the scientists who had experimented on her had said.

"Well, I can't heal you, Samuel. That's not my gift." Suddenly she understood. "Oh, I see. You wanted my DNA."

"I wanted to study your blood. I believed its unique qualities could lead me to a cure." He looked away. "God forgive me, I would never have done any of this to you."

"What did you need from me?" When he shook his head, she said, "Tell me."

"A pint of your blood, and some tissue samples." Self-disgust filled his eyes. "You don't have to worry, Lilah. I will never intrude on your life again."

Lilah went out and found Paul, and brought him back to Samuel's room. "Dr. Jemmet, I need you to take a pint of my blood and a few tissue samples, to send with Mr. Taske when he leaves. Do you have the equipment you need to do that?"

"Over at the sheriff's office I do," the doctor said. "Mr. Findley mentioned driving Mr. Taske back to Denver tomorrow morning, so it would be best to do it right before they leave."

"Thanks." She waited until Paul left before she looked at Samuel. "All you ever had to do was ask, Samuel. Under the circumstances, I would have been happy to help out."

He covered his eyes with one hand. "I can't accept this from you now."

"Then you'll die what sounds like a pretty horrible death, and I'll always wonder if I could have prevented it." She went to the door, and stopped. "Don't do that to me, Samuel. Please."

She joined Guy out in the hall. "Everything okay?"

He nodded. "Nicola and Gabriel have left. They took the GenHance survivors with them." He glanced at Samuel's door. "What did he say to you?"

"He said he was sorry, and he is." She smiled as Paul joined them. "Is there anything else we can do to help, Doctor?"

"As it happens, there is." He gestured toward the back of the inn. "It's time we went back to the caves."

Lilah winced. "You're not going to try to put us in that cage, are you?"

"No, my dear. I'd like to tell you a story about this town." He smiled. "Or, more precisely, I'd like the caves to tell it to you."

Lilah's eyes widened as Paul's face began to distort, and his gray hair rose around his head. "Oh, my God. You're one of the beasts."

"I am not a beast." He didn't shift completely, but retained most of his human features. "I am Ahnclann."

Before he took them up to the caves, Paul shifted his form back into that of the human doctor Lilah was accustomed to. "I don't often change form anymore. I prefer my life as a human, but then, most of us do."

"Most of you," Lilah said uneasily. "How many are there?"

"Do you know, I've never counted," he admitted as he mounted the plateau outside the caves. "We don't often count things unless we have to."

Guy pulled her to a stop, and she saw a gauntlet of silent, staring eyes inside the center cave.

"Don't mind them," Paul said. "No outsider has ever before been permitted to enter the Ahnclann cave, so they have all come out to see this."

"Good Lord," Lilah murmured as the beasts began to shift into human form, and she saw one familiar face after another. "It's everyone in the town." Aghast, she turned to the doctor. "You're *all* werewolves?"

"Technically, no," Paul said. "And we prefer to be called Ahnclann. When we change, we call the process the Fury."

The doctor led them through a labyrinth of tunnels, and at last into a cavern so large it could have comfortably accommodated several football fields. Crystal stalactites hung like enormous, toothy chandeliers overhead, but their corresponding stalagmites had been cleared from the cave floor.

Nathan came out of the shadows, the torch in his hand illuminating his bare, scarred chest. "What?" he said when his father frowned at him. "I'm wearing pants." He winked at Lilah. "This time."

Guy put a protective arm around Lilah. "Why did you bring us here, Paul?"

Nathan swung the torch around. "He wants to show you the story."

The flickering light danced over a long, smooth expanse of stone covered with paintings. The figures nearest Lilah were crudely made, as if by unsteady hands, but they gradually became more sophisticated as they moved down the stone.

"Cave paintings," she murmured. "I didn't think there were any tribes in the area that made them."

"Actually, this was painted by the only true Native Americans in the area." Paul walked up to the first group of paintings, which showed a pack of giant wolf-like creatures hunting game. "This is how it was before people came to the mountain. No names, no cabins, just life as it was in that time. The only things that mattered were hunting and playing and sleeping and breeding."

Lilah stepped close. "They look like giant wolves."

"Most of the creatures of prehistory were very large. We think modern wolves might be distant cousins." Paul moved down the wall and gestured to two-legged stick figures with black hair. "The Anasazi were the first to discover them. They must have seen them hunting, because they called them Chahanat. It means 'the Fury.'"

The doctor showed them paintings that gradually grew more detailed and sophisticated, and illustrated the plight of the Fury.

"Ultimately time and nature decides what lives and what dies out, and the Chahanat were no different than any other creature. Breeding females bore fewer young every year, and many never whelped at all. About the time the first white settlers arrived"—he pointed to a line of canvas-covered wagons—"the Fury were only a few generations away from extinction. No one knew that they would not be the ones to die out."

Nathan stepped up beside his father. "My mother painted these," he told Lilah gruffly, his fingers delicately tracing around the smiling faces of the settlers as they built their cabins and played with their children. "She loved this part of the story. She was crazy about kids."

"The Fury would watch the settlers from the shadows. They weren't afraid of humans, and didn't mind sharing the mountain with them, but they kept their distance." The doctor smiled sadly. "They knew the humans would go on after they died out, and perhaps they were a little jealous, too."

Lilah peered at the next painting, which showed a dark, handsome man dressed in elegant clothing. His mouth was marked with red, and he held the sagging body of a woman whose throat bore terrible wounds. "Is that a vampire?"

"Yeah, he showed up one day, and got stranded here for the winter," Nathan said. "But he didn't suffer."

"The settlers thought he was human, and took him in." Paul walked on to a depiction of countless tiny graves. "By spring he had killed them all. He was trying to flee when the Fury came out of their caves and discovered what he had done. They took justice for his victims by killing him in the same way he had killed."

Lilah looked away from the gory scene of the vampire being torn apart by the giant wolves.

"They ate the body?" Guy asked, his voice sharp.

"The body, the bones, the blood. Every scrap of him was consumed; it was the only way to kill a creature like him." Paul shook his head. "But they were made to pay for it."

Lilah walked down to the next painting, which showed the Fury in the Ahnclann cave. Some were huddled together; others were twisting in agony. In the center of the tormented creatures, one rose up on its hind legs, its face distorted and flattened, its naked skin showing through huge patches in its fur.

"The vampire's flesh made them sick," she guessed. "Was that what finally killed them?"

"No," Guy said as he looked at the last painting. "It changed them."

Lilah caught her breath as she saw the naked figures of humans emerging from the caves. "Oh, no."

"We were highly intelligent, even before the transformation took place." Paul sat down on a flat-topped stone by the last painting. "We understood that by devouring the vampire's immortal being, we had changed ourselves. We just didn't know how much we were altered."

Guy turned to him. "You were the Fury."

"We *are* the Fury," Nathan corrected softly. "Eating that bloodsucker passed on one more gift: his immortality."

His father nodded. "Now each night, when the sun goes down, we can return to what we were before the transformation. Some of us, like Nathan, can make a complete shift from human to Fury. Others cannot, and retain certain humanoid characteristics, as I do. A few cannot change at all, and remain locked in a human body."

"So you're not werewolves," Lilah murmured. "You're werehumans."

Guy gave Nathan a shrewd look. "Your brother is one who cannot change."

"Yeah, it's why Dad let him become a cop," Nathan said. "He never has to worry about Ethan sprouting fur and fangs while handing out speeding tickets."

Suddenly the names she had read on the worn crosses came back to her. "The people buried behind the cabin weren't your ancestors. They were the original settlers. You took their names."

"Their names, their clothes, and their cabins," Annie said as she joined them. "We had to learn how to live in these new bodies, and they didn't need them anymore." She frowned down at the crooked line of her blouse. "Buttons are still my enemy. I can never line up the damn holes."

Lilah had a million questions. "But how did you learn to speak English? Didn't any of the settlers' families try to contact them? How did you keep the other humans from finding out about what happened?"

"We were able to talk, read, and write from the first change," Annie said. "French and English, along with some old tongues no one seemed to speak anymore. We had shared memories of a world we'd never seen, to boot. I may not be able to wrangle buttons or sew a straight stitch, but I can tell you what kings and queens looked like. What it's like to joust across a field and shove a lance through a man's heart." She eyed Guy. "Even how it feels to drain a human being of blood."

"The languages and memories of the rogue they killed," Guy said. "They must have absorbed them along with his body."

"There was no mass travel or technology when we became the Ahnclann," Paul put in, "and only a few trappers and miners traveled around the mountains. We lived in isolation for decades."

"When letters came from back East, we'd answer them by writing things we read in the diaries and un-mailed letters the settlers had left behind," Annie said. "We had to be careful not to make things sound too good here, so that no one would be tempted to visit. Back then people didn't live as long as they do now, so eventually all the folks who knew the settlers died."

"And then you were safe." Lilah shook her head. "But you must have had other outsiders try to settle here."

"Oh, they tried." Nathan showed her his teeth. "We enjoyed their livestock and their women before we sent them on their way."

"Nathan." Paul gave him a stern look before he told Lilah, "We persuaded most of the humans who came through the pass to continue on to Chamberlain, where they could obtain land, jobs, and better supplies. A few staged gunfights convinced the rest that Frenchman's Pass was not the place to raise a family."

"It still isn't." Nathan stalked off.

Paul watched him go. "Nathan was just coming into his breeding years when we became the Ahnclann. Like most of our younger males, he never had the chance to sire young."

"Another gift from the rogue," Guy told him. "The Darkyn cannot have children."

"It is an enduring curse, one that has been slowly eroding away at us," Paul said. "Mating and breeding were two of our most powerful drives, and being changed has not diminished them. But we remain barren."

"That's why Paul sent away for medical books, and taught himself to be a doctor," Annie said. "Someday he's going to find a way to fix that."

"It's taken more than seventy years of study, but with the new advances in genetics and fertility I'm hopeful." He regarded Lilah. "You carry some of the same mutations as the Ahnclann, but you are also human, and you have"—he paused and glanced at Guy—"much insight to offer. I think I can learn a great deal from you, Lilah, if you are willing."

"Insight?" Guy echoed. "What insight?"

Annie nudged Paul with her elbow. "I'd say this is where you and I hightail it out of here."

The doctor and the innkeeper left, and Lilah held out her hand to Guy. "I tried to tell you before, but things were exploding and I got distracted."

He sat down on the stone Paul had vacated, but when he would have drawn her down onto his lap, she tugged her hands away. "Whatever it is, my heart, just tell me. It cannot be as surprising as your talent."

"This might be the one thing that tops it," she admitted. "Paul took some blood samples from me, and that's how he and Ethan and the others knew we were like them. He also ran some standard tests last night, but only one came up positive."

He frowned. "Positive for what?"

"This." She took his hand and guided it to her stomach. When he gave her a bewildered look, she said, "I'm pregnant, Guy."

"No." He stood and took her into his arms. "Lilah, the doctor has made a mistake, telling you this. You cannot be pregnant. The Darkyn cannot have children with humans, or with anyone."

"I know." She gently touched the gash that had already scabbed over on his check. "But you're forgetting two important exceptions. I'm not entirely human, and you're not Darkyn anymore."

He flinched.

"Paul would like to run more tests," she cautioned, "and with all the genetic mutations we have between us, it's probably a good idea. But I'm not worried. I can't say why, but I just know we're going to have a healthy child."

"A child." All around them frost began crawling up the sides of the cavern. "You're having my child."

Lilah didn't feel the cold, not when she looked into his eyes, and not when she merged her thoughts with his. The last of the darkness had gone, and all that was left was Guy, strong and courageous, passionate and possessive, quiet and loving. The enormous, endless love that he felt for her crossed over into her mind and heart, radiating out around them until the frost began to melt.

He dropped down on his knees, spreading his hands over her belly. "I can feel it. So tiny." He looked up at her, concerned. "The heart is not beating."

"That's because it's still forming." She smiled down at him. "We should be able to hear it in about three weeks."

"You will need to see a doctor." He frowned as the reality began to sink in.

"I've already seen one, and I'd like him to be the one who takes care of me." She hesitated, and then said, "I'd like it to be Paul. I'd like to stay here, Guy."

He obviously hadn't given any thought to where they would go. "Because of me?"

"You and me and the baby." She stroked his hair. "Everyone in this town tried to protect us today. Everyone.

They know what we are, but they would never betray us. Where else could we live where people would do that?"

"They are noble creatures." He stood. "But this is such a small, remote place, Lilah. Will you be happy here?"

"As long as I'm with you." She leaned against him and brought his hand to her stomach. "We will be."

Ethan saw his own shadow standing next to the door to his office, and tried to walk past him. The arm that shot out to bar his path bristled for a moment with fur before it dropped.

"Dad probably needs you up at the caves," he told Nathan.

His brother shifted his weight from one leg to the other. "Dad says I can't come back there until I apologize to you."

Ethan frowned. "For what?"

"Letting the Fury come between us." Nathan's teeth flashed. "We were good out there today, you and me."

"You were good." He frowned down at the body that would never change. "I was just adequate."

"I can't ever leave the mountain, Ethan. Not with my temper. You know it. I know it. Hell, I'm lucky if I can spend a full night in town without going over."

He didn't need to be reminded of how easily his brother could change. "So?"

"So you could go anywhere in the world. Do anything, be anything. Have as many women as you like and never have to worry about going Fury on them when things get interesting." His brother leaned close. "So the next time you're hating me for what I got, think about what I didn't."

Nathan strolled past him, and Ethan turned. "I don't."

His brother glanced back. "Don't what?"

"I don't hate you." He stalked into his office and

slammed the door. Once he peeled off his clothes and took a shower, he'd cook up some steaks, pop open a beer, and relive the few moments he'd spent watching her.

When he turned and saw her sitting in his chair with her bare feet propped on his desk, he was so sure it was his imagination that he didn't say anything for a full minute. "Lori?"

"It's Valori," she said, swinging her legs down and standing. "They gave me a last name, but it's just a polite way of saying 'street trash.' Which is what I was. Mama threw me out with the garbage."

He watched her as she walked to him, unsure of what to say but absolutely sure she wasn't getting past him again. "I thought you left with your friends."

"Not my friends. Employers. Former employers." She stopped in front of him and linked her hands together. "I don't have a job, which makes me happy because I couldn't stand it anymore."

"You should always be happy in your work." God, she was prettier than he remembered. "What did you do?"

"I had sex with men I didn't care about. When I wasn't spying on them." She dropped her gaze. "You're the first man I've slept with in ten years who wasn't an assignment."

Ethan considered telling her how his kind felt about sexual experience among females, and how hot imagining her taking on man after man was making him. "I'm flattered."

"Everything was real with you." She frowned. "I don't know why. I don't do real."

He put his hands on her hips and pulled her closer. "Maybe I should run an investigation. See what I can find out." He breathed in her sweet scent. "Can you stick around for a while?"

"I don't have a job, I can't go back to Italy, and that makes me homeless, too." She tilted her head. "So, yes. I can stick around for as long as you'd like."

He lowered his head until his mouth hovered above hers. "I've got a place you can sleep, if you don't mind sharing."

She smiled against his lips. "What would you like to share?"

Turn the page for an excerpt from
Lynn Viehl's next Novel of the Kyndred,

Nightshine

Coming soon from Signet Select

No drug, treatment, or therapy had ever succeeded in completely relieving the pain caused by Samuel Taske's deteriorating spine. He had spent years learning how to rest through meditation and napping for an hour or two, usually in an upright position in one of his custom-built ergonomic chairs. To wake from a deep, satisfying sleep and find himself flat on his back in a real bed was not only a novelty but something of a precious gift.

One he would begin paying for immediately, he thought as he lay as still as possible. As soon as he moved he would likely be in agony. At least Morehouse would arrive soon with his morning tea and paper, and afterward, administering his injection would help him get up and into the whirlpool. . . .

Two fingers pressed against a bone in his wrist while a warm hand settled on his brow. None of them belonged to his house manager.

"No fever, no rash, no arrhythmias," a woman murmured. "So why don't you wake up, *mío*?"

"It usually requires a pot of tea and the *Wall Street Journal*." He looked up at Charlotte Marena's face. Beyond her, he could see bright colors and beautiful furnishings. "Hello again."

"Hey." Her smile lit up her tired face. "Welcome back. How are you feeling?"

"Puzzled." Taske turned his head to the right and left to take in as much as he could, and made another discovery as he felt the smoothness of the linen pillowcase against his cheek. "Someone shaved off my beard."

She nodded. "Wasn't me."

He didn't see any medical equipment around the bed. "We're not at a hospital, are we?"

"I don't where we are, Sam," Charlotte admitted. "I was kind of hoping that you did."

"I'll have to disappoint you." Luxurious and unique as it was, he didn't recognize the room. "How did we come to be here?"

"The last thing I remember was passing out in the back of my unit." She straightened. "Yesterday I woke up here with you. That's all I know."

"Yesterday?" He frowned. "I've been unconscious that long?"

"At least a day." She made a helpless gesture. "Maybe two or three, or even a week." She looked as if she wanted to say more, and then subsided.

"But you woke before me." A vague memory of Charlotte's urgent voice came back to him, and without thinking he reached across his abdomen to touch the wound in his side.

"It's okay. It's already healed." She pulled down the sheet covering him to expose the unmarked skin over his ribs. "The stitches I put in popped out during the night. There isn't even a scar. Maybe you can explain that to me?"

"I'll try." Taske had not enjoyed such a rapid recovery from a serious wound in years, but that was not the only revelation that stunned him. When he had moved, he had felt nothing.

"What is it?"

He frowned as he carefully drew his arm back, and then moved his legs just enough to shift the lower half of his spine. "I don't feel anything."

Charlotte turned and touched his thigh. "You can't feel my hand?"

"No, I have feeling in my legs." Still not trusting his body, he bent his arm to prop his weight on his elbow and roll onto his side. His muscles felt stiff, but the searing coil of nerves around his spine didn't offer even the slightest twinge. "Charlotte." He stared at her. "I need you to tell me precisely what happened to me."

"When I woke up yesterday I found you in shock from the blood loss. You were left here bleeding from a reopened wound." She ducked her head. "Your heart stopped, and I had to perform CPR, but I got you back. I had to give you a vein-to-vein blood transfusion, and then I stitched you up. Fortunately we have the same type. I'm also tested regularly for my job, so don't worry about it. I know I'm clean."

"I remember you asking me about my blood type." She had given him her own blood; no wonder she looked so drawn and pale. "What did you do to my back?"

"Nothing." She put her hand on his arm. "You probably wrenched it on the bridge. I'll see if I can find something for the pain."

"Pain." He laughed a little. "That is the problem. I'm not in pain. I feel no pain whatsoever."

"Okay." She looked uncertain. "This is usually a good thing, right?"

"After fifteen years of enduring crippling pain every day—often every hour of every day—this is an incredible thing," he assured her before he frowned. "An impossible thing."

"Sam, while I was working on you, you had some kind of seizure," she told him. "It could have been a small stroke, and that can cause nerve damage."

"I don't feel any paralysis." He looked down at himself. "Everything seems to be working very well."

"Yeah, but you were in shock, too. Sometimes a combination of these things can do some weird stuff to the body." When he was about to sit up the rest of the way, she pressed his arm. "Take it slow. If you fall, I don't think I can pick you up." She put her arm around his back. "Anytime you want to stop, just tell me."

As he moved into a sitting position, Taske's head remained as clear as his sight. He felt no discomfort, numbness, or any sensation other than that of his muscles coiling and uncoiling to accommodate his movements. As Charlotte stood up and watched him, he eased his legs over the side of the bed, and then slowly rose. Expecting his knees to buckle, he put a hand on her shoulder, but his legs remained strong and steady.

"I've walked with a limp since I was a teenager." He took one step, and then another, and suddenly, effortlessly, he was moving across the room. It had been so long since he'd walked without using a cane that his hand and arm felt odd, but not once did he lose his balance or stagger. Joy rushed through him, a genie released after a thousand years bottled up, granting his dearest wish without his even asking. He turned around and strode to Charlotte, seizing her by the waist and lifting her off her feet to whirl her around.

"Look at me." He laughed. "Charlotte, I can *walk*. I think I can even run."

"That's terrific, Sam." Her hands clamped on his shoulders. "Would you put me down now?"

"I'm sorry." He laughed again as he lowered her back to her feet and pulled her against him in an affectionate hug. "You can't know what this means to me." He cradled her face between his hands. "I thought I was a dead man—God, I knew I was—and now I wake up and

I can walk." He stroked a hand over her hair before he kissed her pretty mouth.

The delight pouring through him grew heated as he tasted the sweetness of her lips, and suddenly his excitement became urgent and dark. He filled his hands with her hair and nudged her lips apart, inhaling her startled breath and tasting her with his tongue. Her hands slid up his chest, pressing for a moment before they curved around his neck. He wanted to laugh again as he splayed his hands over her back and worked them down to the luscious curves of her hips. Before this he could only look at her and wish, but now that he was healed, now that he was strong, he could be like any other man and take her to his bed to give her hours and hours of pleasure. . . .

His bed was in Boston, not here.

Taske lifted his mouth from hers. Charlotte stood very still, her eyes wide and fixed on his face, her cheeks rosy. She looked as appalled as he was astonished. He intended to apologize, instantly and profusely, but the words he spoke had nothing to do with regret.

"I know you." He lifted a length of her hair to his nose, breathing in before he let the golden-shot strands fall back into place. "Your scent, the feel of your skin, everything about you is new to me. We'd never met before I saw you on the bridge. I'd swear to it. But . . . I know you."

She shook her head. "Sorry. I'm pretty sure I would remember meeting a guy your size." She eased out of his arms and turned her face away. "Maybe in another life."

Read on for an excerpt from
Lynn Viehl's

Evermore
A Novel of the Darkyn

where Nottingham was first introduced

"Why did you not come to the hall last night?" Farlae asked as Viviana finished tidying the workroom. "You missed quite a show between Locksley and this Nottingham of Florence."

Viviana had gone to the assembly with Harlech, but had slipped out as soon as Nottingham had arrived.

"I felt weary," she lied. "You have been using us like deck slaves."

"Aye, I have." Farlae's black eye seemed to pierce through her head. "Yet here you are, hard at work with the sun still in the sky."

She gathered the cording for the lord's new bed curtains and sat down well away from the window to work on it. "The work will not do itself."

"Vivi."

"Don't." She did not look up. "I have never asked why you and Rain always go to town on the same night, or come back smelling of each other, have I?"

"If you think to shame me into abandoning my regard for you," the wardrobe keeper advised her, "you will have to work harder than that. Everyone knows about me and Rain. We've been together since the British invaded for the last time."

"Forgive me." She put down the cording and rubbed her irritated eyes. "There is much I have done in my life, before I came here, that I regret. I was reminded of that last night. That is all."

"No, it is not," he said, giving her a wry smile, "but very well. You know where my ears and my shoulder are." He picked up a stack of newly hemmed table coverings and left.

Sewing had always been a mindless, soothing occupation for Viviana, but today the familiar play of needle and fabric gave her little relief from her thoughts. Her mind had become a snarled nest of fear and anger, bound tightly with despair.

Now that he is come, all will be revealed.

She had not wished to keep this secret. Indeed, she had tried to confide in Harlech a thousand times, but the right moment had never presented itself. No, to be brutally honest, she had made excuses so as to keep her husband in ignorance. Harlech would never expose her, but she had feared that the truth would drive him away from her. Surely after all that had happened, after all that she had lost, she deserved some happiness?

The answer to that came from behind her, in a voice that seemed too lovely to belong to a man. "How delightful it is to see a woman at such gentle work."

The hot, heavy scent of aniseed closed around her like a black wool cloak.

She bundled up the satin cord, tangling some of the shining strands she had been wrapping as she went to put the pile into her work basket.

"Ana." A black-gloved hand stopped her, trapping her fingers between the cord and the soft leather. "Are you not happy to see me?"

She faced him. "What would you know of happiness?"

"Not the welcome I expected, but it will do." He straightened. "It is astonishing how well you look. Your pretty face is the same as it was the day that my mother gave you to me."

"I am no longer an ignorant child desperate to feed my family. The family your mother let starve." She lifted her left hand, showing him the plain gold band that Harlech had placed on it. "I have protection now."

"My seneschal told me that you had taken a husband. Interesting news, I thought, considering your past ... and mine." He walked around her, inspecting her as he might a horse. "I feared that time would somehow ravage your beauty, but you truly are as you ever were: a flame among ashes."

"The past is dead, and I belong to another." She felt his hand tug at her headrail, and she grabbed it, outraged. "You will not trifle with me. Not if you wish to continue this obscene charade."

"Why, Ana, was that a threat? You have grown up." He smiled. "I confess, I was shocked that you ran from the room as soon as you laid eyes on me. I expected the charade to end then and there, for you have been made an honest woman. You did tell this husband about me, did you not?" He bent close. "Oh, my. You kept your secrets from him. What a pity."

"Harlech did not know me until after the *jardin* wars were over. We have never discussed what happened to us before we met. It was not important." She refused to cower. "What do you want?"

"Power. Pleasure. Many things." He took a tendril of her hair that had escaped her headrail and tickled the side of her jaw with its ends. "We have so much to talk about, you and I. You will come to my chamber tonight, after your husband retires." His other glove traced the arc of her breast. "I look forward to how we will become reacquainted."

"No."

"That was not a request." He jerked off her hair covering, seized her hair in his fist, and used it to drag her up against him. "You will come to me, Ana, and you will do exactly as I say. Otherwise, your husband will have to be made aware of many things." His hand closed cruel and tight over her breast. "I think I will start with from where you come."

Viviana drew her dagger and pressed it against his ribs. "If you wish me to keep my silence, you stay away from me and mine."

"Or what?" The tip of her blade pierced his tunic and pricked his flesh, but he didn't flinch. "You will expose me? You cannot do that, my love. Not if you wish to go on living. Old memories being what they are."

She knew that if she gave in to his demands, he would take everything from her anyway. "Test me and find out, my lord."

He put his mouth on her cheek, cupped her hand with his, and pushed it against his body, inhaling deeply as the tip of the copper cut through his side. "There, the angle is better. One thrust and you will have my heart. You did covet it once, I think." He held her in place as she jerked. "Don't be timid, Ana," he whispered, his cool breath caressing her ear. "You've held my fate in your hands before this. You've always done the right thing."

Her hand went numb, and distantly she heard her dagger clatter on the stone floor.

Nottingham lowered his head, kissing her stiff lips before he smiled against them and stepped back. "Tonight, in my chambers." He replaced her headrail and arranged the veils around her face. "Wear your hair down for me."

Viviana closed her eyes, and kept them shut until she heard the latch fall. She looked at the cording, which during the struggle had fallen to the floor. Her hands had torn and shredded it beyond repair.